November 2022

Artist's note on the cover image

The cover design of Jane, Frank and Mia is an amalgamation of elements that symbolize the character-driven narrative of the book. The wall background refers to the wall on which Mia drew a drawing of herself as a love-gift to her father, which was not received positively and hence became a critical relational turning-point in the book. The wall also symbolizes the layering of identity, which can be seen through the cracked areas where the Korean flag and tulips are revealed.

The face that unfolds from "behind" the wall represents Mia, a girl with Korean eyes and European reddish-blond hair. Furthermore and perhaps more importantly, the face represents relational connection. The eye can "connect" with the reader by making eye contact. In the reflection of her eye a silhouette of the three main characters holding hands may be observed – this is a detail element that captures the essence of the characters eventual connectedness.

The placing and colours of the names that form the title, Jane (in red), Frank (in off-white / light gray) and Mia (in blue), resemble the flag of The Netherlands, where the essential narrative takes place.

To conclude, the intention behind the design is to communicate the layering and unfolding of the characters involved in this literary narrative.

—Elize Roelofse, founder of Studio Selah, the Netherlands

Jane, Frank and Mia is about three people who cross each other's paths through some unforeseen event. Jane and Frank are seemingly opposites. Jane is a Korean woman who came to the Netherlands to marry Mia's father but is now divorced and raising her 15-year-old daughter Mia. Frank is Mia's chemistry teacher and is famous for his blunt aggressive attitude. As for Mia, she has been feeling lost since her parents' divorce, and unconsciously becomes the pivot of the story as she struggles to find herself. The lives of these three become intertwined as they recognize each other's pain and the obstacles each face, such as discrimination, oppression, misunderstanding, and violence. The author writes, "As a member of a diaspora myself, I love reading books by writers with immigrant backgrounds. War and poverty caused earlier migrations, and often there was no possibility of return. And when you can't go back, it gives the story finality, urgency. Later generations, people like myself, had more choices. They could return to their country of origin or move to yet another country for their career, for profit, or for love. I am intrigued by what makes a home and why people stay or leave. I wanted to tell a story about someone who's left their home."

DAMI JUNG was born in Seoul, South Korea, in 1979, moved to New Zealand with her parents as a girl, and has now been living in The Netherlands since 2006. Encouraged by her parents (her father, a teacher of the Korean Language and her mother, a writer) she read avidly and wrote daily from an early age. Later, music became her equal passion. She attended Sunhwa Arts School, majoring in music composition, and earned a Bachelor of Music (BMus) degree in Musicology from the Korean National University of Arts. In New Zealand, she studied at Victoria University of Wellington (Asian Studies and Women's Studies), and won the Westpac Chamber Music Competition (now the NZCT Chamber Music Contest) with the Ivinkaia trio, appearing on the television programme, Asia Dynamic. Later she worked as an interpreter. Until a few years ago, she wrote primarily in Korean and her first novel was published in that language in 2011. As she has now spent most of her life outside Korea, she has decided to switch to English so that her family and friends can read what she writes. *Jane, Frank and Mia* is her first novel to be published in English. Her wish as a writer is to pour out stories close to her heart which can mean something to others, to help people relate and feel like they're not alone.

Jane, Frank and Mia

Dami Jung

Proverse Prize 2021

Proverse Hong Kong

Jane, Frank and Mia
By Dami Jung
First published in Hong Kong
by Proverse Hong Kong,
under sole and exclusive right and licence,
17 November 2022:

Paperback: ISBN 13: 978-988-8492-64-0

E-book: ISBN 13: 978-988-8492-65-7

Distribution (Hong Kong and worldwide)
The Chinese University of Hong Kong Press,
The Chinese University of Hong Kong,
Shatin, New Territories, Hong Kong SAR.
Email: cup@cuhk.edu.hk; Web: www.cup.cuhk.edu.hk
Distribution (United Kingdom)
Stephen Inman, Worcester, UK.

Enquiries to Proverse Hong Kong
P.O. Box 259, Tung Chung Post Office,
Lantau, NT, Hong Kong SAR, China.
Email: proverse@netvigator.com;
Web: www.proversepublishing.com

British Library Cataloguing in Publication Data
A catalogue record for the first paperback edition
is available from the British Library

ACKNOWLEDGEMENTS

I want to express my deepest gratitude to the Proverse Prize, which brought this book to life. The editors at Proverse Publishing worked with me to make this book as good as it can be, and any errors which may remain are solely mine. I am grateful for this much-needed encouragement as a writer. This opportunity wouldn't have been achievable without the following friends.

Claudia, you've believed in me and been my anchor on this journey. You are one of the most loving people I've ever known. Priti, it means so much to me when you love my stories, and I want to start writing the next one immediately just to hear you say it. Soo-jin, you are my precious reader and friend who goes through the rough first drafts enthusiastically and kindly. And even in that primitive stage, you always understood what I wanted to say. And Young-gi, since I started writing in Korean all those years ago, you've been my biggest cheerleader. Elize, I love the book cover so dearly, and how you made my vision a reality was true artwork. Deimante, thank you for making music with me. It's been inspiring.

Su-kyoung, Eun-joo, Yeoseon, we share the Dutch life as Korean women and, most importantly, delicious Korean food.

Jung-wha in Frankfurt, Hana and Soo-yeon in Seoul, Soomin in the U.K, and Mee-young in the Netherlands; thank you for being there through thick and thin. I've been blessed with you all as my friends for the last two decades.

Michele, Evelien, Felicity, and Francis, thanks for the times we shared coffee, vino, and stories. Our real-life sagas were often more bizarre than fiction, but we could always laugh (and cry) together. And Theo and Christina, thank you for your friendship and support during a difficult time. Frouke, I wish you know that I love you and think of you.

Cecilia, we might make a weird duo, but you've been an important person in my and my girls' life. I am glad you were there at the time, and we've become friends.

Finally, my family, my life. Mom, Dahye, Hyun-soo, Ye-gang, Dad, Min-ok, and Hee-sun, thank you for all the love that you've given me.

Jane, Frank and Mia

Lina, Nara, Euan, and Aaron, sorry for the hours when I nurtured your independence and life skills while working away behind a computer. I hope having a writer mother brings some joy, too, along with the pain you must have experienced.

And Paul, you make everything possible. With you, I don't resent my yesterday, I love my today, and look forward to tomorrow. I've never known such contentment in my life.

To Lina and Nara,
The Three Musketeers in Sneek, once upon a time.

You shouldn't seek to avoid suffering
If you have no suffering, you come to disparage others and become extravagant
That's why the Great Saga says,
We should regard suffering and hardship as the true blessings in our life.
—**Buddhist Wisdom**

JANE, FRANK AND MIA

Dami Jung

Jane, Frank and Mia   10

BEGINNING

It was the middle of February, just before the Crocus holiday. Jane always found "Crocus Holiday" an ironic name for the one-week break in Dutch February. It was too optimistic to believe that spring was just around the corner, and soon would be blooming. But when was it warm in the Netherlands? Only for four months, starting from May until August, Jane felt reasonably content with the temperature. April does what it wants, people here said, but she, by then, would be looking forward to the short, therefore more precious warmer months. September was still primarily pleasant, but Jane started to feel agitated about the coming winter. It was a pleasure that you knew very well that there was an end to it. And she was right. In September, she usually took out her winter coat from the closet in the spare room, and that would be her uniform for the next half year. So much about being fashionable, Jane winced. Even if she wanted to dress up—she couldn't think of what occasion it would be, there wouldn't be much point when you had to cover the lovely dress with her old gray coat.

So on that February afternoon in 2015, Jane was shivering in the cold coming out of the busy supermarket. She regretted not having parked the car near the entrance, but she was in a hurry to get the groceries, and driving around the car park looking for a perfect spot seemed more a waste of time than walking to the car. She passed people at the bike stand, loading their shopping in their panniers, and admired their bravery in this cold. But they were the Dutch, trained from birth in this whimsical weather. It was she who had to adjust to its climate. She heard once from someone that Asian people had a lower body temperature, so Jane was more vulnerable to the cold weather. She doubted if it was a scientifically proven theory, but it was a fact that Jane suffered the cold more than anyone. So it could be a genetic fault on her part, the insufficiency of body heat in her system. Still, the Crocus flower bulbs were grappling hard with the ferocious frost, too. The city council planted them in the middle of the village roundabout, but they weren't precisely flourishing when she drove away from the supermarket. They looked, Jane ruefully noticed, like the spiky new hair on her head that she got after giving birth to her daughter, Mia.

It was fifteen years since Mia was born. This meant that now Jane was a proud parent, no, a slave, no, a co-habitant of the village's most temperamental teenager. A co-habitant whom she had to provide with food, clothing, a roof over her head, and unlimited devotion. Oh, and not to forget measured nonchalance. The balance between dedication and ignorance was challenging to get right, and if Jane messed it up, it most definitely brought down a tantrum.

When she got on the main road after the roundabout, Jane's mobile phone rang. Jane switched on her hand-free and glanced at the screen of the phone. It was Mia as she expected. Mia had an uncanny talent of sensing that Jane had finished her shopping and already vacated the shop and then called her to tell her what she wanted.

"Hi, Mia! What is it that you need this time?"

Jane lightly answered the call, already giving up on the idea of getting annoyed. What's the point, anyway?

Then she immediately felt that something was wrong when Mia didn't bark at her what she so urgently must purchase. Mia was hysterically sobbing.

"Mia! What is it? Why are you crying? Something happened?"

Being a mother, Jane always assumed the worst had happened every time something was up.

"Mom..."

"Are you not well? Please tell me, wait, I am stopping the car."

Jane quickly scanned the road where she could park the car, and the first spot she found, she shoved her little white Kia in the space.

"I have stopped. Please tell me what's happened."

Mia, still sobbing, didn't start telling her the problem.

Jane waited, biting her nail until Mia's sob ceased a bit and she was sniffing.

"It's my Chemistry teacher, Mr. Bloom."

"The Mr. Bully?"

Jane remembered how Mia referred to her Chemistry teacher as Mr. Bully, who unfortunately happened to be her year mentor as well. In Jane's opinion, a man called a bully shouldn't be a mentor to the students at all, but she knew of the shortage of teachers in Dutch schools.

"What about him?"

There again, the worst things that he could have done to Mia passed through her head. Jane tried to calm her breath for the sake of her daughter.

"He failed me!"

Okay, that is not the end of the world, Jane thought. But then, it was, in fact, pretty serious in Mia's circumstances.

"What happened?"

Jane lost count of the times she'd fired that question.

"Mom, I have to pass Chemistry for my profile choice! But he's given me one, and there's no way that I can compensate that next term. The last assignment before the holiday was due last week, and our wifi was playing up. Do you remember? We couldn't fix it ourselves, so I wrote an email to him on your phone that I would hand it in a day later. You remember it, right?"

Jane remembered. She didn't recall any reply from the teacher on that matter, though.

"He didn't say anything then, so I thought it was alright, then he's given me one! Mom, I got one! Can you believe it? And I spent so many hours on that bloody useless assignment!"

'Watch your language,' Jane murmured, but thankfully her lips were stuck to each other. She had to cough her words out.

"That's horrible. But I'm sure we can sort things out with him?"

Jane sounded composed, even to her surprise.

'Keep calm and be a mother.'

She came out of her mantra when Mia shouted at full volume into the speaker.

"Mom!"

Mia sounded incredulous, now angry with Jane.

"You don't understand, do you! I can't catch up with that grade because it was already the most difficult subject for me! And now, with Chemistry failing, I wouldn't be able to go to the next class... I will be separated from Nora and Esther!"

Now, that was a crime that Jane could identify with.

Mia had been struggling ever since Jane and David got divorced eight years ago, and the high school didn't make it any easier. Mia only just made it to the next class for the last three years, and this year for the first time, with help from her good friends Nora and Esther, she was managing a lot better at school. Mia was building up her not so much present self-confidence and feeling good about her improving school grades. It was looking as if she would have less trouble advancing to the next year until this Chemistry debacle was thrown at her.

And just because of the stupid wifi!

"But can't you send him an email? No, better call him this time and explain the situation? We can't do anything about the rubbish wifi service here! I know, Mia. I will call the teacher and tell him that you were not lying about why you had to hand it in a day later. What's his phone number? Wait, I think I must have it somewhere."

"Mom, it won't make a difference. He is ruthless! He is the cruelest teacher I've ever had in my whole life."

Mia sounded like she was going to start to sob again.

Jane's heart broke every time her daughter cried.

Determined to help her daughter out of her misery and take the matter into her hands, Jane said to Mia.

"Don't worry. We all know that from time to time, everyone experiences bad wifi. Any reasonable person would understand that. I'm sure when he hears it from me, the parent, he will re-grade you. I will call him now. See you later at home."

Jane let out a long sigh after she ended the call with Mia.

Jane remembered that she received the school's introductory email at the beginning of the school year and another email from Mia's mentor Mr. Bully, no Mr. Bloom, with his contact details.

There was a parents' meeting a couple of months ago, and as always, David went alone to see Mia's mentor. It wasn't that Jane wasn't interested in Mia's school, quite the opposite. But it was strenuous to be in the same space as David. Until Jane finally gave up going any place where David would be, they used to create the most awkward, entertaining scenes at Mia's elementary school. Jane was confident that all the teachers were talking about them after yet another embarrassing parents' meeting. Jane wondered if they could also see how domineering David was and how she was trying to disguise the ignominy of being belittled in front of other people.

"My ex…" (although Jane was sitting right next to him in the room, he still referred her as a third person) "…doesn't speak Dutch very well. Please talk to me rather than her."

Since moving to the Netherlands from South Korea, she'd always felt like a third-world citizen, but David's remarks were most hurtful. She moved here because of him. If she hadn't so naively fallen in love with him and had a child with him, she wouldn't be here. Even when she did free herself from him, she could not go back home to her family and friends because there was no way that she could take Mia with her. David threatened to report her at the airport if she ever tried to travel with Mia without his permission. Jane had seen enough news about one divorced parent taking a child to their homeland, labeled a kidnapper—and on the Interpol lookout list. Anyway, he kept Mia's passport with him, and she'd given up hope a long time ago of going back home with her daughter.

She finally found the email with Mr. Bloom's phone number, searching through all Mia's school emails.

She dialed the mobile number, praying that he would answer. She wanted to finish the ordeal before she went home and faced her daughter.

Luckily there was a click, and a gruff voice came through the hand-free speaker.

"Bloom."

"Oh, hello, Mr. Bloom, this is Jane Lee, Mia Hollander's mother."

Jane decided to talk in English since she felt much more confident in her English than in Dutch.

"I don't appreciate any parent calling me on my mobile."

His English was like most Dutch people's English, making perfect sense but with a trace of a hard accent.

As if to say, I can speak English no problem, but I only do it if I have to.

"Well, I wouldn't normally call Mia's teacher if it wasn't so important. And,"

She couldn't help it.

"You did send us an email with your contact details, so I assumed that it was for this kind of occasion."

A noise, like Mr. Bloom's grunt, was audible.

"I remember Mia's father told me last time that you didn't speak Dutch. Is that right?"

Jane swallowed almost audibly too.

"I do speak Dutch, but I prefer to talk in English if it is a vital matter."

"You could try. Otherwise, you will never learn."

'Don't patronize me!'

Jane screamed in her head. She still felt mad when people tried to teach her a lesson.

"Well, don't worry about my learning, Mr. Bloom. It is Mia's learning that I am concerned about."

"If you are talking about the grade that I gave her for late hand-in, there's no point, Ms. Lee."

Jane felt the steam was coming out of her head like a pressure cooker. Mr. Bloom sounded more irrational than Jane had expected.

"And can you explain to me, Mr. Bloom, why there is no point?"

"Because it wouldn't be fair for other students. If I let Mia get away with late hand-in, what about other children? A rule is a rule, and it's only valuable if everyone sticks to it."

"I do understand that a rule is a rule. But there are situations when you can't help yourself. Mia finished her assignment on time, but our wifi played up, and she just couldn't send it off. I tried to help her, but it was saved on her laptop. The file was too big on the phone. And..."

"I can assure you, Ms. Lee, that I hear the same excuses every day. And if every parent is going to call me and harass me for the grade, that is another reason why I hate my job."

"Harassing you?"

Jane heard her exasperated voice on the speaker, and she became indignant.

"Excuse me, but I think you were harassing your student here. And if you hate your job, that's because you are not fitted for your job. I can't imagine anyone more un-teacher-like than you!"

This wasn't how Jane was planning to lead the conversation. But this man, Mr. Bully—a perfectly matching nickname for him, now she agreed too- was drawing the blood out of her.

"So you seem to be familiar with the quality of a teacher. What about the quality of a parent? You didn't even show up for the parents' meeting, and according to your ex-husband, that wasn't the first time. But you still decide to call up and demand a higher grade for your daughter who doesn't deserve it."

Jane closed her eyes and swore at David under her breath. Even after eight years apart, he hadn't slowed down with the slandering. And what is sadder, people believed him. He was, after all, one of them, an established and sophisticated fellow

Dutchman whom people had no reason not to trust.

"There are many reasons why I was not there, which I am not going to elaborate because it's personal. All I wanted to ask you was to consider the situation that Mia was in sending the assignment. I didn't ask you to judge me on account of a man who is hostile towards me. I didn't have a chance to defend myself to you, yet you criticize me just like that."

"Well, he described you as an indifferent mother, and you were not there to prove the opposite. He said that he was worried about you overprotecting Mia and spoiling her. If this isn't an example of his concern, I don't know what it is. I'm not saying I believed everything he said, but he even referred you to your fellow countryman, Kim Jong-un. His word, not mine, by the way."

Jane froze since she felt so cold from the anger.

"That is some remark, wrong in so many ways. You take someone's words without any justification, and you teach children at school! I want you, Mr. Bloom, to apologize to me."

"Apologize to you? Why me, not your ex-husband? It was what he said, not what I made up!"

"You did repeat it to me. I didn't have to be confronted with his lies today. I want you to apologize, Mr. Bloom. Otherwise, I will take this matter to the school board."

"You are truly overreacting! This is a free country, and everyone is entitled to their own opinion. You can't stop people saying what they think!"

"I see. So you think it was a perfectly fine remark about a parent, then we will ask the principal and the parents' board their opinions. You will be informed after I raise this matter."

A minute of silence passed in Jane's car.

Good thing that he couldn't see her shaking in her seat.

Then he spat it out.

"All right! I will apologize. How do you want me to do it? Say sorry?"

"You say sorry either to me in person now or later in front of the school board."

Another silence.

"Okay… where? I finish early on Friday and am already home."

"I am coming to you now."

It wasn't how Frank expected the phone call would proceed,

either. Somehow along the line, he'd lost it, again, as he'd done so many times recently.

He was under a lot of pressure at work. He never wanted to be a bloody mentor to the bloody class. And something in Mia's mother's voice got on his nerves. This foreign woman somehow ended up living here, and she was determined to fight for every inch she could win. She sounded like someone who had been oppressed too long and was now so fed up with everything that she had decided to stand up for herself. And that irritated Frank. What was she trying to achieve with that kind of mentality? Relax, he wanted to yell at her. Not all Dutch people are so narrow-minded! But in the end, it was he who was on the wrong foot. He didn't know how he'd done that, but Frank knew that he couldn't afford to cause more problems in his life. He'd already had enough trouble with the principal and the school board.

***

Jane typed Mr. Bully's address on the google map with trembling fingers. He lived just outside the village, and it said 15 minutes from the road she was parked to his house. While she was following the loud voice telling her what route to take, she recalled what Mr. Bully said.

'I'm like Kim Jong-un? You've never experienced a dictator in your life, and you compare me to the biggest bully of the whole wide world? Just because I am from South Korea? You are one of those idiots always asking whether we are from North Korea or South Korea as if anyone from North Korea would be casually sightseeing around the world!'

Then all the assaults that she'd ever received from ignorant European people for the past years came up in her mind. How random people on the street shouted, "Ni Hao!" "Shing, shang, shong!" at her. She usually ignored them and went her way, but she couldn't sustain her annoyance once in a while and stated that she wasn't Chinese. Then they laughed at her over-sensitiveness because 'Ni Hao' was just a hello in Chinese, and why was she so unfriendly to their innocent greeting?

As if Jane would just shout "Guten Tag!" to any European stranger because they looked German.

Oh, Jane, Jane... What is up with you? She asked herself and shook her head dejectedly. What was she doing driving to a man she'd never met, and she already knew how rude he could be.

Her rage shrunk as the air from the pressure cooker escaped. And she felt her eyes were welling up. She was too exhausted for another fight. Her daily life was an ongoing fight with herself, her daughter, and her ex-husband. And with all the misgivings and prejudice she had to face as a third-world citizen in the Netherlands. She once went on a holiday with her family in South Korea when Mia was only three years old. They visited a tiny village on the East Coast, and they stayed in a humble homestay. Jane saw the house's daughter-in-law was from South-East Asia. When Jane asked where she was from, the mother-in-law said she was from Vietnam. More Vietnamese women in the village came to South Korea to arrange marriages and gathered at the house in the afternoon. They worked together, weaving something, and preparing food while watching the children play. None of them spoke any Korean, and it looked like they were living in their own world. Jane was only too aware, whereas her circumstance was different from those ladies, that she wouldn't look very different here. Whether she was from China, South Korea, the Philippines, Thailand, or other Asian countries, it didn't make much difference to most people in Europe. They were all seen in the category of "Asian women who married European men for a better life than home." The possibility that these women all had their own stories and the reality that it wasn't always better than the home was often overlooked.

So... why was she going to Mr. Bully for an apology? To humiliate herself again by another ignorant but, in fact, just an average person?

She considered turning her car back. It would save her time and energy just to raise a white flag. But to what? What had she lost to whom?

She thought of her daughter. What could she tell her if she just went home without an answer for her problem? She didn't even know that her mother deserved an apology for such an outrageous insult...

Jane took a deep breath in. The female voice of the google map said that she was there.

***

When the bell rang at Frank's flat, he glanced at the clock on the wall in shock. He didn't know where Mia's mother was coming from and had no idea how long it would take for her to be here.

It couldn't have been too far since it was only 20 minutes ago that he told her his address and hung up the phone.

Naturally, he had had no time to clean up his place. It was in the normal state of an after-bombing war zone. The sink was overflowing with at least three days worth of dirty dishes, and everywhere was scattered with his stuff—dirty clothing and books and oh shit, what the hell was that clump of tissues doing there?

It was when he just managed to pick up the offending ball of the tissues and put them in the bin that Mia's mother arrived at his door.

He opened the door after picking up more rubbish in the hall and throwing them into his bedroom. He had to blink his eyes a few times before he said, "Hello."

Frank hadn't taken a moment to think about what Mia's mother would look like. Mia looked like a mixed kid, but she had more European features than Asian, except her huge, monolid eyes. He couldn't remember if he had ever met a Korean either, except seeing Kim Jong-un on television. Mia's mother didn't look like Kim Jong-un at all.

She was tall, taller than most Asian women he'd seen, but then he wouldn't have known the difference between Koreans and other Asians, but her height, with her defiant chin-up, threw him a bit.

"Can I come in?"

She asked when Frank didn't invite her in, being stupidly nonplussed.

"Yes, please come in, Ms. Lee."

She took off her gray coat and asked him where she could hang it.

He took the coat from her and hung it on the coat hanger in the hall.

"Have a seat, please. Coffee or tea?"

She tentatively followed him into the lounge, and he could see the disgust on her face when they entered the room.

"Sorry about the mess. I wasn't expecting any visitors. You can move the books on the sofa there and take a seat."

Jane didn't plan to stay long in his flat. She was going to leave as soon as he provided a decent apology. Or even a quick pretentious one. Then she realized that she couldn't just stand there and demand an apology and storm out. So she said, "Coffee would be fine, just black, thanks." and pushed the vast files of books further and sat down.

In the kitchen, Frank put the coffee pods in the machine and contemplated what he could say. What he said to her on the phone was affronting and totally inappropriate, and also arguably racist.

Two cups of strong black coffee were made, and he brought them to the lounge and saw that Mia's mother was intensely staring at his wifi router.

It was…, blinking, which meant it was out, yet again.

Frank coughed to catch her attention, and she turned her face to him, as he was holding out a cup.

"Here, your coffee, Ms. Lee."

"Thank you."

She received the cup in two hands, he noticed.

"Your wifi is not working now?"

Frank thought of lying to her. Yes, it is working fine, thank you very much, none of your business, you nosy mother of a student. But he changed his mind because everyone had the same router, and lying about it would deteriorate his already gravely damaged reputation.

"No. As you see, it is not."

She slowly nodded.

Frank gulped the hot espresso. He could hear what she was thinking. But she made it brief, which was gracious and merciful of her.

"So you agree it is a common problem with wifi, and there are times that things get messed up."

Frank considered his option of answers.

"Yes. I agree."

"Will you reconsider Mia's grade for the assignment? She would understand if you deduct a mark for late hand-in, but if you could just look at what she did, she would be very grateful."

Frank didn't expect Mia's mother to be so matter-of-fact. He was waiting to be burnt on the grill when she demanded to crash his place. Frank had to admit that he didn't actually listen to her when she tried to explain. It was only fair what she pointed out, now that he thought about it.

"I will, Ms. Lee."

Mia's mother's face relaxed then.

"You can call me Jane."

"Call me, Frank, too."

Both of them fell into silence, and Ms. Lee, no Jane, quietly sipped her espresso.

When she put down the little cup, she said.

"Thank you for the coffee, Mr. Bloom."

"Frank."

"Mm, thank you, Frank. I'd better get going. I've still got the groceries in the car. I almost forgot."

Frank somehow didn't want her to go.

"Wait, what about the apology?"

Jane was already standing up, and she stared at Frank. It was a calm but deadly stare, he thought.

"What apology, Frank?"

"The apology that I owe you. About comparing you to... I am sorry. It was wrong of me to say those things."

"But you did."

"Yes..."

"And you didn't think it was something to apologize for. What changed your mind?"

Frank now felt he was being interrogated, calmly but deadly.

"Look, what I think I did was..... not that it was a good excuse, but I do get a lot of phone calls from angry parents who complain about their children's grades. I assumed that you were one of those aggressive ones, and I overreacted in automatic self-defense. What was worse, I counterattacked and used what I heard from your ex-husband as my weapon. It was shameful of me. I do want to apologize, not only because you told me to."

Jane sat down again, and she seemed to be in thought for a while. Then she nodded.

"Apology accepted."

Frank felt half-relieved and half-bewildered by her prompt, no-nonsense acceptance.

"Is that it?"

"Sorry?"

"You are not going to give me any more bollocking?"

"Should I?"

"Well, I do deserve it."

That was the first time Jane smiled since she came to his flat.

'She suddenly looks like a different girl,' Frank registered with an unexplainable delight.

He observed her properly now that she sat on the sofa and looked a bit more at ease.

He couldn't guess her age. He could never guess anyone's age for a start, and people of different races other than his, like Asian and African, were out of his league to make any attempt to guess their age.

She must be at least thirty-something, remembering that she had a teenage daughter, but Jane didn't seem older than thirty to him when she smiled just now.

She was wearing a black woolen dress, with black leggings and black ankle boots. Her shoulder-length hair and eyes were ink-black, so anything that was not black on her was her red lipstick and a thin golden chain over her neck. Oh, and her rather pale face. She had a shadow of light purple colour on her eyelids, so she must have been wearing some make-up, although Frank wasn't an expert on that subject.

"Well, as I said on the phone, I've never called Mia's teacher before."

She sighed and took some time before she went on.

"Usually, I would tell Mia to leave it and get on with other things and try to do better the next time, but she was too distressed, and that also distressed me. She wouldn't be able to make it up with the grade—I know she struggles with Chemistry- and she's been trying so hard to do well at school this year. And since I was there when she was trying to send the assignment, I felt her frustration. I decided to ask you if you would rethink."

Jane was clearly concerned with her daughter's school and interested enough to care so much about her grade. Frank wondered why her ex-husband was slagging about her like that the last time they met.

Jane must have read what he was thinking.

"I'm sure you heard a different story about me."

"Yes. But it seems so unfair because what he said about you made me have a pre-judged mind when I didn't even know you. I wonder why he is behaving like that. It must be so upsetting for you."

Jane looked almost startled to hear the sympathetic words from a stranger. She smiled again, off-guarded.

"It used to upset me a lot more before. It still bothers me, to be frank. But I don't stay awake at night anymore thinking about what he is telling other people. There is simply nothing I can do about it. I can't go around following people he's been in contact with, knock on their door and explain myself. So I try to live my life, which is the only thing I can do."

"That's very mature of you."

Jane just shrugged.

"Why is he so mean to you?"

It came out before Frank could stop himself.

He'd only spent 20 minutes with her, but he couldn't imagine she was so vile and horrible as her ex-husband was making him imagine.

Jane shrugged again.

"I did wonder that too for all this time. But I don't understand him. I don't want to understand him either."

"You don't?"

"No. Because to understand someone, you would have to be like the person. I would have to think like him and feel like him. Full of hatred, bitterness, and disparagement. To understand him would be accepting and acknowledging his logic and action. I can't. I refuse it."

Frank gazed at Jane in perplexity.

"The only answer I can think of is that he is not a good person. Not in heart, and I suspect not in the head either."

Then she shifted uncomfortably on the sofa.

"I don't want to appear to be doing the same thing as him. Bad-mouthing. But that is the only thing I came up with after all these years, and I can't make it nicer than what it is."

Then a slight smile, "As all the Dutch people say, entitled to my opinion, I am too."

Frank smiled after her, but he felt embarrassed.

"Ah, well, that was another stupid comment of me. That I am right to think what I think, and I can say anything I want."

"Oh, no, I am used to that saying. You don't know how many times I've heard it here. In fact, I've come to appreciate that Dutch attitude more than before. I've seen the benefit of such a stance. Because it gives people a voice, doesn't it? Better than the 'keep your mouth shut' attitude."

Frank saw Jane's face crunching as if she was in pain.

"Are you alright? You've gone so pale."

"I..."

Jane's chin, which was so defiant when she came in, dropped to her gold chain.

"Do you want some water?"

"Yes, please."

Jane whispered.

Almost running into the tap in the kitchen, Frank brought the glass of water to Jane.

Jane accepted it gratefully, again in two hands, and took a few sips.

"Thank you. I'm okay now."

Frank wasn't convinced. She still looked like she was going to burst into tears any moment.

"Was it anything I said?"

Frank had never been so self-conscious about what he said. He'd already offended her enough for his lifetime in the first ten minutes of their telephone conversation.

"Oh, no, it wasn't."

Jane smiled faintly.

"Talking about people's attitudes brought me a painful memory."

Then she took a deep breath.

"Do you know that there was a ferry accident in South Korea last year?"

Frank vaguely remembered seeing it on the news.

"Was it when lots of young students died?"

Jane nodded and looked down at her glass.

"Yes. The 16th of April. Do you know what the students on the ferry were told while it was sinking?"

Frank shook his head. Somehow he couldn't bring himself to say anything.

"Stay still."

Jane stayed still. Frank stayed still, too.

"They could have saved everyone on board, but they didn't. For more than a hundred minutes, they told the students to stay still in the sinking ship. The children were just doing what they were told to do."

Frank swallowed hard.

"For many years, I used to find it impossible to say what I thought and do as I believed. Everyone else here was doing so, except for me, and I felt people walked all over me. But seeing these children losing their precious lives made me realize that I needed to speak up too. I can't still do it very well, but I am trying."

"Trying to say what you think?"

"Yes. I am practicing to be more brutish."

Frank raised his eyebrow. He found Jane's determination rather adorable.

He couldn't imagine Jane being brutish as much as he tried, although he now knew she could be fierce when fighting for her daughter.

"I get it. So when you heard this stupid man making awful, misjudged remarks, you saw your chance to stand up for yourself and teach him a lesson."

Jane's eyes were filled with comprehension, and she pretended to look sheepish.

"Was it "that" obvious?"

"I sensed something like that."

Jane chuckled, shaking her head.

"See? I told you that I hadn't mastered it yet. The art of speaking up."

Then Jane thought for a moment.

She picked up the now cold coffee cup with her lipstick mark and then put it down again. She looked around his lounge.

"Can I ask you a question?"

Frank saw the hesitation in her eyes then nodded encouragingly.

"Go on. Don't forget you are practicing."

"You said that you hated your job. What do you hate about it, and why are you there then?"

God, Frank thought, 'This is becoming the most serious conversation I've had since my father tried to discuss contraceptives!'

He looked into Jane's eyes, big and round like Mia's. They were dark as the tree and shining like the moon of Van Gogh's The Starry Night.

"I didn't hate my job always. I used actually to love it very much until a few years ago. But... things happened, and that kind of changed my perspective about my job too."

He waited, but Jane didn't query him further about what changed his perspective. He wasn't sure why he wanted to tell her since he never talked about his personal life with anyone these days. But strangely enough, he felt disappointed when she didn't urge him for more.

"And why I am still there is simply to make a living. I wouldn't know what else I could do since I've always wanted to be a teacher. For now, I just need the job."

"Too bad that you can't enjoy it while you are at it, though."

He was suddenly overwhelmed by sadness.

"Yes, too bad, indeed."

Their eyes locked at that moment, and Frank was unable to move. Neither of them could look away until Jane managed to avert her eyes to the only sound in the flat, the ticking clock on the wall. "I must go," she said.

As she was leaving the flat, she looked around the place again. She'd been fighting the compulsion to clean up while she was there. But thinking of Mia's bedroom in her house, she was not in a position to judge anyone.

Frank took her coat from the hanger and handed it to her. Something caught his eyes when she picked up her black leather bag. Somehow he felt it must mean something.

"What is this?"

He pointed at the yellow ribbon on her bag.

"Oh, it is to remember the Sewol ferry."

"The accident that you were telling me about?"

"Yes. People made it as a symbol of mourning, and I carry one too."

"Isn't it... too painful to be reminded of all the time?"

Frank couldn't understand why anyone would want to be confronted with such a harrowing accident every day.

"Oh, I do want to remember, every single day."

"You do? How come?"

"Do you know what it says on the wall of Auschwitz concentration camp?"

Frank, stunned by what Jane brought up, shook his head.

"Those who cannot remember the past are condemned to repeat it."

After rather long seconds of silence, Frank managed to ask her again.

"So you are actively remembering it not to repeat such an accident."

"Yes. But not only that."

Frank stared at Jane, waiting for more clarification.

"You don't know how many people told me to forget and move on. I tried, but it didn't go away. Time heals many things but not everything. So I decided to live with it. I remember to remember. Otherwise, it would mean nothing, and it is such a shame to waste the suffering."

Frank stood still. He was fighting silently with what he'd forgotten for a long time. He thought that he moved on from the struggle—his grandfather's struggle.

"My grandfather was a Holocaust survivor."

"Oh."

Now Jane stared at Frank perplexed.

"Did he tell you about it?"

Frank shook his head regretfully.

"No. He never wanted to talk about it. He wanted to forget. Otherwise, he couldn't go on with his life, he said."

Jane looked into Frank's eyes, and her eyes were full of solace.

"If we had to and were able to suffer the sufferings of everyone, we could not live." [1]

"Primo Levi."

"You know him too?"

Frank nodded gravely. "Yes. I've read his memoirs and other books. I was grateful that people like him and Anne Frank left us the legacy of what they went through. Imagine no one told their story, and it was all forgotten when they died. What a waste of their suffering would that have been, as you put it. Primo Levi must have gone through another hell reminiscing about his time at the concentration camp. He was also a chemist, and reading his books made me want to study chemistry."

"Everyone had to find a way to fight their war. Your grandfather did what he had to do. We can't expect everyone to go through another hell. People need the mercy of forgetfulness too. I'm sorry that he had to suffer so much."

"Yes. I wish he didn't have to. Because I know it was always

---

[1] Primo Levi, *The Drowned and the Saved*. Simon and Schuster Paperbacks, New York, June 2017, pp.44-45.

there with him whether he talked about it or not."

Then he couldn't say anything anymore.

He was bewildered by this unreal visitor of his, and the only thing going through his disheveled head was, 'What an extraordinary woman!'

Jane woke him up from his mystified admiration.

"Well, thank you for the coffee."

"Thank you for coming."

Frank could hit his head against the wall. As if he had invited her for a nice cup of coffee!

"Well, I think it was needed."

Jane smiled her little smile, and the muscles around Frank's heart twitched.

"Yes, I agree that it was needed."

He murmured when the door closed, and there was a whiff of warm, flowery scent left in his empty hall.

CHAPTER 1
JANE

Jane was driving away from Frank's flat when she remembered it was Friday. That was why she was in such a rush getting the groceries. Every other Friday after dinner, Mia went to stay with David for the weekend. And the dinner before David picked Mia up was the most important meal every two weeks, at least for Jane. Jane finished a few hours early on Friday, so she usually spent the extra hours shopping and preparing dinner. Jane was afraid unless she fed Mia the most delicious meal that her daughter might forget her and not come back.

When Mia was still just a little girl, and the wounds from the divorce were raw, Jane often had to hide her tears while the two of them were eating the last supper. She missed her daughter so excessively when she went away that it physically hurt her. She missed her even before Mia was gone, knowing how much pain she would have for the next 48 hours. It was as excruciating as if her limb was sawed off alive. She also got acute stomachache feeling her navel string was being burnt every time Mia left. But she still tried to talk pleasantly about Mia's school and friends and pretend to be in a jolly mood. Because Jane knew that, once she burst out in tears, she wouldn't be able to close the tear tap for the whole weekend. Jane didn't want to say goodbye to Mia with red eyes and swollen face. That was not how she wished to be remembered by her daughter, in case she lost her daughter for good.

Now the wounds had become half-healed, still open, but had a sort of scaffolding around them. Yet Jane's heart died even after eight years whenever Mia left. She didn't know where this fear and sorrow came from. And if it would ever go away. Jane and Mia used to be best friends, the two hands from one stomach, as the Dutch say about the two persons who can get along very well. Everything changed when Jane and David separated, of course, but to come to think of it, perhaps Jane felt a bit unsure of herself as a mother from the very beginning.

When Mia was born, Jane wanted to talk to her baby in Korean. As comfortable as she was with English, Korean was her mother tongue, and she wanted to sing the lullabies and read the nursery rhymes from her childhood. But David wasn't happy with her talking Korean to his baby daughter.

"I don't want to feel left out by my wife and daughter in my own house. I want to know what you are saying to each other."

Jane did try to convince him that it would only be beneficial for their daughter to be bilingual, but David, as always, never moved from his standpoint.

"It is for your sake too, Jane. You are living and raising a child here in the Netherlands. To take proper care of her, you need to become fluent in Dutch. The best way is to speak Dutch only in the house."

And he was right too. Jane learnt the language quickly, having no other language to rely on. Even when they argued and Jane couldn't remember the words and switched to English to say what she wanted to say, David corrected her.

"Dutch! Speak Dutch!"

It had an abrupt effect to kill Jane's fury when he did. The wrath turned into ineptitude. The dynamic of their discussion could never be on equal ground as Jane lost her language. 'Good for marital peace,' Jane murmured to herself because she soon lost the will to speak. Just too humiliating that he even criticized her pronunciation when they were in the heat of their emotions.

Oblivious to Jane losing her voice, everyone complimented her linguistic talent since Dutch was not easy to master for a foreigner. However, Jane still felt inadequate to fully function as a Dutch mother. Jane was not built to bike in the rain, wind, and snow like other Dutch women. The Dutch mothers were superwomen. Jane believed so because they could easily transport two children, one in front and one at the back, plus a day's groceries in two pannier bags even in the most grueling Dutch weather. Oh, if there were too many children or too much stuff to carry, they also rode a cargo bike. Jane once tried to test it when David said it was one of his ideal parenthood pictures. That was the last time she was on a cargo bike, and she swore 'Never ever!' after she almost hit a parked van and an old lady. You had to steer the handle to the opposite direction you were aiming for, and Jane could never work out that logic. Anyhow, with just one child in the house, she didn't need that monster of a bike, thank goodness.

The whole business with Mia's Chemistry teacher, Frank, was an unanticipated affair that interfered with her plan this Friday afternoon. She wanted to make Japchae, the Korean glass noodles with stir-fried vegetables and marinated beef, Mia's all-time favourite. It was a time-consuming dish to create, to prepare each ingredient separately until she could mix it all with the cooked glass noodles. If she hadn't had to drop by Frank's house, she would have had just enough time to make it before Mia went to David, but now she wasn't sure if that was manageable. She will have to think of another delicious dish quickly. Otherwise, Mia would be grumpy during the dinner, leaving Jane in a gloomy mood for the whole weekend.

'Stop fussing about Mia and live your life!'

That was the advice from her friends Su-kyoung and Sunny. They were good friends of hers, here in the Netherlands, whom Jane met a few years ago after her divorce. They were both married to Dutchmen and had children, two younger than Mia (Su-kyoung's daughters) and two older than Mia (Sunny's sons). They all met at the Korean School of Amsterdam when the children were still young, and the mothers were ambitious to teach their children the Korean language. But as the kids grew up, they lost interest in a language that they couldn't use at school and wanted to do other things on Saturdays instead of going to Korean School. However, the three of them still kept in touch as they got on very well. Now Jane thought they were closer friends than the ones she had in Seoul a long time ago. They shared something unique, the Dutch life, which she couldn't communicate with her old Korean friends.

"It's understandable that you feel guilty about the divorce and try to make it up to Mia, but you've got to stop punishing yourself like that. You are still young and pretty (wink, wink). You've got to find someone again and be happy."

That was a piece of advice from Su-kyoung, who urged Jane to find her happiness in a stable relationship. Sunny had a different idea, though, being as practical and surprisingly honest as anyone could be.

"I don't think the concept of marriage works for women, Jane. After years of observing different married couples around me, I've concluded that women always lose when they marry. No matter your nationality, race, education, financial position, or career, the moment you get married and have children, we all come down to the one title—mother. We get lost in the spiral of motherhood. We blame ourselves if we want anything for ourselves and worry if we are doing enough. Whereas the men just carry on whatever they were doing before children. Motherhood kills. Fatherhood doesn't. So Jane, don't start a serious relationship, just meet as many men as you want and have a ball! Enjoy the time of your life! God, I would if I were you!"

So she should pursue this fruitless business of meeting men, according to her friends, which brought today's other logistic difficulty back to Jane's head. The problem of BF4, as Mia addressed it.

BF was what Mia called Jane's boyfriends. There were only a handful of men with whom Jane had had a couple of dates, so they couldn't practically call them BF, but it had to do with the fact that Mia never wanted to acknowledge them properly with their names. It was either BF1 or BF2, and tonight she was supposed to meet her BF4.

It was the first time Jane invited a man to her house since they met on a dating site—thanks to Sunny's registration for Jane—three months ago. Jane only wanted to see him when Mia stayed with David, which was about twice a month. Jane didn't expect any man to have such patience, and when BF4—in real life, he was called Pieter—didn't get bored and run away after so few opportunities to see each other, Jane thought maybe this time, she could go a bit further than with other dates of hers.

So Pieter was coming after Mia was gone for sure. Jane had bought a bottle of wine and some cheese to go with it, and hopefully, the cold weather today would keep it fresh until she was home. Jane shivered in the car, wondering, 'what the hell was I thinking….. I don't want anything to happen with Pieter. Why did I invite him?'

Jane panicked.

A date, and Mia's dinner. It was all messed up. She felt nervous that today didn't go as she wanted.

What should she feed Mia as "the last supper before the Dad" now? And could she still cancel the date with Pieter?

Then she was home. She gathered all the groceries, including the distressing bottle of wine, and opened the door. She could hear Mia playing music and talking to her friend, probably Nora, or Esther, in the living room. Jane nodded her head at her daughter since she didn't have a free hand to wave and moved her lips to whisper, "Hi," not to disturb the call with her friend and somehow make her angry.

Jane was putting away the food when Mia unexpectedly entered the kitchen.

She thought Mia would be on the phone for a long time.

"Hi, Mom."

Mia started to help her put away the cans of soup and lifted the offending bottle of wine.

"Ooooh, what is this? Wait, is BF4 coming tonight? Are you going to get trashed and be wild?"

"What?"

Despite her shock, Jane smiled at her daughter.

"How did you find about my plan?"

"Oh, Mom, is BF4 really worth throwing yourself at? You've been such a good girl until now. You've been chastening yourself all this time."

"Mia! What do you know about my love life? Besides, with you criticizing every man I came in contact with, I wouldn't have a chance anyway. Oh!"

Jane stopped their silly going at each other.

'How could Mia have forgotten about the Chemistry grade? She was freaking out as if it was the end of the world!'

Amazed by her daughter's speedy recovery, Jane wondered if what she did for her daughter was worth the trouble. Somehow Mia seemed to be in a better mood than usual.

"I talked to Mr. Bloom, well, I met him and talked, and he said that he would reconsider your grade."

"What! Seriously? You actually met him? How? Where?"

"It's a long story."

Jane felt that there was no need to tell Mia about their offense/apology ordeal. It felt now quite childish of both of them to have behaved that way.

"Wow... I never imagined that he would say anything like that. He is the most uptight, indifferent teacher, you know."

"Is he?"

Jane could see that he was uptight, but she didn't think that he was indifferent. Rather volatile, if anything, but he was genuinely interested in what she was telling him.

"Well, this is good news, right?"

"Yes, it's great news! I hope he lets me pass. I would be so happy if I get just six so that I can go to the next class with my friends."

"Well, let's hope for the best."

Then they smiled at each other, a rare moment of compatibility between the two of them.

"Oh, dear!"

Jane shook her head when they resumed putting the groceries in the fridge, and she checked the kitchen clock.

"I was going to make Japchae for dinner, but I don't think there is enough time."

"Oh, I love Japchae!"

Mia looked disappointed for a moment, and then she smiled at her mother again.

"No worries, Mom. We can have it when I am back on Sunday or next week. Oh, can we order pizza tonight? I know we have the frozen ones at home, but I fancy the proper ones, Mom. Can we have it delivered, please?"

Jane nodded in relief. Of course! That's the best thing she'd heard today! Let's do delivery! No need to do the washing up either and that would give her more time to prepare for BF4, Pieter's arrival.

***

When David came to pick up Mia, he sent a text on his arrival, and Mia walked to his car. It was one good thing that Mia was old enough, and Jane and David didn't have to face each other when Mia was switching house. Mia was perfectly able to handle most situations herself and was clear about what she wanted. There was no more need to check with the other parent if it was okay to send her to a birthday party. Mia decided what she wanted to do and where she wanted to be, and they both had to respect their daughter's wishes because she was, no other way to say it, no more a child.

Still, to Jane, Mia was a child, much to Mia's annoyance. Jane tried to suppress her anxiety whenever Mia went out with her mates. She was on good terms with her close friends, Nora and Esther, and their parents too, but Jane had to accept that you could not control or watch your teenage daughter's every movement. Not that Jane wanted to, but the world seemed to have become more violent and crazier. There were people with dangerous minds and intentions for vulnerable children. She remembered once she read an interview with a mother whose two grown-up children both passed away before her. One had an accident, and the other had cancer at a young age. What the mother said to the question of how she felt after all her children died stayed with Jane for years.

"Peace. I used to worry about my children all the time, even when they were all adults and had their own lives. About whether they were safe, healthy, and happy. Not a day passed without worrying about their well-being. Now they are gone, I don't have to worry about them. I know where they are. There is suddenly no more anxiety, only emptiness."

Of course, Jane wanted nothing to happen to her daughter, but she understood the mother's saying. Jane knew for sure she would worry about Mia until the day she was not on the earth anymore. Jane would most definitely worry about Mia even in her afterlife, following Mia on some white cloud everywhere.

With a pang of familiar grief every time Mia left, Jane went into the lounge. After ordering pizza, the only clean-up they had to do was to take the empty pizza boxes to the paper bin in the garden. Although Jane discovered later the rubbish that Mia left on the coffee table, cookie wrappings, and a finished can of coca-cola.

Now the BF4. Discussing the pizza choices, placing the order, and eating the pizza made Jane forget about canceling the appointment with Pieter. A date, but it felt more like an appointment to Jane. She'd had almost no experience regarding a serious relationship with men since her divorce. She wasn't a prude, Jane believed, as many men seemed to think she was. But she had to be careful because many patients of the "yellow fever" were out there. The men with "yellow fever" proudly came out, declaring, "All my girlfriends were Asian," and Jane couldn't run away faster. Those men actively looked for a relationship with Asian women because they had fantasies or fetishes about them. They seemed to imagine Jane being shy and passive in bed, a kitten-like Femme Fatale, or both. This observation came to Jane from listening to them, not sharing the bed with them, though. It put her off when the men she was on a date with started to talk about some Asian food they liked, some Asian countries they visited for a holiday. They then ended the conversation with, "Well, I'm sure you are a wonderful cook, and I hope you will cook your food for me sometime!"

'I'm not any of that!' She wanted to scream. The most horrendous dinner table anecdote in the Netherlands was, "The fruits and food from far away are the most delicious, ha, ha, ha!" Dubious if they were referring to the exotic food or her at the table, Jane wanted to throw the plate to the laughing men.

But then why was she here in the Netherlands? Her choice to marry a European man, a foreigner to her, brought her here. She could have married a Korean man if she didn't like these anecdotes about Asian women.

When she started the long-distance relationship with David, her parents said, "Oh, Jane, I wish you wouldn't marry a foreigner and move far away from us."

She loved her parents and understood their concern, but still, she wanted to move away. She was in love with this great man, the most incredible man she'd ever met. And she also loved the Netherlands.

How could she not fall in love with a country where everyone looked like a superman or superwoman, biking their way along the picturesque canals carrying gorgeous children in their cargo bike?

If Jane had stayed in Seoul, she would have had all her family, friends, and the job she loved. Jane worked hard for her career at the company. Her parents supported her education until she graduated with a bachelor's degree in commerce. Jane had only one older brother who was already married with children when she was growing up. Practically an only child, Jane admitted that her parents used to spoil her, mostly with love. They encouraged her to do everything she wanted to. She believed the world was as kind and limitless as her family showed her. Jane also went to England for a year to master the English language after her study. English was prominently required for a successful business life in the world of international commerce. That was when she changed the spelling of her name from 'Jae-in' to "Jane." She thanked her parent's foresightedness, which gave her a name easy in English too. She was content with her life in Seoul.

But she adored David. How could she not have loved him, too, who was in his immaculate suit and the most fashionable boots on the bike to his work? And he always came home with a bunch of tulips for her. Every time Jane saw him biking back with the flowers in one hand, her heart melted. David carried her in his hands those days. David let her be herself. That was the most crucial thing to Jane in a relationship because there were enough other anecdotes about women and what people expected her to be in Korea.

Before David, Jane had had only Korean boyfriends. As caring as they were, they wanted to design Jane's life. They tried to adjust Jane's studies and then her career to fit in with theirs. They urged Jane to join their family as if she had to leave her own. Jane was too young and ambitious and loved herself too much, so she chose to be free.

Then with David, he had no obligation to change her. David lived a separate life from his family, and only visited them around Christmas. As for Jane's career, he didn't interfere there either, saying, "Do as you want, Jane." Jane thought they were two equally independent people in a relationship.

She was stupidly trapped in the old memories when she was about to meet a new man. Jane felt more and more anxious as eight o'clock, the time when Pieter had agreed to come was getting near. She checked if the white wine she bought earlier the day had cooled enough. Her stomach twisted at the sight of the bottle. 'Please, please let me become normal again.' Jane prayed to someone, something around her that she couldn't quite identify.

When Pieter rang the bell and Jane opened the door, she remembered why she had invited him. For the last three months, Jane had known him as a very compliant, rather sombre man after his divorce. Whenever they met, they talked about nothing other than broken homes and uncontrollable teenage children. How they felt guilty towards their children, how they regretted their mistakes in their marriages, and how they didn't feel hopeful things would improve soon. When Pieter dissolved into tears at the café the last time they met up, Jane decided to invite him to her house so that they could talk without people peering at his distorted face.

It was understandable. Pieter had only been divorced for two years, and his two daughters were still just twelve and eight. Having gone through her very own hell called divorce, Jane didn't want to change with Pieter. Every divorce was different as every marriage was, and Pieter's divorce was another drama than hers.

Pieter and his ex-wife sold their massive house in a famously affluent village, and Pieter moved into a modest flat. He was paying the maximum alimony to his ex and children and practically had just enough to live on by himself. But what he missed more than his enormous house and the opulent salary was his children.

Being a devoted father, he used to spend all his time with his daughters after work, and now he only saw them for two days every two weeks. The daughters missed him too and cried when he took them back to their mother's house after the weekend, but things had changed recently when his eldest turned twelve.

She heard from her mother that Pieter had had an affair before they got divorced, and she blamed him for the breakup. Whereas, as far as Pieter was concerned, their marriage had already been broken for a long time, but he couldn't really explain it to his daughter. The little sister also joined her sister's front line, and now they refused to see him, which caused him to break down without warning.

"Hi, Jane," Pieter smiled woefully and gave her three kisses. "I've brought you some flowers."

"Oh, thank you. Come in."

Jane quickly put the flowers in the vase and asked Pieter, who sat obediently on the sofa, "Would you like to have coffee or something else?" 'Please say coffee, please!' she thought.

Pieter must have heard her plea and said, "Coffee would be fine, Jane."

Jane, feeling a lot more at ease now that Pieter settled for coffee, brought out some biscuits with it and sat next to him.

"How are you Jane, is your daughter at your ex?"

Jane almost felt guilty to say yes.

"He is lucky that he can still see his daughter."

'I don't know how long that will last, though,' Jane thought, but she didn't express her doubt to Pieter.

"I still don't know why Miriam told the girls about my affair. She acknowledged at the time that it had nothing to do with our divorce. She even said that she caused it as much as I committed it."

Pieter put his head in the hands.

"I mean, what good would it do to two little girls like ours... I am so miserable about it."

Jane had heard this about thirty times now. But she still dutifully nodded comfortingly. "It is difficult, Pieter. We can't always explain to children what happened in our marriage and how we got divorced. They wouldn't have understood, and it would only have made them more confused. And it is a difficult age too. I remember when Mia was twelve. Nothing I said made sense to her, and everything made her angry."

"Did it get better now that she is older?"

Jane thought about it.

"In some ways, yes. She is fifteen now, no more a child. She might understand things if I told her, but still, you don't want to burden your child with your story. Your daughters will come around because they know what a loving father you've been to them all these years. Keep your faith and hang around. Let them know that you are always there. I'm sure they miss you. Sadly, the grown-ups mess up for children and try to influence their loyalty, but the children always love both parents."

Jane put her hand on his shoulder confidently.

Pieter took her hand and held it in his hands.

"You always make me feel better when I talk to you. I wonder why more ex-partners couldn't think like you. Most people turn into enemies when they get divorced. I feel so hopeless sometimes. We are still fighting over the same things even after the divorce."

Jane squeezed his hand in agreement.

"I know. It is a shame. I am talking about it like it was easy, but of course, it wasn't... Oh!"

Jane stopped talking when Pieter pulled her hand tenderly towards him and kissed her full on the lips.

It was the first time Pieter kissed her properly, and Jane wasn't sure if she was pleased. She wasn't disgusted, but she didn't feel her head spinning or her knees weakening.

When Pieter's hand moved down from her shoulder, Jane extracted herself from him and gently took his hand off her.

Pieter seemed more disappointed than Jane could estimate.

He wiped his face helplessly.

"I'm sorry. I didn't know how you would feel about me kissing you."

"It's okay. I wasn't sure either until you did."

Jane smiled, and Pieter did his best to smile back, but it didn't work very well.

"You don't like me that way, I guess? I must have bored you witlessly with my pathetic divorce sagas every time we met."

"Oh no, you didn't bore me. I offered to listen to you because I felt for you. I found it hard to be a divorced parent and hard to date as a divorced parent. We always ended up talking about our children and ex's, didn't we? I think the time when we talk about other things will come, and then we must be ready for a new relationship. I've been divorced for much longer than you, but I realize I can't do that yet."

"But it's been ages for you, Jane! Does that mean I've got another six years until someone likes me?"

Pieter pretended to look horrified, but Jane saw that he was making a joke.

"You know very well there are plenty of people who also find a new love or enjoy a series of exciting relationships soon after divorce. I am a disaster when it comes to having fun, not a good example for you."

"I would miss talking to you, though."

Pieter smiled a little bigger smile than before.

"Me too. We can still talk when you need to."

"I wish you'd want to be something else than just my therapist."

"I'm not a therapist! I've got more issues than most people, and I struggle too."

"But how come you are so self-sufficient? You don't look like you need a pep-talk from anyone. How do you do that?"

"Oh... I don't know, Pieter. I didn't have anyone to talk to for a long time and just read books and listened to songs. Other than that, I don't know how I got through it."

"Books and songs... Maybe I should try that too, although I've never been into reading or music. Have you got a piece of advice for a lazy bum like me?"

"This too will pass...."

"This will pass?"

"Yes, Pieter. It's Peter Himmelman's song. Listen to it when you are home, and don't lose your faith in your daughters."

Jane was reading a book in bed later, and when she was turning off the bedside light, she saw a message from Pieter.

Hi, Jane, thank you for the best piece of advice that anyone's given me. I will be playing this song over and over, and I will be thinking of you too. I hope you find someone as kind and wise as you soon. Xxx Pieter."

CHAPTER 2
FRANK

Frank was discombobulated when Jane left him in the hall. It was as if she had come and thrown some random balls at him. One had hit him hard in the face, and he was lying on the floor with some head injuries.

Who was this woman firing such deep, soul-provoking questions at a stranger? How come he felt that he could talk with her about his life when he couldn't talk to anyone closer to him?

Not that he had lots of close friends. Frank had always been a bit of a cynic, whereas other people were concerned. Perhaps it had to do with his family atmosphere that they couldn't talk about what his grandfather went through. Frank felt that there was always a dark cloud hanging over their house.

'Just tell us about the time, please, granddad. You are suffocating us like this!'

Frank was sullen about his grandfather's inability to talk until he read Italian chemist Primo Levi's books at the age of fourteen.

"We who survived the Camps are not true witnesses... We are those who, through prevarication, skill, or luck, never touched the bottom. Those who have, and who have seen the face of the Gorgon, did not return, or returned wordless."[2]

Only then could Frank understand his grandfather's silence and grief, so great that no-one else could imagine its depth.

Frank gorged on Levi's books as a boy would indulge himself at a sweet shop. And just like Levi, he decided to study Chemistry. It was impossible not to be captivated by chemistry when Frank read Levi's book, *The Periodic Table* − the best science book ever.

He threw himself into books and studying, and people only thought of him as a bookworm and uninterested in other matters. But Levi's words touched him in a way that he desired to touch the world. He wanted to go out of the lab and be with people. He wished to ignite that Chemistry in other students so he'd become

---

[2] Primo Levi, *The Drowned and the Saved*. Simon and Schuster Paperbacks, New York, June 2017, p. 70.

a teacher in the end, and he loved his job.

He wondered what kind of woman read Primo Levi. Frank would never have expected that he and Jane had anything in common. Did Jane have a partner? What did she do for work? What happened in her marriage with Mia's father that he was so aggressive towards her? What kind of kid was Mia at school?

He tried to remember what he saw of Mia in the class. She was one of the quiet ones and didn't stand out much. That wasn't a bad thing because usually, you stood out if you were attracting negative attention. In that sense, Mia was just an average kid, Frank thought.

But then, how could he know when he was deliberately trying not to get familiar with the students? It was now five years ago when it all happened, but Frank still felt all kinds of emotions coming up, just by thinking of how things went wrong, terribly wrong.

* * *

Jesse was in his last year's class. Frank had still been an enthusiastic teacher until then, and he noticed when Jesse seemed to struggle with his grades. Jesse had been one of the best students for the last five years, and Frank knew that Jesse liked Chemistry and wanted to study Science at university.

Frank asked Jesse if he could stay after the lessons and talk.

Just the two of them in an empty classroom, and Frank said, "Is everything alright with you, Jesse? You seemed distracted, I thought. With your grades, and also how you looked in the class."

Jesse was perplexed when Frank prompted him. Jesse never got extra attention from a teacher. He probably didn't need it being the model student.

After some reluctance, Jesse decided to open himself up. Because there was no one else he could talk to, and it was pressing him so gravely.

"Mr. Bloom, I'm... confused."

Frank raised his eyebrows. He anticipated that Jesse spent too much time at his football team. Jesse was a good player but had no intention to be a professional player, so Frank wanted to remind him of school's importance at this critical moment. Jesse needed to pass the exam at the end of the year and get his diploma to enter university. Somehow Jesse's confusion didn't sound like it was between school and football.

"What are you confused about?"

Jesse looked up into Frank's eyes. Jesse was tall, but Frank was taller. Jesse's agonizing eyes seemed to ask, "Can I trust you? Can I tell you about my troubles?"

Then Jesse nodded as if he was saying, "Yes, I trust you. You are different. You showed me how Chemistry was fascinating, which used to be my least favourite subject before you."

So he told Frank.

"I am confused about who I am. Whom I like, actually. I had a girlfriend last year, and I did not doubt that I liked girls. Then..."

Jesse's eyes dropped down to the floor.

"I have this feeling for Mark."

"Mark? In our class?"

Jesse nodded resignedly.

"Yes."

"What kind of feeling is it?"

"I... I think I fancy him."

Frank swallowed quietly. This wasn't really his area of expertise, but he had to try to help Jesse.

"But, there's nothing wrong with it?"

"No?"

Jesse looked surprised and relieved at the same time.

"Of course not. Nothing is wrong when a person likes the other person, whether they are of the same sex, different sex, or both."

"Well, not according to my parents, though."

Frank knew that Jesse's parents were religious and strict Christians.

"Have you talked to your parents about it?"

Jesse let out a nervous laugh.

"As if! They would send me straight to the church to 'cure' me. They think homosexuality is a disease."

Frank was aware that although the Netherlands was one of the most tolerant countries towards homosexuality and other sexual orientations, in real life, even here and in the year 2010, it was a struggle for many people to come out of the closet.

"So, what do you wish to do with your feelings then, Jesse?"

"Well, nothing, I guess. I know that my parents will kick me out of their house, and my football team will also shun me. It is such a macho world, you know. No football player has dared to come out all these years, which doesn't even make sense if you think about it. I can't tell anyone about it, for now, well, except you, Mr. Bloom."

Frank nodded at Jesse solemnly. He understood Jesse's fear. Frank, as a bit of the black sheep of the family himself, knew how it felt when you were not accepted as you were. But he was glad that Jesse had confided in him. Now Frank took him under his wing, and they would think of the best strategy for Jesse.

Frank didn't believe a hard way of coming out in Jesse's case was a good idea. Jesse wasn't sure of his feelings 100 percent. He could both like men and women. He was still very young, only seventeen, and had all the time ahead of him to explore and find out. Soon. Not now. It would be easier to investigate his sexuality if he was not dependent on his religious parents and living in their house. When Jesse finished high school successfully in the coming year and went to university—where he would be studying Science—Jesse could experiment and discover who he was and what he wanted.

"I've got an idea."

Jesse looked up at Frank hopefully.

"Why don't we wait, just for now, to search who you are or whom you like, as you said. I can't imagine the trouble with your parents when they find out. I don't think their belief that it is wrong to like a man, or both a man and a woman would do you any good. You need the time and freedom to explore your preference, and for that, you need to leave your house. Once you are at the university, you will be able to do all that. Let's call it your "escape plan." What would you say?"

Jesse seemed relieved that Frank was not urging him to go out and fight with the whole world. He nodded at Frank eagerly and smiled for the first time since they started the conversation.

"Yes. I think that is a good idea. If I told my parents now, it would only make things worse."

"I think so too. You have all the time of the world once you are out of the house and live independently."

"Thank you, Mr. Bloom. I don't know what I would have done if it wasn't for you."

"I'm always here if you want to talk to me. Let me know how things go, okay?"

"Yes, I will. Thank you, Mr. Bloom."

"You can call me Frank."

Jesse smiled and left the classroom with a much more relaxed face and confident posture.

For the rest of the year, Frank and Jesse stayed close. Frank found it fulfilling that he was the listening ear to a student in need.

Frank checked with Jesse regularly if he was feeling good and doing well with school. Jesse sent him messages if he felt insecure about his future, and Frank tried to assure him that everything would be fine.

"Hi, Frank, I felt a little down today. Wondering if our 'escape plan' will work out well. It disturbs me that nobody knows who I am, how I am."

"Hey Jesse, of course it will, and you will have a great life soon. It's just a bit of 'Grit your teeth and bear it' time at the moment, I know, but in a few months you will be exploring and experimenting with who you really are. Hold on there, and believe in yourself. I do."

The exams were coming closer, and Jesse engaged in the final sprint. Frank thought that Jesse would tell him if something was up. Frank wasn't overly concerned when Jesse went quiet for a while because he knew Jesse was studying diligently. Jesse was on track.

But he wasn't. Frank found out that Jesse had fallen in love hard with a boy, his teammate on the football team. Other teammates caught them in the changing room. The two of them were humiliated and kicked out of the group. The boy whom Jesse wanted to risk it all for said he didn't have the courage to be gay. When Jesse came home, his parents heard what happened. They said they would pray for forgiveness for Jesse's sin, and Jesse would be cured of his illness. Their son—a perfect son for any Dutch Christian parent—couldn't be gay. He was just confused, that was all. When Jesse didn't come down for dinner that evening, his parents found him in the attic. He had used his scarf from the football club.

Frank's friendship with Jesse became a subject of speculation. Jesse's parents found Jesse's diary which said that Frank was the only one he could talk to. Jesse wrote that Frank encouraged him to be himself. And Jesse felt that he could confide in Frank about anything. Then there were many text messages which Jesse and

Frank had exchanged after school about exploring and experimenting. About leaving his parents and their house.

Jesse's parents concluded that Frank got the idea of homosexuality into Jesse because he liked the boy. Frank was responsible for their son's death. Frank protested for all that his life was worth against the accusation. As much as he was fond of Jesse, he had never thought of him in that way. Frank lived with a girlfriend, and what better evidence could there be that he was heterosexual?

But people talked. So much so, Jesse's death was investigated by police. Mr. Bos, the school principal, was one of the few people who believed that Frank had nothing to do with Jesse's death. According to the principal, the only thing Frank did was to listen to the boy and be there for him. Even if the principal's trust in Frank was due to his (heterosexual) shenanigans that he'd witnessed at Christmas staff parties, Frank was grateful for his faith. Most people started to see him differently. Frank's whole life, from his childhood until adulthood, was examined through the magnifying glass. Was he tempted to experiment with his sexuality too? Was he also hiding his true identity, and was that why he encouraged Jesse to be himself? Did Frank fancy his student, who was only a minor? Why would there be smoke when there was no fire?

Frank had always believed in the fairness of Dutch pragmatism—until he was being judged. He would have agreed with everyone that there were always two sides to a story, and both accounts should be weighed equally.

'But what if my story is the right one? How come I should prove to the world that I am wrongly accused?'

Even he could see his pathetic reflection in other people's eyes, so he stopped whining for justice.

Then Else, Frank's girlfriend, said she couldn't go on like this. Not that she wasn't convinced of his side of the story, she emphasized. But the stress caused by the investigation and people's speculation was becoming too much for her. Frank felt failed as a man when she left, wondering if he wasn't masculine enough for his girlfriend, so that she couldn't be sure of his sexuality.

It never seemed like it was going to end. Frank seriously considered finishing his life as Jesse did. He didn't because if he did kill himself, people would think that he was responsible for the whole thing. Frank would not be able to defend himself anymore. The other thing that kept him just hanging on was, again, Primo Levi's words. Frank knew, as excruciating as his pain was, it was nothing compared with Levi's. Levi had experienced, more than anyone, how fragile man's humanity was in this world.

Nearly two years after Jesse's death, the police closed the case. Jesse's parents, still convinced of Frank's involvement and disappointed with the dropped claim, moved to a different part of the Netherlands. It looked like things were slowly getting back to normal to the outside world, but Frank didn't buy it. He still heard gossip flowing around between colleagues, students and parents of the school, and even the village people. Frank could feel it in the air. But he had no choice. He couldn't flee because then it wouldn't just be in the air, it would become the solid truth. He'd seen how ruthless people could be. He'd learnt who his real friends were and who were not. He had only four people who were still left from his old life, his parents, his older brother, and Mr. Bos—Ron, as he insisted on being called. Everyone else had turned their back on him, and he didn't want them either.

So here he was, more cynical than ever. He couldn't love his job as he did before. Deep in his heart, he knew he still wanted to be a teacher, but he could not admit it to himself. Wasn't that what caused the problem, too, because he wanted to help Jesse in the first place as a good teacher? Three more years passed now, and he didn't feel a grudge against Jesse anymore. There were times that he was angry about the black hole that Jesse had pushed him into, but he was primarily sad for the boy. How Jesse must have been devastated that day. His love abandoned him, and his parents would never understand him. Frank stopped blaming Jesse long ago, and only sorrow and pain were left in him.

***

Frank stayed where Jane made the space for sitting on the couch. For hours in the dark after Jane had gone. What happened in the last five years flashed through his head. When she asked questions, "Why do you not like your job?" and "Why are you still there?" it shook him as a storm shakes a tree.

And he'd wanted to tell her. He'd only just met her, and she was there for some hideous reason, caused by his reckless self-defense mechanism. But by some unexplainable urge, he wanted to rip his heart out to her. He wasn't prepared to be touched by such a gentle yet firm soul. He wasn't sure if it was lust, what he felt for Jane. Frank wanted to rip off his clothes for her, too, so it could have been just that. But he most wanted to bury himself in her arms. He longed to stroke, smoothen, and feel her woollen dress and silky black hair.

He wanted to tell her that he was miserable at his work because he couldn't be himself. After Jesse died, the last thing he wanted was to connect with the students. He was there to teach them Chemistry but nothing else. Frank built a wall around him so no student would ask him for advice or help. To keep him safe, he behaved more unfriendly and impossible. He counter-attacked if he felt threatened. He knew it had made him a very unpleasant person to be around as it had led Jane to his apartment that afternoon.

And he also wanted to tell her why he was still there at school. He couldn't leave and become guilty. He wasn't responsible for Jesse's death, and he couldn't give in to people who didn't believe him. Maybe that was what Frank saw and felt with Jane. They were the same, fighting to stay against all odds. For Jane and Frank, life would be a lot easier if they just went away. Jane could go back to her country and not have to face her angry badmouthing ex-husband. Frank could get another job and leave this place and start again. But they were still here, to preserve something. It was, Frank realized, their integrity.

CHAPTER 3
MIA

Mia arrived at David's house, a quarter of an hour drive from her mother's little cottage. Dad lived in the house where her mother and Mia used to live together before the divorce. Their old family home was a much grander place, in an area full of freestanding villas with private driveways. Dad also drove a much bigger car, he was a fervent lover of fancy sports cars, and he changed his vehicles every few years in the same way as he did his GF's.

If only had he had a big enough heart, too, Mia wished. Since the divorce, she had never felt at home in her dad's house, except the time when Monica was there. She felt like a guest even in her old room, where she had spent the first seven years of her life. Nora and Esther would freak out if they saw her dad's house. But Mia didn't plan to take them here. Her father said to bring her friends, but couldn't he imagine how much Mia would be sweating, paranoid in case her friends spilled some juice on his precious couch? David must be unaware of this obvious reason because he kept asking when he could meet Mia's friends. He could take them somewhere really lovely, too, and they would have lots of fun. A kind offer from her father, but Mia never wanted to show her father to her friends. Not that he would embarrass her by flashing his money, but by slagging about her mother. David never stopped saying bad things about Mia's mother. It didn't matter whether they were close acquaintances or strangers whom he had just met in a barbershop, whether they were interested in his story nor not. He would grab every chance, every ear, as long as they could hear him. That embarrassed Mia more than anything in the world. She could see some people cringe at his words. David always told the same stories and made people agree that Mia's mother was the most disgraceful woman in the whole wide world, even when they had never met her. That her mother was a South Korean didn't help either; some idiots immediately put her mother in the same category as Kim Jong-un when David revealed his ex-wife's ethnicity. The two fixed things that her father repeatedly advertised about her mother were that her mom was a slut who would sleep with anyone and a thief who stole his money. He told people this even when Mia was there.

Mia was amazed that people believed his account. To Mia, it didn't make any sense. Suppose her mother was all that, why would she be still here, raising Mia alone and having to put up with this witch hunt around her? Where was the money that she allegedly had stolen, and where were the men? Mia hadn't seen any trace of hidden money or men in her mother's life. Mia was old enough now to laugh at her father's fables behind his back. Still, it disturbed her endlessly. It used to really upset her when she was little, mostly just after they got divorced. Whenever she went to her father, she cried with her head under her pillow, missing her mother and being scared of his anger and bitterness. Mia couldn't believe that what her father was accusing her mother of was true, but why would a big and important man like her father say such horrible things about her mother? Her mother had been only loving and kind to her all of Mia's life.

Well, maybe too loving and too kind sometimes, Mia sighed. Mia had read in a book—she couldn't remember which one anymore—that God gave mothers because he couldn't be everywhere. Mia couldn't agree more. It felt like Jane was around, even when she was physically somewhere else. Her mother seemed capable of getting in the back of Mia's head too. Jane detected when Mia was hurt, sad, or upset from miles away. Mia wondered as a little child if Jane had inserted some kind of chip in Mia's body. The chip must have told what was up with Mia since her mother seemed to know "everything" that happened at school. But thankfully, Mia grew up, and the chip must have expired. Now there were parts of Mia's life that Jane didn't know anymore. Because if Jane still knew everything, there wouldn't be any life for Mia, would there?

Mia wanted to go straight to her room when her father let them in and turned off the alarm. Dad asked if she wanted to watch a film with him, and she said no, she was tired and going to bed. He looked unhappy, but instead of getting angry with her, he made a sad face.

"You never want to spend any time with me these days. What is up with you? You don't love your father anymore? After everything that I have done for you. For fifteen years, I've been looking after you."

Mia by now knew how to handle the situation when he was

playing this sort of card.

"Don't be silly, Dad. I am just tired. I am usually tired when I come here because I had the whole week of school. I will see you tomorrow. Sleep well."

Then she gave him a quick kiss and went to her room.

Once in her room, Mia shuddered behind the closed door and let a long sigh out. Even giving a peck on his cheek was getting too dreary.

When did this all happen? Mia used to worship her father. She still remembered the shock when her mother came to pick her up from a sleepover at her best friend's house eight years ago. When Mia got in the car with Gomi—her teddy bear—in her arms, she saw that her other stuffed animal friends were sitting in the back of her mother's car as if they were all going on a road trip. Then her mother told Mia that they were not going home but to a holiday house and would stay there for the whole summer holiday.

"But what about papa?"

Mia cried when her mother said no, it would be just the two of them.

Mia saw that her mother got distraught when she begged her to go back and pick daddy up and drive to the holiday house together. Her mother stopped the car at the side of the motorway, on the hard shoulder. Mia was stunned to see her mother was crying too.

"Mia, I'm sorry that daddy cannot come with us. I'm sorry that we won't be living together anymore. I know how much you love your dad... and your school and friends. I promise it won't change. After this holiday, you will see your dad and go to him and stay in your old room regularly."

"But, why, mama? Why are we not together anymore?"

Mia had never seen her mother so devastated.

Her mother closed her eyes and didn't say anything, just held Mia to her chest and stroked her hair.

Mia pulled away because she couldn't breathe in her mother's tight hug. Her mother whispered, "Mama doesn't love papa anymore. And you need to love each other when you live together."

Mama not loving papa any more? This was unthinkable!

Mia had never seen her mother arguing with her father. She

had never even raised her voice to him. Her mother's announcement was unimaginable. It felt like the end of the world to Mia.

"But, why do you not love papa then? I love papa, and I love you. I want both of you to stay together with me!"

"I know you do, Mia. But I want to be a good mama to you, the best I can, and I can't do that with papa. I can't."

"But papa still loves you, right? Papa doesn't want you to go away?"

Mia's mother stared into the car window. The other cars were passing them fast, making lots of noise, while her mother's little car trilled like a mournful melody.

"Papa might think he loves me, but it is not love to me. Papa's love is not good to me."

"But, poor papa!" Poor papa. That was the thought that overwhelmed Mia for so long.

"I don't understand what you are saying, mama. I don't know why you are leaving papa, but I don't want to lose him."

"You won't lose him, Mia. We are not going anywhere. You will see him as much as you want, and you won't lose your father. It's only natural that you don't understand this big people stuff. You will understand more when you are older."

***

When Mia went back to her old house after the summer holiday, everything was changed. The house felt empty, her father was a broken man, and he cried when he saw Mia.

"Oh, my little girl! I thought I'd never see you. I thought your mother had taken you away from me forever. How much I missed you and how much you have grown in the last six weeks!"

Mia's heart went out to him.

It was weird in the beginning at the holiday house, and Mia missed him. But soon, Mia got used to having just her mother with her because it often used to be just the two of them. Her mother took Mia to South Korea every few years, and it was always her mother who was home and looked after her. So after the first week, Mia made new friends at the holiday park and almost had forgotten about her father.

But when she came back and saw how much her father had changed, Mia felt guilty that she had got used to not having him

Jane, Frank and Mia   54

around. He had diminished to a shadow of the great man Mia had once looked up so much. Mia saw that her mother had taken the photo of her that had hung in the lounge. Mia's photo had been taken in a professional studio and was one of the few items that her father allowed on his modern lounge wall.

She felt so bad at her father losing the picture.

'Poor papa is all alone!'

So when he disappeared into the kitchen to make their dinner, Mia grabbed her crayons. Daddy put her favourite programme on the television, but Mia had a more important task. She drew her father and her in a big red heart on the wall where the picture frame had been.

The first time Mia went to see her father alone was also the first time she'd seen a different side of him. Mia understood that she shouldn't have drawn on his wall, but she still couldn't understand why he didn't see what Mia was trying to do, showing her love for him. Now Mia was fifteen, but she still didn't understand it.

***

After throwing herself on the bed, Mia took out her mobile phone and hesitated.

Can she text Daan now? It wasn't that late. But she knew he would be hanging out with mates in the city, and she didn't want to get disappointed when he couldn't talk to her on the phone.

Instead, she texted Nora.

"At Dad's now, rescue me!"

Nora answered her straight away.

"Poor you, I wish you were at your mom's, and we could hang out tomorrow."

"It will have to wait until next week. How are you?"

"The same, watching the series at home."

"Okay, won't disturb you. Enjoy the series. Xxx"

"xxx. It can't be that bad there, can it? Hang on there, girl."

Mia turned off the phone and thought of Daan again. She never told Nora and Esther about Daan.

She knew that they would be shocked if they found out Mia had something going on with Daan. Not that Daan was a bad boy or anything. He was the sweetest boy Mia had ever talked to. But Daan's mates, the gang, as he called them, had a bit of reputation. Mia didn't know what exactly they had a reputation for. Daan said he wasn't telling her if she didn't know by herself. But he did say that he didn't want to show Mia to his mates because some of them were indeed bay boys.

Daan was two years older, and he was in the last year of high school. Mia got to know Daan on Instagram when he sent a dm, a private message four months ago.

"Hi! You also go to Maerlant High School, right? I thought I recognized you. I saw you on Milan's posting and wanted to say hi."

Mia's heart jumped at the message. It was the first time that she'd got a dm from a proper, real-life boy. Her heart was on a rollercoaster when she checked his account and saw his photos. He was so good-looking! Mia couldn't believe anyone so gorgeous would show an interest in her.

Because she didn't think she was pretty. She looked different if anything. She had her mother's eyes, big brown monolid eyes like Mulan. Her hair was blond when she was born, like her father's, but became redder as she got older. The combination of her Asian eyes and non-Asian hair made a weird effect, Mia grimaced. People didn't know where to place her. Her eyes screamed clearly Asian, Chinese! But her strawberry-blond hair and complexion that was fairer than any pure Caucasian person were confusing. Mia's mother said she thought Mia was enchanting, but Mia hated how she looked. She didn't think anyone would find her beautiful.

So Daan's messages delighted Mia. What's more, he said that he'd noticed her at school long before he dared to send the message. He said she was eye-catching and prettier than anyone he'd seen. He loved her eyes. Enchanting was the exact words he used, just like Mia's mother.

Their messaging went on obsessively, and they met each other secretly outside school. Mia closed her eyes when she thought of the kiss yesterday. It was Mia's first kiss, and she was still trilling when she remembered how it felt. Daan said last night that he wished that they were older.

"Older? How come?"

Daan sighed, and Mia knew that he was longing for her, wishing she was right in front of him to kiss again.

"So that we can live together."

Mia smiled at the thought. She didn't want to admit that she'd love that too, not too quickly.

"Won't you go away to a college and leave me alone then? You would meet more interesting girls at the college."

Mia teased Daan just to hear that he wouldn't think of it.

Daan laughed at Mia's provocation.

"No. I'm not going to a college, but not because of that. I never wanted to go to study. I wanted to work. So I can stand on my own feet and leave the house."

Daan told Mia briefly that his family struggled after his father's accident, and he wanted to be independent.

"I'm going to work for my uncle next year. He's got a private building company. As soon as I have my high school diploma, I will be earning my living."

Mia sighed in despair.

"God, I've got another two years until I can do that... how dreadful."

"That's why I said I wished we were older. But when I have my own place and earn enough money next year, you should come with me, and let's stay together."

"I will be only sixteen then, you're crazy!"

Mia laughed at his optimism affectionately. But to be honest, there was nothing she desired more. She wanted to get away from her father's bitter sentiment towards her mother and get at a distance from her mother's undivided devotion. To be on her own. To be a grown-up!

The time that Mia never wanted to be apart from her parents was gone. She was tired of them, both of them. Mia admired her father when she was little and thought he was a superhero who could do anything. And she loved her mother so much. So much so it hurt when she thought of her mother, mostly when Mia was away from her. But when they got divorced, they destroyed everything. They ripped her world apart.

How could they? Mia used to feel enraged at their selfishness. Mia had a perfect world, with a dashing father and a beautiful mother, and she loved them more than anything. They lived in this splendid house 'together.' Her father, whom she was so proud of, changed into a grumpy, sour man who would only slander her mother for everything she did and everything she didn't do. He'd simply become a toxic man. And her mother...

Mia didn't know what to feel about her mother. Before the

divorce, her mother was Mia's favourite person. Jane was different from other mothers at school, but it didn't bother Mia at all. Of course, Mom looked different from being a Korean, but Mia still thought her mother was the loveliest mother of all. Jane always looked after herself very well. She said it was her being a Korean. She said that the South Korean people put more effort into their appearance, and all those years of growing up in a society where 'the look is everything,' Jane still took great care of her clothing and religiously used the Korean skincare products that Mia loved trying on too. But it wasn't only in her looks that her mother was different. Mia was always wearing most clothing layers in the class because her mother thought it was a freezing day, whereas all the other children turned up in their t-shirts and shorts. Mia was the last one in the pre-school who could do her laces, much to the teacher's concern because her mother insisted on doing it for her. Jane was a Korean mother, physically and mentally, which meant an overprotective mother.

Now Mia was fifteen, almost a grown-up, and her mother's over-protectiveness got on her nerves. Mia wanted to break out of Jane's nest. Mia had always been independent, and Jane knew it because she told Mia the story when Mia was only two years old. Jane took Mia to a playground on the way home from a supermarket. Mia loved climbing the slide and coming down with an unstoppable giggle. They had fun for half an hour, and her mother wanted to go home, but Mia disagreed with her. After urging Mia to come with her for another half an hour—pleading then negotiating with sweets and all the other things that Mia liked, Jane gave up. Her mother decided to pretend that she was leaving and hid behind a tree in the playground. Mia's mother thought that Mia would change her mind if she disappeared from sight and would look for her mother. Her mother waited and waited, watching her daughter climbing up the slide for the hundredth time. She waited for her daughter to realize that her mom was gone and call out for her. No such thing happened for another fifteen minutes. It was Jane who got terrified that Mia had just forgotten her and would stay there forever. She came out from behind the tree, almost in tears, and begged her daughter to come with her. Mia did, thank god, only because she was done with the slide and wanted to have the soft ice cream that Jane had previously offered her from the nearby snack bar.

***

Mia snuggled against Gomi (Gom means "bear" in Korean, and Jane named Mia's teddy bear "Gomi") and thought again about Daan's kiss. When they left the bench in the park and started to walk towards the school, Daan's mate Simon spotted them.

"Hey, Danny boy! I see why you haven't been around! Is she your girlfriend?"

He gazed at Mia shamelessly. Mia didn't like the look that Simon gave her and almost visibly shuddered.

Simon was one of the bad boys, not even going to school anymore but still hanging out with his mates who did. He was the leader of the gang. He whistled and slapped Daan's back.

"Is she wicked! Is she real? I've never seen Chinese ginger!"

Mia stood frozen and now really shuddered from a fit of anger. She'd heard many things, but this was new and more offensive in many ways.

"And what are you? Are you real? You'd better shut your foul mouth if you can't say one decent word!" Mia snapped at Simon, and all the boys there now turned around to check her out.

"You'd better say sorry, Simon. She is my girlfriend and doesn't deserve your rudeness." Daan's usually friendly face changed red, and he looked furious.

"Ah, okay, I will say sorry to you. Only because this Danny boy is my best mate and I know how he is when he is angry. Sorry!"

Simon didn't look sorry at all, but Daan turned to Mia and said.

"Let's go. Your lesson is starting."

Still unsure whether she had to accept such an insincere apology, but at the same time, too intimidated to talk to Simon, Mia left the gang with Daan.

When Mia expressed her anxiety about Simon, Daan said not to worry about his mate.

"He's usually harmless, Mia. Anyhow, he has nothing to do with you. Let's not waste our precious time together talking about him."

Daan was good at comforting Mia. He was also brilliant when she called him after crying to Mom about Mr. Bully on the phone.

"Don't worry about Mr. Bloom, Mia. I know him since two years ago, and he's not as bad as everyone thinks. I'm sure he will come around when your mother talks to him. It will be fine."

Daan made her feel so much better, and by the time Mom got home, she almost forgot about the horrible teacher.

Mia sighed in Gomi's ear. As soon as Daan had his own place, she would leave her parents and live with him. When her parents demolished her ideal world, they lost their entitlement to Mia's life, and Mia was going to disentangle herself from both of them. Mia found her father poisonous, an awful person to be around, and that was regretful and unfortunate. And her mother was pathetic. She had been sacrificing her life and happiness just to be near Mia.

The life and happiness that Mia had taken away from her mother. But Mia would not give up on 'her' life and happiness because of her selfless mother.

CHAPTER 4
JANE

At six forty in the morning precisely, David came down the stairs. All ready to go, in his navy striped suit. Jane was breastfeeding Mia, who was now seven months old. She said, "Good morning," and David came to the sofa and gave Jane and Mia a kiss.

He went to the breakfast bar, and there were muesli, yogurt, and fruits that Jane put out for him before she fed Mia. This was his weekday breakfast—whereas he would enjoy fresh warm croissants at the weekend—and he asked Jane while he was mixing everything in a bowl.

"Have you got a plan for today?"

Jane shook her head. There usually was no plan, and David knew it well.

"No, nothing. Except for going to the supermarket. What would you like to have for dinner?"

The same question every day.

"I saw that they had a special deal on beef at Albert Hein. Probably with potatoes?"

"Sure. I will get those. Anything else?"

David finished his breakfast in less than ten minutes and stood up.

"No. Just the usual."

He brought the bowl into the sink and had a glass of water.

"Gotta go. See you later. Have a good day."

He came to give the last kiss to Jane, and he thought of holding Mia before he went but knowing that Mia had just had her milk and was most likely to throw a bit on one of his best suits, he just kissed the baby girl's head.

"Bye, honey."

"Bye!"

When she heard the door closed in the hall, Jane whispered as an afterthought, "Have a good day too."

***

When Mia did her burp as expected and spilled some milk on Jane's worn-out top, Jane carefully put her daughter down in the spare baby cot next to the sofa. Mia was already asleep.

Jane moved with purpose as she planned her every movement

per second. David was always on time to leave at seven if the weather permitted. He was biking to his office in the city unless it was raining cats and dogs. Then he would go 20 minutes later in his car.

Jane walked to the hall and opened the cupboard under the stairs. There she picked a backpack, a similar design as David's one with the laptop pouch but slightly bigger. The bag was already half-filled.

Jane brought the backpack to the kitchen. She opened the fridge and got five little plastic bottles with her breast milk that she pumped out yesterday. She put those in a plastic bag in case they spilled. She took out a couple of ready-made baby food jars and wrapped Mia's spoon in a kitchen towel. She checked the time on the clock. She had to hurry.

She filled the rest of the bag with nappies and put wet wipes on top of them. Experience had taught her to have the wet wipes— the most essential item when you were out with a baby—within reach of her hand. She filled her plastic bottle with tap water. It would be very challenging to go to the toilet alone with Mia, so she wouldn't drink anything if she could help it, but you never know, she might get really thirsty.

That reminded her to visit the toilet before she left. After washing her hands, she stood before the mirror in the hall. Jane didn't recognize the woman in the mirror. She looked blank, as if she had forgotten how to feel anything. Even her tears had dried up, so Jane couldn't cry anymore. She needed to fill this woman with a life as she filled the backpack with Mia's necessary things.

Mia. She had to do this for both herself and Mia. She couldn't be a good mother and look after her well in this state. She had to go back home and become herself again.

Jane wore the baby carrier over her shoulder and waist. Then she put the backpack on her back. Jane wobbled a bit when it was a lot heavier than she wanted. Should she take some stuff out of the bag? But they were all basic things that Mia couldn't do without. She would have to carry them all. And Mia too. Baby on her front, backpack on her back.

Jane dragged her feet, walking to the baby cot where Mia was still blissfully sleeping, unaware of her mother's preparations. Jane lifted her daughter as carefully as if she was a glass doll and sniffed the baby's neck as she always did. She put Mia in the carrier, and her chunky legs dangled over Jane's nervous stomach.

She glanced at the clock again. Good, she was on time. The weight of the bag and the baby together pressed her down to the depth of the ground, but she took the step. When she closed the door and locked it with the key, something closed in her existence.

Jane waited for the bus to the train station. She had a plan and hoped it would work out. It had to work out. She couldn't buy any ticket beforehand in case David found out. She didn't have her own bank account since she stopped working when she was pregnant with Mia. Mia had almost been born two months too early, and the doctors had to stop her premature birth with an infusion of medicine. Jane was then bedridden until Mia came at around the expected date. Luckily Jane still had a bit of savings in her Korean account which she still kept from her working days in Seoul, and she took that cash out over the last few days when she went to the supermarket. She wouldn't use her bank card. That way, David couldn't track her down.

Or could he?

Jane knew that David of capable of many things. Things that she didn't know that he was capable of. In fact, she didn't know him until they got married and she moved to the Netherlands two years ago.

***

Jane met David when she was twenty-four years old. She was working for a Dutch insurance company in their Seoul office. They sent her to the headquarter office in Amsterdam for two-month-long training. She was staying in a nice hotel in the city center, and she had the time of her life exploring Amsterdam. When you hadn't got any strings attached, life was fun. She got on with her Dutch colleagues surprisingly well. With their directness, it was easier for her to know where she stood. She would have struggled if people had a hidden agenda in the office, but everyone just said what they thought, without much filter. Jane, already tired of the office politics back at home, loved the atmosphere at work. She felt the Dutch and the Koreans were a good match. After all, the Koreans were not called the Italians of Asia for nothing, with their pronounced emotions. The most frequent exclamation that Jane heard from her Dutch colleagues was, "You are so different from our Japanese colleagues!" Jane replied with a wink, "Yes, we have a bigger mouth than the Japanese, but not as big as yours!"

She devoured Amsterdam after work. She strolled the fascinating Jordaan area, flourishing with hip cafes and restaurants and exciting flea markets and antique shops. There were often wine and food festivals, and she was obsessed with the museums in the city. On the weekend, she enjoyed the nightlife with Mariska, one of the office's young colleagues. Together they visited the famous trendy clubs in Leidseplein and had loads of laughs. On one of these wild nights out, she bumped into David, a noticeable figure in his business attire among the drunken tourists.

The club where they met was new in the town, and everyone in the office talked about it. When Jane and Mariska arrived in front of "Billy Whoo" in Rembrandtplein after the usual Friday afternoon drinks with colleagues, there was a long line of people waiting to be admitted. It was only June, but Jane still shivered when the sun went down. Jane was dressed in the little black dress that she changed into after work. Jane didn't want to stand in the line and get frozen. She said to Mariska, "Let's go somewhere else," and the two of them left the queue. They walked towards the other clubs next to the Billy Whoo. When they passed the bouncer, a vast dark guy covered in black sunglasses and a black suit, he stopped them.

"Hey, you can go in right now."

And he made way for just the two of them.

Stunned by this sudden regal entry, they giggled and felt special.

'Maybe it was this black dress,' Jane was almost convinced.

They entered the place with great expectation. It was full of glittery people, and the music was deafening. The theme of the club was doubtlessly oriental. Mariska left Jane to fetch their drinks, and Jane leaned on the wall avoiding having the dancing crowd bumping into her. Standing alone, she felt awkward with people staring at her and the wall. When one of the drunk men winked at her, gazing at her and then the wall, Jane turned around. And she spotted what was painted on the wall.

It was a massive portrait of an Asian woman, like a doll. Her slanted eyes were accentuated, and she looked as if startled by something. The woman was wearing an exposing gown that looked like a kimono, and her ample breasts were luscious. Her face was glowing, like snow white, her lips full and dangerously red, and her hair darker than a raven. The woman on the wall looked like Jane.

When Jane realized the uncanny similarity between her and the painting, she didn't want to stand there anymore. She didn't want to be in this club where all the men were staring at her with apparent amusement.

She went to look for Mariska, and on her way to the bar, several drunk men stopped her, grabbed her shoulder, and swayed "Oooooh," like they found their toy.

"Get off me!"

Jane shook off the arms, finally reached the bar, and saw Marisake conversing with a man. They were shouting into each other's ears. She saw that Mariska was still holding the drinks in her hand.

She tapped Mariska's shoulder and took a ten euro note from her clutch. She also had to shout into Mariska's ear.

"For the drink! You have it for me. I'm going back!"

Mariska looked at her disbelievingly. "Really? How come? This is the best place we've been to lately!"

There was no point in explaining why Jane didn't like the club in this crazily overwhelming chaos.

"Never mind, you have fun! See you on Monday in the office. Get home safe, would you?"

"Yes! Shame that you are going. You get home safe, too."

Mariska seemed to be attracted to the man she talked to, so Jane just gave her three kisses quickly and left the bar.

Unfortunately, to leave the club, she had to pass the offending wall. She had to stop and wait for other people to pass when sturdy, clammy hands wrapped her waist from behind. The forceful fingers pushed her into the end of the wall, and she was gagging from her offender's horrible breath with alcohol. He was whispering something in Dutch in her ear while pushing her to the wall. He held her waist tightly, and Jane, even with her height, couldn't free herself from his grip.

Then the man turned her around under the painting, and she saw his face. Drooling under the glittering ball of light in the club, he smiled at Jane. Jane felt sick, looking into his frantic state. Jane realized that he was not only drunk but must have taken something else too.

She screamed for help, but the loud music muted it. No one was paying attention to them, and Jane was invisible inside man's grip. His dribbling mouth came close to her. Even when she knew it was useless, Jane screamed, "Don't! Help!" in her desperation.

His face almost touched her, and she closed her eyes, not wanting to acknowledge what was happening.

Smack!

Someone had pulled off the man, and he was mercilessly thumped on the floor. Only then people got interested and stepped behind to watch Jane, whose body was shaking and face covered in tears, the man on the floor, and another man, who must have thrown the guy to the ground.

The other man, the rescuer, put his hand gently on her arm and asked in English, "Are you okay? Do you know this man?"

Jane shook her head, but her legs were trembling more than her head.

"If you want to, I will take you home. You'd better leave here."

She nodded. She wanted to leave and wanted this man to bring her to safety. She was scared to be alone on the street and travel on the tram. The night scene of Amsterdam city overflowed with drunkards at its best.

"Okay, let's go."

The man held her arms, not as the other man did, and his touch was reassuring and steady.

He made the way easily. People seemed to recognize his air of superiority, and Jane was impressed even in her delirium.

Out on the street, Jane was freezing in her short dress again and shivered uncontrollably. Her teeth clattered, probably from shock too.

The man took off the suit jacket that he was wearing and placed it over her shoulders.

Then he led her to the taxi stand just a few meters away and opened the first taxi door in the line.

"Where to go?"

"The NH Hotel, please."

He repeated it in Dutch to the taxi driver.

She realized that he was still holding her hand in the car, and she couldn't remember how that happened. But she felt safe, protected by his hand's solid presence on her.

"Are you sure you are okay?"

He gazed at her with concern.

She nodded.

"Yes."

"In shock, though."

"Yes."

"Were you alone?"

Jane shook her head again.

"No, I came with a friend, but I wanted to leave."

"You didn't like the place?"

"No."

"I can imagine."

She looked up.

"You can?"

"Yes. The painting. It is in bad taste, to start with, and thoughtless and insulting in your case."

"It was. I didn't feel comfortable there. It made me a mere object in other people's eyes."

"Yes, I hope the club closes down soon."

Jane felt her body start to relax a bit from the shock. She smiled weakly at him.

"Thank you so much for helping me. I never had a problem like that until tonight, well, not to this extent. I didn't feel confident going home alone. Thank you."

He smiled too and said, "You're welcome."

After a few seconds of silence, he asked.

"Are you travelling?"

The hotel was only fifteen minutes away from the Rembrandtplein on the tram, and the taxi was even quicker. The car was nearly stopping at the entrance of her—now so familiar after two months—hotel. The man stopped Jane when she took out her purse to pay the driver.

"Don't."

"But,"

The look on his face made her give up protesting. He was oddly authoritative, but it wasn't unpleasant.

'Where is the "Going Dutch"?' Jane murmured in her head.

"Are you staying here for some time?"

Jane remembered his question and answered him just before she got off.

"Not anymore. I was here for training. It's almost finished, though. I am okay to go now. Thank you very much."

"Wait! I'm coming out to say goodbye. I don't even know your name yet."

It was the first time that Jane had looked at him properly. Under the bright light of the hotel entrance, he was tall, blond, and, well, quite handsome. A typical Dutchman, actually.

"Jane. Jane Lee. And yours?"

"David. David Hollander."

Jane smiled impetuously.

"That's a self-explanatory surname."

"Well, I thought better not leave any doubt about that."

He smiled at Jane, too.

"Then I am Jane, Jane South Korea."

"Lovely."

She felt something on her shoulder hanging and remembered his jacket.

"Oh, here you go. Your jacket. Thank you very much, again, for lending it to me."

"No problem."

With David Hollander's jacket off her, Jane was shivering again.

"You'd better go in before you freeze to death. That would be a shame after I saved you tonight. It's only June, though."

"I've been cold since I got here a couple of months ago, which was annoying. Well, goodbye, David. Thank you."

"No worries."

She went into the hotel. When she turned around, David waved and got in the taxi they came with, and it drove away.

The next day Jane woke up with a stiff body. She must have been in such a shock, and that must have impacted the muscles. She tried to roll from side to side on the bed and groaned from the pain.

Hotel breakfast was until 11 o'clock in the weekend, and when she saw the time, she gave up getting up for it. It was quarter to 11. Instead, she had a long shower, dried her hair, and put some moisturizer on her face. She would go out and have a brunch in the café near the hotel.

When she was getting dressed, the telephone in her room rang.

She almost dropped the cloth hanger because nobody called her in the room. Her company would usually contact her on the mobile phone, and it was the weekend too.

"Hello?"

"Jane? It's David. We met last night."

"David? How come are you calling me?"

"Well, I just wanted to check if you were okay."

"That's very kind of you. I am fine. Wait, where are you calling from?"

"I am at the reception of the hotel. I wondered if you'd come down to have lunch or coffee with me?"

Jane considered his offer and thought, why not? She was on her way out for lunch anyhow. And he had saved her from that dirty, drunken, stoned man. It was only fair that she treat him for lunch.

"Only if you let me buy lunch for you. It's the least I can do."

"I can let you do no such thing, Jane. It would be like I have invited myself for you to treat me. I will buy this one, and if you still want to buy me lunch, you can do that next time."

"Next time? But I will be leaving in ten days!"

Jane exclaimed in surprise.

"Still enough time for another lunch, I believe."

There wasn't really much point in arguing with him.

"Alright, I am coming down in a bit."

Jane decided to ditch her original outfit plan—a white shirt, jeans, and the red cardigan—since it resembled the Dutch flag, she realized. Perhaps David would see it as an homage to him. She quickly threw her cardigan on the bed and chose the beige trench coat. It was a light one that you could wear on a rainy day in the summer.

When she took the lift from the fourth floor, she inhaled deep in front of the mirror. She wasn't sure if this was some kind of date or not, and not knowing the nature of his interest made her anxious. But then, she wouldn't be in Amsterdam for long. "So, no pressure," Jane reminded it to herself.

There he was, in the lobby of the bustling hotel. He rose from a lounge chair when he saw Jane, and he looked genuinely pleased to see her.

'How can he remember me in bright daylight?' Jane wondered since he also looked different now from last night's goodbye scene. Of course, David would recognize Jane. Jane laughed at herself. She was the only Asian woman in the lobby.

He was still tall and blond, but his facial expression was much relaxed. Jane could see that he was excited too. He must also have been tense last night in a situation like that. Maybe that wasn't his thing either.

"Hi, Jane! How are you? You look fine, as you said."

He kissed her cheek three times, the Dutch ritual.

She gave him three kisses too.

"I'm good. How are you? It must have been some night for you, too."

"Well, I'm good. Although it's not every night that I save a lady in a club."

"I'm glad to hear that. I was concerned about the safety of nightlife in Amsterdam."

"I would still be careful if I were you. Enough crazy people out there, like everywhere else."

"Yes, I did find out."

Jane felt a bit awkward, standing there like they knew each other. She didn't know anything about him, and she just prayed he wasn't another weirdo in disguise, like a wolf in sheep's clothing.

But Jane already decided to take the risk with her rescuer. She was a risk-taker. That was how she lived until then, going to England to study English and accepting this job sending her to the Netherlands.

"Where shall we go? Are you familiar with the location?"

Jane shrugged, "I've only been to a few cafés here. I am happy to go anywhere."

David's face brightened at her answer.

"Then let's go to one of my favourite places. It's only a ten-minute walk from here. They have the most delicious sandwiches in Amsterdam."

"So, tell me about yourself."

They ordered their sandwiches, Jane the goat cheese with walnut and honey from the oven, and David salmon and cream cheese with chives. Sipping the fresh orange juice mixed with some vitamins, David gazed at Jane and smiled.

"Well, what do you want to know?"

Still unsure of this meeting's nature, Jane was cautious to open up too much to a stranger.

"I know you are from South Korea and here for training. What kind of training brought you here?"

"I work for a Dutch insurance company in their Seoul office. I had just started a year ago, and this was the training every outstation employee needed to take after their first year at the company."

"Did you say that you were going back in ten days?"

"Correct."

"Shame that we didn't meet earlier."

Jane looked at him in surprise. What did he mean by that, exactly?

"Well, if we had, it might have put me off from clubbing in Amsterdam, for sure."

Jane kept her tone light since she didn't want to fill in his intention, whatever it was.

"Well, that's not a bad thing, I guess. It could have saved you from more troubles."

"You don't sound very enthusiastic about the nightlife in Amsterdam. How come you were there last night?"

Jane didn't want to be lectured by anyone about what she should and shouldn't have done.

David seemed a bit taken by her challenging stare and stared back at her in amusement.

"Business. Business brings me to the weirdest places."

"So, what do you do?"

"I work in finance. Stock and investment, that kind of boring stuff."

"I see. Do you like what you do?"

It could have been a bold question if it was anywhere else, but this was the Netherlands, and Jane found this directness disengaging from the mundane going around the bush conversation.

David nodded.

"Yes. It earns me enough money that I can do pretty much anything I want to do."

"That's... good for you."

"Yes. And you? Do you like your job?"

Jane's face became animated.

"I do. I can't wait to go back to the Seoul office, although this was great too."

"Do you like Amsterdam?"

"I love it!"

"What do you love about it?"

"Oh, almost everything! The culture, the history, the buildings, and canals... The museums!"

"You are lucky that Rijksmuseum (the museum of the Netherlands) is finally open after such a long renovation. I had clients from other countries who wanted to visit it and complained, 'Is it still going on? It's taking forever!' Did you see it? Did you like it?"

"I did. But I loved the Van Gogh Museum better. I found Rijksmuseum too overwhelming, whereas the Van Gogh museum was more manageable and therefore for me more enjoyable."

"So, where is your favourite place in Amsterdam?"

Jane didn't need to hesitate.

"Anne Frank House."

"Really? Was it also 'enjoyable'?"

Jane shook her head thoughtfully.

"No, not in that sense. You just feel what was happening there all these years ago when you stepped in. It makes you feel humble to remember those who suffered. You must have been there, too, living here all your life?"

David nodded.

"Yes, vaguely. I think we went there with school. And I have to confess that I wasn't paying as much attention as you."

The café was packed, and their sandwiches arrived much later than expected. Jane felt ravenous, and they both finished their lunch without further interrogation.

"Did you like yours?"

David asked when she sighed in satisfaction.

"Yes. It was amazing. Yours looked nice too."

"It was. Coffee?"

"Yes, please."

"Which one would you like?"

"Small latte, please."

One large latte and one small latte arrived, and David resumed his questions.

"Are you seeing anyone in Seoul or maybe even here?"

Jane was startled by his inquiry and shook her head.

"No. And you?"

"No. That's wonderful news."

"Oh. Why?"

"I wanted to ask you out."

"Really? How come?"

"Well, I think you are gorgeous. I felt so when I saw you last night."

"I don't think it was a pretty sight, though."

"Not what happened, but you were, nevertheless."

"Oh."

"And I feel this massive responsibility to keep you safe from all those crazy people. I don't want to think what would have happened to you if I hadn't intervened."

Jane shuddered at the thought too.

"I'm grateful that you saw me there and helped me out. I screamed for help, but of course, no one could hear it. How did you hear me?"

"I didn't. I just happened to be watching you because I thought you were beautiful."

"Oh."

Jane was flattered by his remark but didn't know what to say.

"What kind of man are you looking for?"

David smiled at her inquisitively.

"Well, the truth was that I wasn't looking for a man at all."

David raised his eyebrow disbelievably.

"You didn't go to club for that?"

"No! Of course not!"

Jane was exasperated at his assumption but then saw that he was just challenging her.

"I love going out to dance. I love to dance."

"Then let's go dancing together."

Jane stared at him hard.

'Do I like this man or not? I can't really decide.'

Jane wasn't sure what she wanted to do.

David was an attractive man, no doubt, and different from any of her ex-boyfriends, who were just boys compared to David. But he was also slightly more authoritative and protective.

"What kind of woman were you looking for?"

Jane asked him back to save time to think of an answer.

"I didn't know until I met you. I found out that I was looking for you."

After they left the cafe, David walked her to the hotel. When they said goodbye in the lobby, he said, "I know a place to take you. When can you come out with me next week?"

"Where is it?"

"It's a secret."

They met two days later, and he took Jane to Anne Frank House. Jane didn't know where they were going and was wearing her usual high heels. Walking cautiously on the narrow, old, steep stairs, Jane felt his hand on her arms, steadying her steps.

She stood in front of a wall and read what it said.

Ik weet wat ik wil (I know what I want)

Heb een doel, heb een mening (I have a goal, I have an opinion,)

Heb een geloof en een liefde (I have a religion and love.)

Laat mij mezelf zijn dan ben ik tevreden (If only I can be myself I'll be satisfied.)

"Are you okay?"

David asked Jane when she didn't move from the wall for so long.

Jane nodded and whispered, "I'm trying to memorize her words."

David's face came down to her ears, and his breath made her shiver, not from cold but from something else.

He whispered too.

"Don't need to. I will take you here as often as you want. Come back to me, Jane."

By the end of the following week, when Jane had to leave, he said, "You should come back, Jane. Is there any possibility, any chance at all, that they can bring you here? Please say yes, Jane."

Jane just smiled, thinking of the proposition that the headquarter office informed her last week. In a few months, they needed someone from the Seoul office and asked her if she would consider the position. She wasn't going to tell David yet, though. They've only just met. Or she might. She decided that she liked him quite a lot after all.

***

The bus to Amsterdam Central Station arrived, and Jane was abruptly pulled out of the reverie. She got on the bus with Mia on her front and the backpack on her back. She was relieved to find a seat with no other passenger. She sat with the bag on her back. If she took off her backpack, she wouldn't be able to put it on again. But she couldn't sit comfortably, and it was dangerous for Mia to be so close to the seat in front of her, so she took off the backpack in the end. Mia also seemed uncomfortable and woke up, but she fell asleep again when the bus started off.

Already exhausted on the first part of her itinerary, Jane doubted her plan. How ambitious was she to think that she could run away? How did she think she could manage the bus, two international train journeys—first to Brussels and then London, and another long-haul flight? She would have had to find a place in London to stay overnight with Mia and buy the flight ticket to Seoul from the airport. She had it all planned in her head and believed she could do it. She used to do things like this. She went on adventures. If she was still the same Jane before she came here, if Jane wasn't twisted and weakened in the course of her marriage, she could do it. Mia started to wake up and wiggled and cried in the carrier. Jane's breast was full and getting sore. She thought they were like two balloons about to burst. But she couldn't breastfeed her on the bus, so she tried to find one of the bottles in her backpack. Jane lifted the heavy bag beside her foot with one hand while holding the back of Mia's head with the other hand. She was self-conscious of her baby disturbing the peace of other passengers on the bus and was desperate to still Mia's hunger.

Struggling to fish out the bottle from a fully packed bag with one hand (impossible to use both hands sitting with a baby on your chest) with Mia screaming louder and louder as Jane couldn't locate one, Jane felt despair simmering from her belly. It was where Mia came from, where she and her daughter were connected. And the simmering misery soon swayed her whole existence like lava out of a volcano. She sobbed on the bus with Mia wailing and strapped on her sore breast, and that was when she decided to go back to their house.

* * *

By the time David came home in the evening, there was nothing to tell him about his wife and daughter's temporary deviation. David loved coming home every day and had a habit of stopping for a second when he got on his driveway. He stood there to admire his house. This house was his pride and joy. He'd constantly desired to live in a 1930s style old house with a character. When they found out Jane was pregnant, David decided to leave his downtown luxury apartment in Amsterdam and moved to this mansion in Amstelveen, a prosperous village just outside Amsterdam.

He let out a sigh in satisfaction. Everything was as it should be in the house too. Jane got the grocery from the Albert Hein supermarket and bought the beef on the offer. David preferred to handle the meat himself because he was better at grilling a steak. But Jane had already boiled the potatoes to perfection, and the broccoli was ready to be cooked briefly by the time David was done with the steak. While David had his dinner, Jane mashed the potatoes and broccoli and fed Mia on her IKEA baby chair— the only time David bought anything from there because the baby stuff was not fixed features in his house and disposable. Jane said she had a late lunch and wasn't hungry yet. David poured red wine into his glass, the same Chilean that was his favourite, and enjoyed the familiar taste. Life was good, as the slogan of Korean electronics company LG says.

David smiled lovingly at his wife, feeding his daughter and making the baby laugh with the airplane sound. David loved the fact that Jane needed him. He was the one who saved her from the beginning. She was where every man was circling her and eyeing her as an object of lust. She needed him here because she didn't speak the language and didn't know how things worked. She couldn't even make a call when she got a letter from the city council or tax office. He was her hero, savior, and guardian. She was nothing, no one at all without him in his home ground. And David loved that.

***

Many times since that day, Jane dreamt of escape. In fact, she escaped into that dream whenever she couldn't bear her reality. Her only lifeline was her daughter, her light and joy. Jane did her best not to show her grief in front of her child. Every day Jane knew that she'd made the right choice watching Mia growing. To her daughter, papa and mama were everything. Their daughter grew up in a house and a neighbourhood that everyone was envious of, and Mia had everything she needed. David and Jane were the fences that safeguarded little Mia's life. Together, the three of them were a picture of the perfect family.

At the beginning of their marriage, David and Jane fought often, but thankfully Mia didn't get any of that period. The first couple of years were tiresome as Jane tried to adjust to her marriage, motherhood, and the new country. Jane had to rely on David for everything, and she hated it. She used to protest when their way of doing things was different, but she could never win. Jane couldn't argue when David said that this was his country. He was the one who knew best, even if it was the most mundane, petty things like groceries and maintaining the household.

"Jane! How many times have I said we should only buy the food we are going to eat today? I want to have the freshest products every day, and we don't need to stock up our cupboard like it is wartime. And haven't I told you not to use toilet paper and wet wipes to clean things up? It's a waste of money, and you are too extravagant!"

"David, I don't want to go to the supermarket every day to provide the freshest products for you. You are not a sheik, and I'm not your servant, although you seem to believe we are. I have a baby to look after! All by myself! And that's also why I use those to clean up simply because I don't even have the time and energy to find the mop and leave the baby alone while cleaning. I don't even know why I have to defend myself for this!"

"God, Jane, why don't you just listen to what I say and do as I say? What do you know about life here? If you followed my instruction, you would have saved yourself from making mistakes. Why are you always making it an issue?"

"Because I have my opinions too. You might know more about life here than me, but I also have a brain to think and am equipped with common sense. Don't say that I only have to listen to you. You need to listen to me, too! We are equals. Just because I am living in your country, you can't control what I believe and feel. I decide for myself!"

"I don't need you to play the smart pants with me. I needed a wife who would follow me and be compliant. I thought you, considering where you're from, would be different from a Dutch woman. I was so sick of their attitude—"I don't need a man, I can do anything better than you" attitude—and now see what I've got!"

"What? So you wanted to marry me because you thought I was

this obedient Asain woman you had in your primitive mind? What do you know about where I am from? What do you know about its people? I never tried to be someone else when I was with you. The only thing I did was to try to understand you and adjust what I could to you. But I can't just erase myself as you want me to. You've married a wrong Asian woman!"

"Well, I will make you the right one then!"

They yelled at each other, blamed each other, and often despised each other. But when Jane realized that it was like pouring water into a broken bucket, she gave up on her marital war. Because, as annoying as it was, she had to admit that many times David knew better than her. And even if he was wrong, he never changed his opinion or wanted to acknowledge it, not for once. It was just too exhausting and destroying Jane's soul because she wasn't built for this cockfighting. The day she went back to the house with Mia was the day she stopped fighting for good.

So she stayed for her daughter. And she tried so hard to look happy around her daughter. But there were still times that the little girl came to her and said to Jane totally off-guard.

"Smile, mama. Smile," Then she would touch Jane's mouth with her tiny fingers to spread a smile.

Feeling guilty that Mia noticed her sadness, Jane plastered a smile on her face with Mia. But Jane discovered whatever she did that she couldn't put a fake smile in her eyes. You really had to smile for real for that. That wasn't easy when there was nothing else to laugh at in your life. She was alone with a small child all day, without any grown-ups to pour her heart out to. International calls were unaffordable those days when Jane didn't have her own money, and over the years, she'd lost contact with her friends in Seoul. So instead, Jane found her shelter in songs, books, and films. Jane played her favourite song repeatedly in her head and often sang it aloud to her baby daughter.

It was the first English song that she learnt from heart in Seoul. Every morning she got up at six to go to her high school and listened to the radio programme called "Learning English with Pop songs." They had a song each week to study the lyrics. One of the songs that Jane loved and memorized was "The Greatest Love of All" by Whitney Houston.

After all these years, she still remembered every word of it. And she remembered the old Jane, a sixteen-year-old high school student, full of hope and ambitions for the future. Her dreams and laughter. The sense of freedom. Now married with a child but never so desolate in her life, she brought up the song out of her memory box, sang it with her heart, and cried. That song must have been written for Jane. She was absolutely sure of it. It was her only way to keep sane and have faith in a lonely world.

CHAPTER 5
FRANK

Frank couldn't get Jane out of his head.

He thought of her all the time, and it'd become an obsession.

He thought of her delicate face, her skin like white jade, and her eyes like onyx.

He was staring out at the window in the school staff room, and there was a blackbird that was staring right back at him. His black coat was smooth and shiny, and the eyes were like black marbles. He thought Jane was like a blackbird, his merel (blackbird in Dutch). The merel snorted at him and flew away. Frank said to himself, "You must be going mad, you hopeless eejit!"

He contemplated calling Jane and asking her out, but that sounded even to him, outrageous beyond. What did she know about him, and how could he explain what he felt for her? No doubt that she didn't think anything about their meeting. He would be glad if she remembered him at all if he called.

So calling Jane out of the blue was out of the question. The only thing he could do with his obsession was to keep an eye on Mia instead of Jane. He gave her six in the end for her assignment. He didn't expect Jane would call and thank him, and she didn't. Honestly, he didn't give Mia six to please Jane but because Mia's assignment deserved it. But he couldn't help himself longing for Jane's call.

He might find a legitimate reason to call Jane if he observed her daughter closely. That was Frank's secret intention. He taught Mia's class Chemistry, and he looked for her when there were breaks between the lessons. And he noticed that Mia was sneaking away more often from her group of friends, Nora and Esther and a few other girls. His eyes followed when he spotted Mia walking to the bike stand and vanishing behind it. There was a little park around the school and a walking path to it. Frank waited to see when she came back because their lunch break would be up in 20 minutes.

Indeed Mia returned just before the break ended. Frank saw that her face was flustered, and her big round eyes sparked even from a distance. It hit Frank at that precise moment that Mia resembled someone in love. He'd seen it in Jesse's face when he first confided in him. Jesse's eyes also radiated when he talked about this boy who made him confused about his sexuality.

Frank lingered to find out whom Mia was seeing. Mia wasn't aware of Frank standing there and watching her and rushed back to her class before being reported late. Frank had no lesson after the lunch break and waited for some more time. When no one appeared, he walked to the bike stand and carried on to the park's walking path. Frank pretended he was going for a walk in his free hour. And when he entered the park, he saw a group of boys, well, some of them were too big and vicious to be called boys. He recognized Daan, who used to be his student, and Simon, a famous drop-out among the teachers, for his brutality. Daan was the only one who smiled at Frank and said, "Hello, Mr. Bloom." All his other friends ignored Frank and kept on smoking.

"Hello, Daan, no lesson now?"

"Ah, well, actually yes, I was about to return to school. Sorry."

Frank didn't bother to confront other boys. He didn't want to get murdered in the park. What a sad world it had become, Frank thought regretfully. Then he prayed fiercely that it was Daan whom Mia was meeting in secret.

***

Frank didn't have any hobbies these days. When he came home, he had too much time on his hands, and he couldn't escape from his obsession with Jane. By now, he had recalled their conversation thousands of times. And it made him discover a different perspective about himself and the place he was living. What Jane said made him see his culture and social habits from an outsider's eyes. Until then, he'd never considered what people said and did from such a perspective.

He listened to his colleagues in the staff room with an interest he'd never had before. Ever since Jane told him how often she'd heard the typical Dutch saying, "I can say whatever I want to say," he was staggered to witness how true it was. It was an attitude programmed into their brain, so people didn't even have to point it out. They just lived it. Most of his colleagues among the high school teachers got on well with each other, and different opinions were respected. Still, Frank wondered how often this typical attitude hurt other people's feelings if you were not programmed in the same way.

He remembered a discussion that had started a few years ago in the Netherlands and was also a subject of debate at his school. Every year on the 5th of December, the Dutch celebrated "Sinterklaas"—the Dutch version of Christmas. It was the night before Saint Nicholas's birthday, the patron saint of children. He traditionally appeared on a white horse and had as his assistants Zwarte Piets (Black Piets). They carried a bag full of cookies and candies for the children. The Piets were dressed in Moorish custom and had their faces painted black. And it was this blackface that made people suddenly (in Frank's opinion) see the Piets as racist. The discussions and demonstrations about whether this children's festivity was racist or not became so vehement that they often got out of hand. There was violence, arrests, hatred from both sides.

As long as Frank could remember, for those few weeks before Sinterklass—a folk festival rather than a religious one—the whole country got into one big party mood. Frank's family too. His grandparents and parents lived and raised their children as more Dutch than Jewish, and Frank never learnt to feel his root strongly when he was growing up. Like any Dutch kid, Sinterklass was his favourite time of year. It was the only occasion except for their birthday when children were shamelessly spoiled. He had only good memories of the Sinterklass, and he felt upset that some people made a problem out of nothing and were ruining its joy. As far as Frank was concerned, nobody had any issues with Black Piet until people from outside, like immigrants or ex-pats from other countries, raised the racist debate and criticized it.

"It is our tradition! Shut up and leave if you don't like it. Don't try to take away our children's pleasure!"

Frank was more on the side of "Keep Our Black Piet" than "Kick Out Black Piet." For him, Sinterklass had lost its shine when they started showing "Roetpiet (sooty Piet)" instead of "Black Piet".

At his school, some students started a support group for "Kick Out Black Piet" last year, and it divided the whole school, even the teachers. Frank initially thought the majority of the Black Piet opponents would be people from ethnic groups associated with the blackface, but he was surprised that they were more diverse than that. Nevertheless, Frank stayed out of the discussion in the staff room or classrooms. He didn't want to get involved in any controversial argument.

After he met Jane and had a glimpse of a different perspective, he wondered if he had always been right. What would Jane have thought of Black Piet? Would she have agreed that it was racist? But she wasn't black. She was...what was she? Do we say Asians are yellow? But she wasn't yellow. She had fairer skin than Frank!

She had been married to a Dutchman with a Dutch child. Did she go along with their tradition and didn't mind it at all? On which side was Mia, as she was half Korean and half Dutch? Frank was suddenly dying to know Jane's opinions on these random issues and just talk to her.

He remembered that one of his students, Mae-lee, had started the "Kick Out Black Piet" pressure group. He was her mentor, but he hadn't shown any interest in his pupil's social activities up to now. Mae-lee's parents were from China, and she was born in the Netherlands. She was one of the top students, and Frank was surprised that she had the time and passion for anything other than studying. Angelo, whose parents were from Surinam (one of the Dutch colonies), was another group member, Frank remembered.

When his students had a self-study hour in the classroom, Frank stayed to supervise. He usually let them get on with their stuff, but he approached Mae-lee studying diligently, looking focused.

"Hi, Mae-lee, how's it going?"

"Oh, Mr. Bloom, I'm good."

Mae-lee seemed alarmed when he talked to her since it had rarely happened before, and soon her face became worried. She must have thought that she was in trouble.

"Is there something?"

"No, no. I just wanted to talk to you."

"Okay... About what?"

"About Black Piet."

Mae-lee's face got even paler. She'd had a lot of challenges at school ever since she started the pressure group. Some children even threatened to hurt her if she carried on. Some told her to go back to her country. But she was born here and this was her country too.

"Why do you want to talk about it?" Sinterklass wouldn't be here for another seven or eight months, she thought. Why start the trouble now?

"Well, recently, I started to wonder what made you feel that Black Piet was racist. You see, I am only a Kaaskop (Cheese Head, meaning Dutch person, but also a stupid person) and couldn't see the problem with Black Piet. It was something I grew up with, and you'd heard the stories hundreds of times. They were my childhood figures, no harm intended."

"But Mr. Bloom, when you were a child, wasn't the story also a bit different? I heard from my parents and friends' parents that they used to be scared of Sinterklass and Black Piet when they were young. Sinterklass had a birch rod, and he kept his Great Book with all the details of what children did. If you were naughty, they would take you in the bag all the way to Spain, where they came from. The naughty children were taken away from their parents."

Frank nodded, surprised to remember the story. Those were indeed the stories that he was told as a boy.

But, wait, why was it different now?

"So you see, the children nowadays don't get told that story. Because it makes children fearful, and the moral of abduction and punishment is utterly wrong. So although it was a tradition, it needed to evolve with time."

Frank stared at the girl in amazement. How could she be so intelligent and logical? That was the best point made so far, clearer than any aggressive protest.

Feeling much more confident that she wasn't in trouble, Mae-lee called out to her friend.

"Angelo! Come here. Tell Mr. Bloom what you had gone through every year with Sinterklaas."

Angelo, a dark boy who was gentle and friendly, came over to Mae-lee's desk.

"I didn't know you were interested in our story, Mr. Bloom. It isn't even Sinterklass yet."

Angelo grinned and sat on the empty seat next to Mae-lee.

A few students in the class were eavesdropping on their conversation. Most were uninterested and used this opportunity to look on their phones.

"Well, I think it started as early as at toddler school. When Sinterklass and Black Piets came to visit and gave us the pepernoten(Dutch Sinterklass cookie), all the children stared at Piets and me and started to call me Black Piet. I wouldn't have been too traumatized if Piets weren't so ridiculed. They were always messing things up and talked like they were not very sharp. It didn't stop until I went to high school. Then you are older and kind of lose your enthusiasm about Sinterklaas because you stop believing in it, like Christmas and Santa Claus. But I could never really enjoy Sinterklass like other kids. It was a period that I despised how I looked, something I couldn't do anything about, and that made my parents sad too. They had similar experiences. I wished it was done and over quickly."

"People say if we change the tradition, it will destroy the children's joy. But what is good about children's festivity if it doesn't include all the children? What about the children who were teased as Black Piet because of their skin colour? Where was their joy? All the children were taught what the tradition was. It is not something they had invented themselves. The fun and joy of Sinterklass is coming from celebrating the special occasion, and mainly from getting presents. It doesn't matter which colour of skin Piets have!"

Frank stood astonished. Why hadn't he deepen himself in the discussion before? Why did he not bother to listen to the other side? "It is our tradition, don't touch it!" Frank felt ashamed of his previous misgivings. These students were more mature than he was.

"Hey, what have 'you' got to say about blackface? You are not even black! Don't say things that you know nothing about!"

That was Hugo, one of the cool boys, whom Frank found rather arrogant.

Mae-lee didn't even blink her eyes. She must have had these arguments countless times before.

"It is not like you have to be black to understand. We can all put ourselves in someone else's shoes. That is called Empathy and Humanity. We didn't have to be Jewish to know what happened to them was wrong and inhumane."

Frank froze.

'My grandfather survived from the concentration camp, and yet I didn't think this was discrimination.'

Frank was in shock, suddenly realizing these complicated, often invisible layers of different discrimination.

"As a child of Chinese parents, I've had my own experiences growing up here, and I can understand how Black Piets can be offending to some of us. And you can do it too, Hugo, if you wanted to."

Frank clapped silently in his head. He then asked Mae-lee.

"Will you tell us what you experienced as a Chinese-Dutch kid?"

"Of course, Mr. Bloom. You must all have learnt to sing "Hanky Panky Shanghai" on the birthdays at school, right? And make 'slanted eyes' using your index fingers?"

Guilty. Everyone had that one at elementary school.

"And learning rhymes with the sentence "Shing, shang, shong plays ping-pong in Hong Kong?" There was always a ridiculous cartoon of a Chinese man in a colonial era in the textbook. And not to forget making 'slanted eyes,' naturally."

Guilty, again.

"I mean, when you learn these stereotypes at school at such a young age, what kind of messages are you giving the children? Every Asian is a unique person like every other person on the earth, some with slanted eyes and some not. The 'slanted eyes' gesture is always used to ridicule people in a negative context. All my life, I had children around me making 'slanted eyes' with their fingers. Even random strangers in random places do that and start to chant "Shing, shang, shong." It's something you would not have experienced if you were not Asian in the Netherlands."

Now it seemed everyone was listening to Mae-lee. Mae-lee would be a great speaker, whichever direction she decided to go, Frank was sure. He felt the old excitement that he used to feel when he discovered something extraordinary about a student, a talent.

"But what else can you call 'slanted eyes' other than 'slanted eyes'? It is just a fact! Should I then get offended if someone calls me 'white'? You guys are just creating a problem for the sake of creating a problem! Wait, what about Mia? I wonder what she thinks about all this?"

Hugo, clearly a bad loser, was still trying to make a point, which was not even relevant.

'What about Mia?'

Frank turned around to see Mia. Mia seemed as startled as Frank that she was now involved in the discussion.

"What do you want me to say?" Mia asked Hugo coolly.

"If you felt the same way as Mae-Lee. Since you're half Dutch."

"Mae-lee is also Dutch, you know. She was born here just like you."

"Yeah, but she obviously feels different from the rest of us, minding all this."

"But she wouldn't have felt different if no one treated her differently."

"I was talking about you, Mia. I've heard enough about that Chinese girl!" Hugo wagged his finger at Mae-lee.

Frank decided to wait without interfering. Mia seemed able to say what she thought.

"For someone like you, it doesn't matter if our parents were Chinese or Korean, or half of anything. Because you just can't see it, can you? What you think as a stupid joke could hurt someone's feelings. Have you ever heard of the saying, "You can kill a frog when you throw a stone for fun?" And as for what I feel, I feel all that Mae-lee feels too. I have 'slanted eyes' after all."

What started as a simple question to his students had become a heated hour-long discussion that everyone had something to say about in the end. Frank asked the class to share any kind of discrimination they had experienced in their life.

Ali, whose parents were Moroccan, said he was sick and tired of how the media presented the Muslims in the Netherlands. He felt that people saw him as a potential terrorist and would always point their fingers at him in any suspicious situation. Other Muslim boys all agreed with him.

Sienna, a girl with Moluks parents (coming from Maluku, Indonesia), said people lump them together with Indonesians as a whole, whereas they had a significant culture and history of their own.

"It's the same for all Allochtoons,[3] isn't it?" Juan, whose parents

---

[3] Allochtoon: a Dutch word from a Greek term, with the literal meaning, "emerging from another soil", used in the Netherlands to mean "person with migration background" and/or "person who has at least one parent who was born in another country than the Netherlands." Those with Dutch nationality can still be

came from Aruba, looked around the class. "It doesn't matter where you or your parents came from. We are all labeled, "Allochtoons," and we are represented as "inferior" and "problematic." We are more likely to have a low income, low education, low loyalty to the Netherlands, but high criminality, aren't we?"

"Yes, that there are terms like 'Allochtoon' and 'Autochtoon'[4] is shocking."

Frank nodded at Mae-lee's comment.

"As far as I'm concerned, the city council of Amsterdam decided to stop using the terms because of their divisive effect. But we still have a long way to go."

Jeanine, a shy Autochtoon-girl, raised her hand.

Delighted to see her participation Frank exclaimed in excitement.

"Jeanine! Tell us what you think."

"Well, I am 'Autochtoon', but I feel discriminated against, too." The other "coloured" children of the class all turned their heads and stared at her.

"Because I am fat." Jeanine looked up at Frank and asked tentatively. "Body shaming is also a form of discrimination?"

Frank nodded solemnly. "It is, Jeanine. A good point. Thank you for sharing."

Then Ben, another quiet Autochtoon boy muttered, "People think that there is no poverty in the Netherlands, but there is. People are ignored and shamed for lack of money. I was teased because I always wore out-of-fashion second-hand clothing and old shoes. I never joined any sports club and learnt swimming at

---

"allochtoon" because they are immigrants or the descendants of immigrants.

[4] Autochtoon: a Dutch word from a Greek term, with the literal meaning, "emerging from this soil". It has an opposite meaning to "Allochtoon", and is used in the Netherlands to mean "Dutch person" and/or "ethnic Dutch."

In 2016, the Dutch government decided to stop using both terms but they are still commonly used.

school when everyone else got their first diplomas when they were four. I was the only big kid in the A diploma class, and I would rather have drowned myself."

Everyone fell into deep thought, and some looked upset because they rarely talked about what they were struggling with.

After the silence and collective contemplation had lasted long enough, Frank looked around at the serious faces of his students.

"So, can we all agree that discrimination is a very complex matter? It can come from anywhere and target anyone. There are various layers, different sorts, and many directions in it. So we can't just look at everyone and judge everything with the same eyes. After listening to all your stories, I've realized that our country's biggest problem is not the racism and discrimination itself, but our belief that it doesn't exist here. We consider ourselves open-minded and tolerant and refuse to hear different opinions about us, but we should not think that we are untouchable. We are as faulty as everyone else in this world."

Frank was in awe of his students and fascinated by all their different experiences growing up in the Netherlands. Also, it was the first time that he had interacted with his students as their mentor. Ever since Ron had urged—no almost forced—Frank to take the mentorship of this Year 4 class, Frank wanted to do only the very least. He kept an eye on their overall grades and focused on whether a student did well enough to go to the next class.

Frank wasn't sure if this was a positive turn-around in his career. The last time he got close to his students, it ended in tragedy.

"Why are you still there if you hate your job so much?" Jane had asked him. But it wasn't that he hated his job. He hated the unfairness of what he had had to go through because of one of his students.

'But I am still here. I'm not going anywhere,' he thought. So if he wasn't going anywhere, what should he do?

"What a shame you can't enjoy it while you are there." Jane said. What a shame, indeed. Frank might just as well enjoy it and do it properly.

***

Late that afternoon, Frank was the last person leaving school. As he passed the bike stand, he recognized Mia's bike from the plastic flowers on the handlebars. Was Mia in the park? It was going to be dark soon. He decided to check on Mia before heading home.

As he reached the place where he saw the boys the last time, he could see Mia's reddish-blond hair. She was cuddled up in Daan's arms, and he caught them kissing briefly when the other boys were busy distributing something. He hoped it was only cigarettes.

But Simon caught Mia and Daan kissing too. He said something, and Mia looked at him in disbelief.

She stood up and said something to Simon and Daan. Without being noticed by them, Frank walked back until he was at the school.

A few minutes later, Mia arrived at the bike stand, too. She was so stunned to see Frank standing there, that she froze.

"Hi, Mia."

"Hi, Mr. Bloom."

Mia put her key in her bike lock.

"It's a bit late, isn't it?"

"It's only six."

"Does your Mom know where you are?"

Mia's eyes flamed when she heard Frank.

"What's all this? It's none of your business!"

"Well, I can ask you, since I am your mentor, how things are for you."

"And that includes checking on me if I go home on time?"

"Your mother might be worried if you are very late."

"She won't notice because she gets home after six anyhow. And I did text her."

"Great. And where were you?"

"God! What the?"

Mia almost stamped her foot on the ground.

"Why should I tell you that? I haven't done anything wrong."

"Are you together with Daan?"

Mia gasped. Her mouth stayed wide open.

"Daan is a nice boy, but I can't say that about his mates."

Mia just stood there, her face as white as the moon.

"I strongly suspect that they are dealing in drugs too."

Mia's hands started to twitch, and she dropped her school bag.

Frank stepped closer and lifted her bag from the ground.

"I just want you to be safe. Those boys are dangerous to hang out with. Especially when you are so young, I would be worried about you."

"I'm not into drugs," Mia managed to mutter.

"I didn't think you were. But they are. You might get into trouble if you hang out with them."

Mia's lips trembled. Then she looked into Frank's eyes. The fear in Mia's eyes struck him. He realized how vulnerable the girl was.

"But I like Daan."

Frank's heart broke.

He suddenly saw Jesse's face in the attic. He must have had the same look when he said, "But I like him," to his parents before he went up to the attic.

Frank opened his arms without thinking, and Mia broke down.

"I can't think of not seeing Daan, Mr. Bloom. I just can't."

He held the girl and let her cry out. It would have raised some suspicious eyebrows if anyone had seen them there, but luckily Frank knew that he was the last one, and honestly, he didn't care.

"Then we will have to think of a way of seeing Daan, but not his friends."

Mia nodded, looking instantly better—no, relieved—when Frank said that after a while.

Frank wasn't sure if what he said was the best thing for Mia, but he didn't want Mia to be cornered like Jesse. Not having hope pushed Jesse to the end.

"Will you not tell my parents about it, Mr. Bloom? My father will probably kill me. He wouldn't like me having a boyfriend at all. Even if Daan were the kind of boy that he would approve."

"What about your mom?"

Frank studied Mia's tearful face. "Your mother seemed pretty understanding to me. Isn't she? Can't you talk to her?"

Mia's eyes were frightened when she talked about her father, but when Frank mentioned her mother, her expression changed to something else. Something Frank struggled to identify. He hadn't seen such emotions before.

"My mom... I can't."

Was it pain that Frank saw in her eyes?

"Why?" He whispered, touched by what he'd seen.

"Because I've hurt her enough. I've ruined her life. She is here because of me, even when she doesn't want to be. I am the reason for her sadness."

CHAPTER 6
MIA

It was such a weird day. First, there was the discussion with the whole class about Black Piet. Then Mia met Mr. Bloom at the bike stand when she thought no one would be at school. She never imagined she would be talking to Mr. Bloom like that, let alone cry in his arms. But she felt lost, more than ever in her life. She felt like her name, Mia.

When she asked her mother what her name meant in Korean, her mother said, "A beautiful child," and kissed her head. Mia had always believed her mother's explanation. But when she was twelve years old, she found the truth about her name. Mia went to South Korea with her mom to visit her grandparents. Mia didn't understand anything her grandparents said, but she still liked to be with them. If Mia concentrated really hard to listen to them, she might start understanding Korean.

Her mom used to say that she regretted not talking Korean to Mia. But Mia knew the reason, and that was because her father didn't want her to. And his wish was the law in their house. Mia was going to a high school after that holiday in Seoul, and she was old enough to see that. As time passed after her parents' divorce and Mia got older, she started to see what went wrong. She didn't understand in the beginning, but now she did.

On their last day before returning to the Netherlands, Mia sat with her grandfather on the lounge sofa. They were waiting for the dinner that her grandmother and mother were cooking for hours in the kitchen. Mia was afraid she might explode because her grandparents always fed Mia too much. It was the only thing they did with Mia, cooking and eating. Mia couldn't eat as much as they wanted since food never stopped coming. And they kept stroking Mia's face and smiled and cried a lot, too. Mia didn't know what to do then. Mia just squeezed their wrinkly, dry hands on those occasions.

Her grandfather turned on the television, and she didn't catch what programme her grandfather was watching. Mia started to recall the last three weeks she and her mother spent in Seoul. Mia noticed that her mother changed when she was in South Korea. Ironically that was how Mia found out that her mother wasn't happy in the Netherlands. Her mother never said she wasn't happy there to Mia, though. Her mother had an okay job as an administrative secretary at one of the Korean logistic companies near Schiphol Airport. Mom said it wasn't what she had studied for, but the commute and working hours were manageable, and she could earn a living for the two of them. She had her friends, Su-kyoung Imo (aunt in Korean) and Sunny Imo. Mom still looked after herself and was as pretty as when Mia was young.

But Mia knew that her mother wasn't as happy as she should be. It wasn't only that her mother never had a proper boyfriend since her divorce. It was because Mia's mother had become someone else when she went back to South Korea.

Her mother walked differently, talked differently, laughed differently. Her back was straight, which made her look taller, and when she spoke, her face was full of expressions. And she laughed a lot. Loud and free. Like a young girl. She was animated instantly when the plane landed on Korean soil. Her skin glowed with excitement, and her blood seemed to circulate faster since her cheeks got more colour in them. Mom was a different woman! Mia realized this unfamiliar, passionate woman was her mother, who she really was.

As the day they had to go back to the Netherlands got closer, her mother became quieter. It was as if she was mentally preparing her departure. It was like her mother thought, okay, now I have to stop being so ecstatic and excited because otherwise, I wouldn't be able to cope when I go back.

Her mother tried not to cry when they left, but Mia knew her heart was bleeding under her serene appearance. Her mother almost broke down when she said goodbye to her aging mother, who seemed to have shrunk even more each time they visited her. Mom's chin was stiff as she was determined not to show her grief. With Mia, her mother tried extra hard to compose herself. More so this time, because Mia had been so angry the night before.

***

Mia did her best to stuff herself at dinner for the sake of her grandmother. Then she plopped on the sofa again with her grandfather. Mia was always flabbergasted about how much Korean people could eat. In the Netherlands, people only had one hot meal a day, and here the Koreans treated each meal as a feast. Too full to think anything, Mia stared blankly at the television screen. She still didn't get what it was about. But there was music, and Mia liked listening to Korean songs even if she didn't know what they were singing. Then came some children's photos, and each had numbers, like telephone numbers and things written in Korean. She heard her name being called repeatedly by the presenter.

"Mia..." Then again, "Mia...."

Mia turned to her grandfather.

"Granddad? Why are they saying my name?"

"Huh? What did you say...? I wish you spoke Korean, or I spoke your language... Jane?" Grandfather called her mother, helping her grandmother clear the dishes and tidy up in the kitchen.

"Yes, Dad?"

When Mia's mother came to the living room, her grandfather helplessly pointed to the television screen and Mia. "We were watching television, and Mia asked something, but I don't understand what she said."

Her mother asked Mia, "Did you ask granddad something?"

"Mom, I heard my name many times on television. What is it about?"

Mom turned to see what was on television. Then she understood. "Oh, it is to find lost children. If anyone has seen them, they should call."

"But why my name then?"

"Ah, it's because Mi-A also means a lost child."

It shocked Mia more that her mother didn't seem bothered even a little bit. How could she say such a world-shattering thing so matter-of-factly, as if nothing was wrong?

"A lost child? But, but you said it meant 'a beautiful child!'"

"It does. In Korean, a letter has more than one meaning in many cases, depending on which Chinese character they are using. In your case, it was a beautiful child."

Mia had never been as upset with her mother as she was then.

"But it is the same! It sounds the same! If you just heard it, you would not know if it was a beautiful child or lost child!'

"But Mia, nobody would use 'lost child' for a name. It is only logical!"

"Not to me! I don't see any logic in that! How can I tell my friends!" Mia was always proud to tell her friends that her name

meant 'a beautiful child' in Korean whenever they asked. "How could you? How could you give me such a devastating name!"
Her grandfather was astonished by Mia's outburst, and her grandmother came running to see what was going on.
Her mother came to hug her, but Mia shook her mother's arms vehemently, "I hate it! I hate you! I hate my name!"
Child after child passed on the screen, all lost, and Mia closed her eyes.
It was as if Mia had lost her name. She initially loved her name very much, but now she despised it very much. Her mother repeatedly tried to explain how it wasn't anything like she thought, but Mia didn't want to listen because Mia wouldn't understand. She couldn't because she wasn't Korean. Well, only half, but it wasn't enough to comprehend a complicated matter like this.
Mia got over the shock eventually as time went on, and a few years passed. But she still felt sullen about her name. Whenever Mia felt alone in the world, she remembered her name. She hardly felt like a beautiful child. She felt more often like a lost child. Then she felt angry again with her mother. How could she! How could she give such a name to her child!
And today, biking back home in the early sunset of March and thinking about what had just happened at the bike stand, Mia felt like her true name, a lost child.

***

When Mia arrived home, her mother was already back. Mia saw her mother glancing at the clock in the kitchen when she entered.
"Hi! You okay?"
"What do you mean?"
"Since you are later than when you said you'd be home. Is everything fine?"
"Why wouldn't it be?" Mia couldn't help being sulky with her mother. Was it because she was thinking of her name again? She didn't know.
Her mother sighed softly. "Well, if you say so. How were Nora and Esther?"
"Huh? What about them?"
"You texted that you were with them?"
Oh, bollocks. Mia almost forgot what she said to her mother.
"They are fine. What's the dinner?" Mia changed the subject and

sat at the table.

"I thought we'd better use up the vegetables in the fridge. I've made Bibimbap."

"Oh, yummy."

Mia wondered if Daan would like Korean food. He said he'd never had any before but wanted to try it. Mia watched her mother finishing off frying two eggs in the pan. Mia stood up and washed her hands at the sink.

"Will you get something to drink? I think I might open that white wine if you'd take it out for me."

Mia opened the fridge, got the sparkling water for herself, and picked up the bottle next to it. She recognized the label. "Wait, isn't that the wine you bought when BF4 came?"

Jane looked up from the bowl where she was assembling the vegetables on rice. "Ah, yes, I think so."

"How come you didn't open it? Didn't it go well?"

"We just had coffee, and he didn't stay long."

Mia realized that she didn't ask her mother how it went with BF4 when she returned on Sunday evening. She was too preoccupied with her love interest, Daan, and she'd forgotten about her mother's.

"I think we will just stay friends," her mother added with no trace of regret.

"Why? What did you not like about him? Did you just dump him after you invited him here?"

Jane brought two bowls to the table, and she poured the white wine in her glass.

Then she raised her glass and clinked it to Mia's sparkling water. Jane smiled and said, "Gun-bae ('Cheers' in Korean)!"

Despite her earlier grumpiness, Mia smiled at her mother's rare playfulness. "Gun-bae for what? What are we toasting to?"

"To us. You and me. The Thelma and Louise of Amstelveen."

Mia giggled at her mother's old favourite phrase.

"You should have been drinking that wine with BF4."

"That is exactly my point. I don't need any BFs. Done with it now."

"How come?"

"Because I realized, again, that I don't need a man in my life. I've got you."

"Oh, Mom! Stop saying that. It's creepy! I can't and don't want to be your boyfriend. I'm your daughter, and I've got my own life!" 'And Daan,' Mia silently added.

"I'm not saying that you should be anything other than my daughter. There's no pressure to be anything else. It's just... So far, every man I met has missed that 2%."

"Oh, Mom, not that crazy theory again!" Her mother's 2% story exasperated Mia.

2% was Mom's favourite Korean drink. It was transparent and peach-flavoured, subtly sweet water. Mia also liked to drink it when they went to Korea. Her mother told her about the drink's advertising slogan when Mia tried it for the first time

"When you miss that 2% in your body, this drink fills it."

And her mother used to say to Mia whenever she found something not quite complete or perfect, that it just missed the 2%. Now that was almost a permanent analysis for any of her BFs.

But Mia agreed that none of them were quite right. Mixing the thinly sliced vegetables and adding more chili sauce and sesame oil into her bowl, Mia thought about the men her mother had briefly dated over the last eight years.

There was BF1, the most horrible man of all four, from Mia's point of view. Perhaps she saw him as so bad because she was very young, and he was the first man other than her father who'd come into their life. Mia was only eight, and she still missed their old life. This man, whose name was Gus, was too eager and wanted to please her mother and Mia.

'I've already got my father! I don't need another dad!' Mia physically screamed it a few times into his face too.

But what Mia hated more than having another dad was sharing her mother with someone else.

Pretty soon, it became clear to her mother that it was too much to juggle between her daughter and a new boyfriend. They both demanded Jane's undivided attention and had the mental age of eight years olds.

After him, it was more or less the same story. There was this BF2, who was as gruesome as BF1 and as childish as 9-year-old Mia. Mia and BF2 got into a near fight. When the three of them went to the zoo, he hissed into Mia's ear, and he looked just like that otter that they passed. "I didn't come all the way here to walk behind your mom!"—Only because Mia wouldn't let him hold her mother's hand.

By the time BF3 made an appearance, Mia was a bit older, almost thirteen, and had a lot more interest in her own life than in her mother's. She now wouldn't mind a man who would take some of her mother's attention from her. She would love it if her mother went out in the evenings and at the weekend. The BF could hold her mother's hand as long as he wanted.

But her mother always said that they all missed the 2%.

When Mia inquired what the 2% consisted of, Jane couldn't explain it either.

"Did dad have that 2%?" Mia asked her mother boldly over the bowl of Bibimbap.

Mia's question nonplused her mother, but Jane had always been honest with Mia. Mia would give her mother that.

"There were times that I thought he had in the beginning. There were times that I thought he was perfect."

"Then, what changed?"

Her mother stopped eating her food and thought about it. "Well, everything. I changed, too. Changes can be good for a person, but often it breaks the relationship if you don't change in the same way as the other person."

Then her mother smiled her smile. A little restrained, a rueful and beautiful smile. It was the smile that only her mother smiled. That made her mother her mother.

***

After dinner, her mother started to clean up the kitchen and asked Mia, "Have you got lots of homework?"

Mia sighed at the mention of homework. She was sure there was a lot but couldn't remember what it was. "Yes, as always."

"Then better finish it first before you do other things? It's quite late already."

It was only eight-thirty, but her mother was right. By the time she did everything she had to do for school, it would be midnight.

"Go, I will finish everything here."

Mia retreated to her room. She wanted to stay back and ask her mother more questions about her father and their marriage. But she also wanted to talk to Daan.

She sent a WhatsApp message to him, but Daan didn't answer her immediately.

When he didn't react to her message straight away, Mia got worried.

She hoped that Daan was not with Simon and his other friends. Mia's thoughts went back to the afternoon and the talk with Mr. Bloom.

Mr. Bloom was right. Mia knew that Simon dealt drugs. And his other friends were all Simon's pawns. Daan swore that he didn't have anything to do with it. Simon asked Daan to join him many times, but Daan said no. He had no intention to get into trouble. Daan had his plans all set, working for his uncle's company from next year. Simon liked Daan because they grew up in the same neighbourhood, but he knew that Daan wasn't interested in his business.

Her phone pinged. Expecting Daan's message Mia went for her phone with joy, but she was puzzled to see who had sent her a message.

Talk about the devil, it was Simon. But how did he find her number? Did Daan give it to him?

He had been very rude today in the park, and she had left them in frustration.

He saw Daan kissing her when the other boys were rolling cigarettes and discussing their drug-dealing business.

Simon looked right into Mia's eyes, and she felt uncomfortable at the way he was eyeing her.

His eyes glowed with savage amusement and also twinkled with something dark and dangerous. "You know that Daan and I share everything, don't you? Hey, Danny boy, did you tell your girl that we used to share absolutely everything? What was mine was Daan's, and what was Daan's, was mine. You got to know that when you are Daan's girl, you will also be mine."

It was outrageous, what Simon told her. She looked at Daan indignantly, asking for some clarification. A denial.

"What the hell is he saying, Daan? It can't be right, seriously?"

Daan glared at Simon, who just laughed at the two of them and moved back to his pawns.

"Of course not. He is just making up silly things. You are mine, only mine."

"But why is he claiming that everything yours is his?"

Daan shrugged and held out his hand to her.

Reluctantly she stretched her hand to him.

"He did help me a lot in the past, that is true. He even gave me some money when things were really rough at home, which I will pay him back. But don't worry about what he said. He likes to tease people. Nothing to worry about!"

So what did Simon want from her now? Why did he text her?

Only one way to find out. She opened the message.

"Hey, Mia, Daan went off like a bomb after you left and told me to set things right with you. I'm saying sorry because I care about Daan. He is like my little brother. He likes you a lot, and that's why I should also care about you too. Anyway, take care, see you around."

Oh. This wasn't what Mia expected at all. She let out a deep sigh of relief.

So maybe this Simon wasn't such a bad person. Everyone was overreacting about him. Mia was, and Mr. Bloom was too.

Another ping on her telephone, and this time it was Daan.

She smiled and settled into a long and secret messaging session in bed that would put some serious blushes on her cream face. Her homework could be damned. What was the point of going to the next class when Daan would have a job and earn his living? He would take care of her, he said. And Nora and Esther wouldn't even miss her in the next class because she hardly spent any time with them to keep her secret safe. She only needed Daan. He filled her 2%.

CHAPTER 7
JANE

The kitchen was back to how it was, clean and everything orderly put in place. When Jane finished her first glass of wine, she poured some more and stored the bottle back in the fridge. She sat at the table with her glass.

She was worried about Mia, but she wasn't sure about what. Her daughter came home late, more often these days than before. Jane believed her daughter when Mia said she was with Nora and Esther. She didn't have to call their parents to check on her story. How embarrassing that would be for Mia! Jane shuddered.

"Did Dad fill that 2%?" Mia asked.

He did once. And Jane did once too, filled his 2%.

What had happened? What changed them? She asked that question thousands of times over the years.

Or perhaps nothing changed, and they just didn't know who they were.

***

When Jane returned to Seoul after their first lunch, followed by the visit to the Anne Frank House and dinner and a few more dates, she was already lightheaded and in love with David. The distance between them only enhanced their desire for each other. They emailed, called—the telephone bills! David was gallant, and he insisted that he would call her back every time she called, missing him so much.

After half a year of sleepless nights due to the time difference and the telephone bill up to Mount Everest, Jane managed to get the post in Amsterdam. The position was contracted for a year, and she had the advantage of no family attached. David was waiting for her at Schiphol Airport with an extravagant bouquet of tulips. Jane's company offered either a flat to rent or a housing allowance. She chose the money and practically moved in with David once she arrived in the Netherlands.

They worked, they biked, and they loved. Jane still met up with Mariska for a coffee during the lunch break, but she stopped going to clubs. There was no time or need for it. She had enough fun exploring Amsterdam, as David knew it. She followed him to his favourite spots and accepted the things he loved to do. Amsterdam was best seen by bike or boat. Every weekend they looked for hidden gems of places. David owned a shiny sloop, and if the weather was pleasant, he took her around the canals of Amsterdam.

The tall and narrow houses looked like they had just come out of a picture book, and appeared higher and more mysterious from the water level. But on the ground, you could see inside the Dutch homes because the Dutch never closed their curtains. Jane was fascinated when she got a glimpse of the lives inside the houses, people cooking, reading, and talking. She wondered if she would fit in with those lives in the Dutch houses. It was different from her life in Seoul, and it felt special, especially next to a man who was so content with himself and a perfect part of this ideal world.

Jane wondered what would happen when her contract ended, and she would have to go back to her old life. The long and strenuous commute to her work, squashed in a metro train like a bean sprout in cultivation, was something she looked less forward to. But her beloved family was waiting for her. And she missed her colleagues with whom she worked hard and partied hard. As tough as life was in South Korea, it was addictively exciting.

But after half a year of a blissfully coupled-up life with David, what Jane missed most from her old life was freedom. She was only 25 years old and felt she was too young to settle down. As luxurious and comfortable as the life with David was, she wanted to explore the world on her own terms. She wanted to experiment, fail, and succeed by herself. Not to be led by someone who'd already been there and told her what to do. Because that was what David had been doing all the time since they got together.

David was 34 years old, and he was well into his career as a financial advisor. He didn't want to take a risk and fail for the sake of failing, as he pointed it out. David wouldn't let Jane go out on her own because he didn't wish his girlfriend to be seen as an object of lust like the first time they met. He didn't want to share Jane with anyone. He pleaded to Jane, "I love you so much. I don't want to spend my time with anyone else. I only need you!"

Jane loved David too, and she felt torn apart. She also found out that she didn't know herself well enough. Before Jane came to stay in the Netherlands, she considered herself unbiased, and she didn't want to believe in stereotypes. But perhaps she had some stereotypical prejudice about European men in general.

Jane imagined every European man would be liberal and feminist. That was the image she developed from brief encounters with fellow students and professors at the English school and colleagues at work. But she'd never actually lived with one. What do they do in their house? How do they treat their wives and girlfriends? How do they love, and more importantly, how do they fight? These things were not something she could notice at a university lecture or office. They were, Jane now realized, not very different from any other men, even Korean men.

There were possessive men everywhere in the world. Men who dominated and got angry when things didn't go the way they wanted. Men who got so grumpy and miserable when their women rejected them that the women almost wished they had just given in to his needs. Men who oppressed their women and isolated them from the world, so the women could turn to no one. Some men called their women a whore because they took them easily. Some called their woman a nympho when she took the initiative. It was not about the nationality, race, age, social status, or wealth of the men, Jane learnt. It was about whether the man was a good man, had a good heart. Nothing else mattered to the compatibility of the relationship.

Three months before the end of her contract, her company informed Jane that her post in Amsterdam would be terminated as initially planned, and she could carry on with her original position in Seoul. She said to her boss that she would miss Amsterdam, and that was true. But when she came out of his office, she was relieved. Almost in tears, suddenly she was able to breathe more freely. Then she realized that she'd been walking on her toes and feeling suffocated for months. She was going back! To her own life! Thank god, thank god....

Jane had detected that something had changed with David too. He probably felt that Jane was yearning for her old life. He was ever more obsessed with Jane's whereabouts and continuously checked her diary and phone. He urged Jane to ask for a reposition to the Amsterdam office, and she said it all depended on what the company was planning in the future. She didn't want to promise anything. She couldn't wait to be herself and not be scrutinized all the time. David's love smothered her.

Then one morning, when Jane got up, she felt a violent reflux of nothing, and she ran into the bathroom and threw up all the liquid out of her body. She was holding on to the toilet and thought, 'I am leaving in a month.' She had a vague idea of what it could be. Jane was pregnant.

She'd always suffered severely from the side-effect of the pill, and when David saw how Jane had to lie down from massive headache and nausea during the day, he offered to take the protection. Released from the suffering, Jane was ever so grateful. But something must have gone wrong with his protection, and now she had a baby. David's baby. She never had a great desire to be a mother before and was certainly not planning to have one in the near future. But she sensed something moved in her uterus. She swore that she felt it fluttering, and she wasn't sure what to do.

When Jane told David and asked if he knew something went wrong, he shook his head, looking so austere. Thinking of her options, she burst into tears. David gazed at her with stern eyes and said.

"It was your responsibility, too, as much as it was mine. You can't just rely on me using the protection."

'But you offered.'

Jane whispered in her head but didn't say it aloud. Because whatever they were going to do with the baby, showing any regret felt like offending the little life inside her, and she didn't want the baby to hear it.

A week later, David proposed to her. It wasn't anything spectacular, her friends in South Korea would be appalled if she accepted such a matter-of-fact proposition, but Jane didn't care.

It was a choice between her and the baby. If she went back to Seoul, she was sure that her relationship with David wouldn't survive. Raising a child as an unmarried single mother was taboo in South Korea, and she would have to depend on her old parents. Jane's baby was a mixed kid too, and in a racially homogenous country like Korea, she could imagine her child, as well as her innocent parents, would live in speculation and scrutiny. If she wanted to keep the baby, she had to stay with David. Still, Jane didn't want to marry David just because of the baby.

When David asked over the dinner at home, with a ring in the box, "Would you want to marry me?" Jane stared at him for a long moment.

Then she asked, "Do you want to marry me?"

David looked bewildered.

"Of course! Why else would I ask you?"

"Well, because I am pregnant? Also, a good reason?"

"No. That's not a good enough reason for me. I wouldn't just want to marry you because you are pregnant."

"Then, why?"

"Do I need to give you reasons? You don't know why?"

"Why?"

David looked almost furious.

"Because I love you. And I want to spend our life together."

"Would you have asked me if I wasn't pregnant too?"

David gazed at her in silence.

"I was going to ask you. That was always my plan before you had to go back. I wasn't sure if you'd say yes because I felt you were drifting away. I was worried that maybe you didn't want to be with me anymore. But on my part, that has always been the plan."

"Okay."

"Okay?"

"Yes."

"Yes?"

"I will marry you. If that was what you wanted all along."

Her answer was as matter-of-fact as his proposal, but David seemed happy enough and relieved that she said yes. They were going to marry and have this baby. They were going to be a family!

"I hope you are not making a mistake, Jane. You can come back and bring the baby up here if that's what you want. It's not going to be easy, and I can't lie about it. But you were so excited to come home!"

Her best friend, Seri, begged Jane on the telephone when she called and told her news. She was the only one Jane told about how she felt about David before finding out she was pregnant.

"You were only talking about David this, and David that, all the time. It pained me that you were only living his life. Where was 'Jane'? You can't live your life as his little trophy forever. Sorry to be so cruel, but I fear that your baby would drag you down to his well."

When Seri didn't seem enthusiastic at all as Jane wished about the baby, Jane found her talking less and less to her friend.

The sudden surge of mother instinct in Jane was a shock to herself. She was amazed that there was a life, a little person growing inside her. Jane was so conscious of the baby's presence, and it frustrated her when no one could see her miracle. She wondered when her belly would grow, and she could show off her bump with pride. Jane was in a bubble, she and the baby were one, and she never felt alone since she was pregnant. The bubble she was in improved her relationship with David too. Now he was the father of her child, and his protectedness was not an obsession but the most beneficial virtue. The two of them went baby-shopping and cooked healthy food every day. When they went out, David was on a constant guard if anything would harm Jane and the baby. Once a biker wasn't looking where he was going and almost hit Jane. To avoid the collision, Jane made a haste step and missed it. David caught her elbow just in time.

"Watch out where you go, aso![5] She is pregnant! She has a baby!"

Jane had never seen David losing his composure like that. His face was red and his veins were almost popping, Jane looked at him in awe. What more evidence did she need about David's love for both Jane and the baby? How could it be a mistake when she felt this happy with the baby? At some point in her life, she'd have settled down and probably had a baby. Why not now? Why not with this man?

Still, when she went to the office and handed in her notice, she was deeply traumatized. She felt the door of her life was closed. For good. She wouldn't be able to open the door again and go back. She returned to David's apartment like a lost soldier and cried her eyes out. When it was time for David to come home, she washed her face and told herself.

'This is part of your life. You are growing up. You've lived your

---

[5] Aso: Dutch swearword meaning an asocial person

life up to now only for yourself and now you need to live for someone else, your child. You are becoming mature. You are a mother.'

She didn't know how many times she would hear this from that moment on, from herself and David, that she was a mother.

***

Years later, Jane wondered if she should have left there and then. She knew that she'd never want a life without Mia, but couldn't she just go back to her country and raise her alone? Perhaps she shouldn't have told David she was pregnant and should just have vanished from his life. He wouldn't have found out, would he? As a father loves his beloved daughter, David loved Mia, but maybe it would have been better for Mia if they could have saved her from all the misery brought by their divorce. Did Jane make a wise decision then?

It was the best she could do at the time, but she felt trapped in her marriage to David and her love for her daughter. She could not move on, but she couldn't go back either.

When Mia was a little girl, Jane thought of the stories she heard at Mia's age growing up in South Korea. Now she was a mother and wife in a foreign country, and the old familiar stories came back to her in a different light.

Jane recalled one of the tales in particular, "The fairy and the lumberjack," and thought about it a lot. Once upon a time, there lived a lumberjack with his widowed mother deep in the mountain. The good-natured man was so impoverished nobody wanted to marry him. One day he helped a deer hide from a hunter, and in its gratitude, the deer told the lumberjack the following. "The fairies come down to the pond at the summit to take a bath. Hide one of their celestial robes. She won't be able to return to heaven, and you can marry her. Never give her robe back until you have three children."

The lumberjack followed the deer's instructions. But when the fairy and the lumberjack had two children, the fairy missed her family very much. He couldn't bear to see her so sad and gave her the robe contrary to his original plan. The fairy took one child in each arm and flew back to heaven. Hence the three children! She couldn't have taken three children and flown away with all three. The lumberjack was later reunited with his wife in heaven with further help from the deer. However, the story had a tragic ending. He went back to see his mother, and things went wrong, and he died. The myth says that he became a rooster and cried every day.

Returning to this story after many years, Jane was struck by how full this children's tale was of injustice and irony. There were so many examples that Jane now looked at it from a new perspective.

Like... How the fairy was forced to marry the lumberjack because he'd hidden her robe. She had no choice! It was a crime! She couldn't fly back without her robe! And how awful of him to have held her hostage with their children. The story said they were happy in their marriage but did anyone ask the fairy? How could you make someone happy when you took her to prison, away from her home? The most idiotic part of the story was, once he was finally reunited with his wife and children, why did he have to go back to his mother and die? Jane was sure that his poor old widowed mother would have wanted her son to live happily ever after in heaven with his family rather than coming down and dying in front of her. Was this lumberjack the first line ancestor of Korean mama boys? What a messed-up fairytale, Jane acknowledged sadly.

Jane thought of the fairy often when she, too, felt like a hostage in her new life. Jane was the fairy. She wished that she had the celestial robe back to take Mia home. But Jane knew she couldn't go without David's permission. She chose this life herself, and she had to live with it.

"Too bad you can't enjoy it while you are there."

Didn't Jane say something like that to someone?

But that was what she'd been telling herself all these years.

Oh dear, did she say that to Mr. Bloom?

Jane suddenly remembered their encounter with more clarity. The tall and lanky man with curly dark hair and even darker green eyes gave her a cranky first impression, but he was transformed when he talked about Primo Levi. Mr. Bloom. What else did she say to him?

CHAPTER 8
FRANK

Frank wished he could talk to Jane about something else. Like what is your favourite music, book, film, and food? What is your hobby? Can I join you—whatever it is? Would you like to go out with me?

Frank sighed. He did try to find a reason to call her, but he didn't want it to be anything grave or worrying. Frank knew another parents' meeting was coming up next month, but he decided this talk couldn't wait.

He was still in shock when he came home after talking to Mia at the bike stand. Mia's emotions left a profound impact on Frank. What he heard was heartbreaking, that Mia thought her mother's sadness was because of her.

Was Jane sad? She didn't look precisely ecstatic or jolly when he met her, understandably due to the circumstances. But he wasn't sure if Jane was sad. It was a bit different from sadness, he thought. He couldn't put his finger on it, what he felt from her. If anything, other than sadness, it was close to... endurance.

He felt that Jane was enduring. It could be her broken marriage, the bad relationship with her ex, bringing up a teenage girl on your own, or all of it. Or that she was living in a foreign country. But what was striking about her endurance was her acceptance. She somehow didn't seem to mind it. She seemed to have made peace with a life full of faults and the fact that you could not have everything right. Didn't she say that she didn't want to waste the suffering and tried to remember it every day? What kind of person would think like that? Everyone Frank met, including himself, wanted to forget the unpleasant parts of their life. This woman lived to remember. Did that make her sad?

He might find out if he got to know Jane better, but there was this matter with Mia for now. He was concerned, almost sickened by the thought that Mia could get involved with Simon. Daan was a gentle boy and wouldn't be able to stop Simon if anything happened.

It was nearly nine o'clock and probably not an appropriate time for a teacher to call a parent. But they'd better talk when Mia was not around, and Frank thought he would give it a go. Hopefully, Jane was still up.

When she answered, her voice sounded startled and anxious.

"Hello? Mr. Bloom?"

She must have kept his number on her phone, and he felt a bit uplifted about this. However, the reason could be because he was Mia's mentor.

"Hello, Jane. And it is just Frank, not Mr. Bloom, please."

"Oh, yes. Frank. Is everything alright? Is this about Mia?"

Jane sounded deeply worried. Frank swallowed hard.

"Well, yes. I just wanted to talk to you for a bit. Are you okay to talk now?"

"Yes, of course."

'I actually want to talk to you for a long time.' Frank corrected in his head and went on.

"I've noticed that Mia's grades have gone down recently, especially the last two months."

Frank could hear Jane's breathing. She was waiting and contemplating. "She got six for her assignment, so her Chemistry is okay."

'There, just boasting about yourself, aren't you.'

Frank was embarrassed, but the damage was already done.

"But her other subjects, the ones that she usually gets a good grade for without much trouble, are not as they used to be. Like English, it is one of her best subjects, partly due to you speaking English with her; but because she hasn't been doing any homework, she got an inadequate mark. And maths and geography too. Were you aware of it?"

Frank didn't mean to interrogate Jane but realized that it sounded like he was. 'Oh, dear, this isn't going well. It's harder than I thought.'

"I didn't know how bad her grades have got, to be honest. I was worried about her, although I couldn't think of why."

"What made you worry about her?"

"It was... I don't know. I can't explain. She came home late today and the last few days too. She said she was with Nora and Esther, and I didn't want to embarrass her by checking it with her friends, but I had this feeling... that she wasn't telling me everything."

Frank nodded as if Jane could see him.

"I agree that it would not have worked very well if you did check on her. But still, I think you should know where she was. I've only found it out today, and it will have to be confidential between you and me."

Jane sighed and closed the kitchen door. Mia wouldn't usually come down when she was doing her homework, wait, it must be something else that was keeping her upstairs, she realized now that Jane heard from Frank that Mia hadn't been doing her homework.

"Yes, I won't share what you tell me with Mia."

"Good. So... Did you know that Mia has a boyfriend?"

"Bo... boyfriend?"

"Yes. Did Mia ever tell you?"

"No... She didn't."

Jane sounded abashed to hear this from Frank. Probably she thought more in the line of school problems, with grades, teachers, or friends. But naturally, Mia could have a boyfriend whom Jane didn't know about. Most teenagers didn't run to their parents to tell them the news firsthand. Frank hoped that Jane didn't think it was anything wrong. Perhaps it was not allowed in her culture? He had no idea. Because it was a big thing for anyone, wasn't it? Your daughter's first boyfriend, possibly her first love.

"Of course, having a boyfriend itself is not a crime," Frank added cautiously, then hesitated a bit. "I wouldn't call a parent every time I see a girl hanging out with a boy. I was just concerned because of who he was. Well, more with who his mates were."

"Oh..." Now Jane sounded truly scared.

"Who is he?" Jane managed to ask after Frank waited for her to say something.

"The boy Mia was seeing is Daan. I know him a bit. He used to be my student two years ago. He is a nice boy."

"But his friends are not?"

Frank inhaled a long breath before he carried on. "No. I can't say that they are. In fact, I believe that the group of Daan's friends has had trouble with the police for some while. That's what I heard from other teachers and students. The leader of the group makes the others join in dealing drugs."

"Drugs?" Jane's voice was trembling as if she was going to start crying.

"Daan seems to be out of the business. But he still hangs out with them and is a close friend with Simon, the leader. I talked to Mia today when I found out whom she was seeing after school. Mia said she understood my concern and would stay out of Simon's business."

Silence from Jane's side.

"And I hope that Simon stays out of Mia's life too." That was what Frank was more worried about.

"Should I... What should I do about it, I mean, with Mia? Should I talk to her?"

"Well... I'm not sure if I'm the one to judge anything... but how close are you to Mia? I'm only asking because I know how the relationship with your child changes when they become teenagers. Does she usually talk to you about stuff?"

Somehow he could see Jane shaking her head regretfully to the telephone. "She used to when she was younger. Since she went to high school, she started keeping things from me. Which I understood she would naturally do as a teenager, and I didn't want to make it worse by pushing her too much."

"She does love you. A lot."

That seemed to have thrown Jane out. "What made you think so?"

Frank heard her chocked voice. "I could see it. When we talked today."

"Did she say something about me?"

"Yes."

"What did she say?" Jane was whispering, and Frank wondered if he should tell her. In his opinion, this was an even more weighty issue than the Simon problem, so he encouraged himself to speak to her.

"She said she couldn't tell you because it would make you even sadder. She said she was the reason for your sadness."

Then something happened that Frank never expected to happen.

Jane broke down. The second time today, a woman, a girl, the mother, and the daughter had cried on him. Frank was so stunned by what happened he fell into a sort of shock.

"Jane?" He could only murmur after at least ten minutes when Jane's sobbing had gone down a bit. "Are you alright? Has what I said upset you?"

Still lots of sniffing going on behind the telephone line, but Jane managed to answer his question. "I'm sorry... It's not you. It's...

what Mia said."

Frank's heart ached for her. He wished he could put his arms around her and hold her tightly. "I'm sorry to have told you."

"No, no. You had to tell me. Thank you."

Frank wasn't sure that he'd done anything to be thanked for. But he understood what she meant. "When Mia said it, I saw how much pain she was in, truly believing what she was saying. Which also showed the amount of love she had for you. I just felt that I had to share that with you."

"Yes..."

"Are you okay? Were you shocked?"

"Shocked? No... not shocked. She's never said that to me or confronted me with her thoughts, but I have felt it somehow, to be honest."

"Then what made you...." Frank gulped his words back, 'break down like that.'

"Is Mia right? To think like that?" It was a daring question from Frank. Maybe he crossed a line there with Jane as a practically unknown outsider.

"It is not true. But I can imagine why she thought like that."

"So you were sad, but not because of Mia. Is that what you're saying?"

A long silence. Then Jane admitted to Frank.

"Yes. That was how it was."

Frank felt that the atmosphere of their conversation had changed after Jane acknowledged how she was feeling.

Frank's voice got softer as he longed to be there for her. "If it's not because of Mia, why were you sad, Jane?"

'And why should she tell me such an intimate story? But please', Frank prayed, 'please tell me your story, Jane'.

"I was sad for lots of reasons, but none of them was Mia's fault. If I didn't have Mia, I don't think I would be here."

"Here, in the Netherlands?"

"No. Here in life."

It was Frank's turn to be speechless. He thought he felt how profound Jane's endurance was, but it was agonizing to hear the extent of it.

"What happened?"

"Ha!" Jane exclaimed faintly as if she heard something mad. "What has not happened is a more appropriate question. So many things happened, and everything changed. But that's life, don't you think?"

Then she seemed to be lost in her thoughts. Frank didn't want to interrupt her, in case she changed her mind and stopped talking to him.

"But it's not anyone else's fault. I made the choices, and I had to live with the decisions."

"What choices and what decisions?"

"To stay here. To marry Mia's father and stay with him."

"Was it a bad decision? So you regretted it, and that was why you were sad?"

"It's not as simple as that, at all. I wish I could simplify things like that."

"Sorry. I didn't mean to underestimate any of your burdens."

"But I didn't think it was a burden. At least, I didn't consciously think so. I just wasn't aware that other people saw that I suffered too, and Mia thought it was her fault. That's clearly my fault."

"You didn't mean to show it."

"No... I didn't, and perhaps that was the problem too. Frank, do you want to hear a Korean tale?"

Frank smiled at the sudden change in her subject.

"I'd love to hear the Korean tale."

"It is called the Dangun Story, and it's the founding myth of Korea."

Then Jane started to tell Frank the tale. Frank was mesmerized by her dreamy voice, and he could just see what she was describing in front of him.

A god's son, Hwan-woong wanted to help people and govern them in a way benefiting people. He came down, with his aides, to Mount Taebaek, a prominent, long mountain range running along the east coast of South Korea. A bear and tiger came to him because they wanted to become humans. Hwan-woong told them that if they truly wanted to be humans, they had to stay for one hundred days in a cave, avoiding sunlight and eating only mugwort and garlic. The tiger lasted only twenty-one days, but the bear persisted and turned into a beautiful woman! The woman conceived Hwan-woong's son, and the son, Dangun, established the kingdom of Korea. He ruled the country in a humanitarian way.

"Weird story, right?"

Frank didn't want her story to end. He loved listening to her dainty voice, and he was almost in a trance. "It *is* a bit weird but entrancing, nevertheless."

Frank could hear light amusement in Jane's voice. "You must be wondering why I was telling you this story?"

"I am waiting for that part."

Jane giggled. It sounded lovely when she did that.

"I couldn't explain how I felt in the past, how I lived through it. I used to think that I was the bear woman. It felt as if I was eating mugwort and garlic alone in a dark cave. That was how I felt for some years of my life. The bear had to go through it to become a human being. I had to go through it to be a mother. And my reward was Mia."

Frank gazed at the emptiness in his lounge. He felt the overwhelming presence of Jane's solitude filling his heart.

"But I haven't done an outstanding job being Mia's mother after all. Even after all that self-control. Mia felt it all, and she thinks it was because of her. Oh, Frank..." Jane's voice started to waver again. "I don't know what to do anymore. What if Mia throws herself onto someone else because she blames herself for her mother's shortcomings? What if these boys, who are not so innocent, take advantage of her? How can I help her?"

"Jane, first of all, don't think you've done a bad job as a mother. I think it's the opposite. You didn't see how much Mia just wanted you to be happy. Even I saw it today, and that's why we are having this talk." 'Also, because I was dying to listen to your voice again.'

"But how can I let her know that she was not to blame? That our life can't be explained in one simple sentence. Even with the best intentions, people fail, and it's not just one person or one mistake that breaks a relationship. Often we can't describe why love dies, either. How can I make her understand all that? I know that, for the last few years, I haven't explicitly been celebrating my life, but then, I have always been a modest person. I am not talking about being humble but being moderate in showing my feelings. That was how I was raised too... But I haven't been depressed or anything, at least not for some time now."

Frank was cautious about saying so, but he wanted to think with her and help her. "Maybe Mia remembered when you were very sad a long time ago."

"She must have."

"And for now... maybe she thinks you are here because of her while you'd rather be somewhere else, like your home country."

"But that's what I have been struggling to explain to her. We understand each other a lot, but there are a few things about which we—I, as a Korean, and Mia, as a Dutch kid—can't really get close to each other. There was this thing with her name... Oh, never mind. I don't know why I am telling you all this. Well, I know, it's because you are helping Mia and me."

"Tell me about her name."

Jane sighed. "Mia means 'a beautiful child' in Korean. When she was born, I thought that was the perfect name for the most beautiful baby in the world. You see, when I was pregnant with Mia, I had this talk with David about whether we should wish her to be beautiful or smart. It was a silly discussion. We were in a silly mood. We knew that it was not us who would have any influence on that. David said he wished Mia to be beautiful, and I hoped for intelligence because that would get you far in life even if you were not attractive. Then when I saw her, she was so beautiful, I had to give her that name. It staggers me now when I hear Mia saying that she doesn't think she is pretty. She thinks she looks freaky—her words—with her red-blond hair and different eyes. I am astounded that she doesn't see her beauty!"

"But what was the issue with the name then? Doesn't she like her name?" Frank was so intrigued with their conversation he'd forgotten what time it was. Not that he cared.

"When we went to Korea to visit my family, she heard her name on television. She found out that 'Mia' had another meaning, 'a lost child.' She was furious that I'd given her such a name." Jane let a long sigh of frustration. "I couldn't explain adequately enough that it's common for Korean words to have more than one meaning. People would only use a certain meaning for names, so nobody would think of a lost child when they hear Mia, but for Mia, it was something incomprehensible."

"It is quite a complicated concept if you're not familiar with it. I can easily understand Mia got confused because it is confusing to me too."

"But it would never have meant a lost child! But I seem to have failed to make that point to Mia, and now Mia hates her name as well." Jane still sounded flushed and went on. "Well, her name wasn't the only thing that we couldn't understand, of course. You see, unlike what Mia believes, it was never a sacrifice to stay here with Mia. So many people would love to live in the Netherlands, and I consider myself lucky too. From the moment I found out I was pregnant with Mia, we were here together. It's true, I'd have gone back to my country if I wasn't pregnant, but where Mia is, that's the only place I want to be."

"Mia knows that. She is a smart girl and a beautiful girl, and I can imagine she sometimes feels lost too, being a teenager. For you, it was never even an issue, being here with her, but maybe she felt the pressure."

"So what can I do to make Mia understand that it wasn't her fault?"

"I can only think of one solution."

"What is it?" Jane sounded hopeful for the first time since she answered his call.

"By being real happy right here, right now."

Jane swallowed hard.

"Then, Mia would know that she wasn't making you sad. She wouldn't feel guilty. And that's what you told me too. That it was a shame if you weren't happy while you were here."

By the time Frank put his now stone-hot telephone down, it was midnight. He had to charge it too somewhere in the middle of their conversation. They'd been talking for three solid hours!

Frank's head was full. It was enthralling to hear Jane talk, and there was so much to contemplate. Frank told Jane not to confront Mia at home yet about her boyfriend. He would keep an eye on Mia at school. If anything raised his concern regarding her boyfriend—now Jane knew he was called Daan—or other issues, he would call Jane.

Jane said that she was grateful for his help, and he should call her anytime when needed.

Frank thought of saying to her that they could also meet sometime to talk about things. But he didn't bring it up because he was glad that she was so open to him and didn't want to lose her trust by looking too eager. He shouldn't look like he was coming on to her, although he was. Instead, Frank invited her to the following parents' meeting.

"But... David would be there too." Jane sounded genuinely terrified by the thought, and Frank wondered why she was so intimidated by him. After so many years apart, Jane still seemed scared of him. That was the last thing that Frank wanted to expose Jane to.

"I've got an idea. When the email from school is sent to all the parents, I will write David another email. That I, as Mia's mentor, want to meet her mother this time. And he can come to the next meeting after that."

"Will he accept it, do you think?"

"Well, you know him better than I do."

"I doubt if he'll stay away. He doesn't like to be excluded."

"Well, anyone who has a bit of common sense would see that it's only logical."

Jane still sounded doubtful.

"I will clearly state that he isn't to come this time. Leave it with me, Jane."

So he had something to look forwards to now, seeing Jane in a few weeks, and he couldn't wait.

Although the things they talked about were anything but light and carefree, he was exuberant about their depth. Jane was such a spellbinding creature, and Frank had never encountered someone like her. Jane was his mystical merel.

CHAPTER 9
MIA

This weekend, Mia had to go to her father. She dreaded it because Serena, David's girlfriend, would be there too. Serena was not a mean step-mother type of a bitch. She was actually pretty nice. But Monica, one of her father's previous girlfriends, was Mia's favourite, and since Monica left, Mia had lost interest in any of his girlfriends.

Initially, Mia was on her guard with Monica too, because the girlfriend just before Monica only stayed for a couple of months. Mia was sure that the girlfriend—Mia forgot her name now—didn't like her. The girlfriend got angry if Mia said anything about her mother and told her not to do so in her presence. The girlfriend also had a daughter of the same age as Mia, and she could see the girlfriend constantly comparing Mia to her daughter. According to the girlfriend, David spoiled Mia due to the divorce.

"David darling, I know when your daughter comes here that you want to compensate for lost time and pamper her. But you've got to be careful. Otherwise, she might grow into a spoiled monster! My ex used to take my daughter, whom I raised with only the best things in the world, to McDonald's and order pizzas for dinner when he had her for the weekend. He let her stay late at night watching inappropriate films and bought loads of rubbish presents! Whenever she came back to me, I had to detox her from her father. You shouldn't overindulge your child."

As if he would indulge Mia! Mia sighed when she overheard the girlfriend complain. Her father was a sucker to have exorbitant stuff for himself and his house, but since the divorce, for anything Mia needed, he said, "Go and ask your mother. I've paid her enough money!"

The only thing that the girlfriend wasn't aware of was that David didn't like to be criticized, so thankfully, the relationship didn't last long.

Then Monica came along when Mia was nine years old, and she was different. Monica was younger than the other girlfriend and didn't have any children of her own. Monica didn't frown when Mia talked about her mother and was absorbed in Mia's story. Once Mia told Monica one of her mother's Korean fairytales,

"Kong-jwi, Pat-jwi."

"Look, Monica, it is just like Cinderella. Kong-jwi is the poor daughter whose mother died, and Pat-jwi is the bad stepsister. The horrible stepmother and Pat-jwi did everything to make Kong-jwi's life hard, but Kong-jwi ended up marrying the lord. But mama said in the Korean version that there was another story after that. The stepmother and stepsister tried to take over Kong-jwi's place but got caught and punished. Mama said that part of the story was not nice for children at all. Mama said fairytales were not always good stories. Do you agree, Monica?"

Monica listened to Mia's story attentively and nodded.

"I think your mother is right. I don't believe all fairytales are good stories, either. We need to make good stories ourselves."

"So, there can also be good stepmothers?"

Monica smiled at Mia. "Of course, not all stepmothers are like the ones in the story. They could love you a lot and become a good friend in your life."

"Do you think you can do that, Monica?" Mia looked up at Monica, full of hope.

"I believe I could. If we want to make this a good story, and we do our best, then I'm sure you and I can do this."

Then Monica added, "How lucky you are to have a mother like yours. It must be lovely to hear all these different, special stories!"

Astonished by Monica's good nature, Mia opened herself to her. At the time, Mia's mother had been overly tired, working hard to build a stable life for the two of them without her father's help. Even Mia knew how her father had made it impossible for her mother, refusing to pay alimony and hiring the most expensive solicitors to fight her. His reason for being unreasonable was that her mother contributed nothing to the household.

"What has she done for the seven years she lived in my house? Nothing! Nothing at all! She enjoyed the most luxurious life at my expense. That woman is a parasite!"

Mia heard her father ranting like this to Monica many times. He said the same to everyone around him. He also told Mia that her mother was stealing his money. "Your mother might go to jail."

When her father warned Mia in this way, Mia heard Monica gasping next to him. That was the scariest thing that her father had ever said to Mia, and Mia burst out crying. What should she do if mama went to jail? Did mama really do such a bad thing? Monica held Mia in her arms and told Mia's father in a stern voice that Mia had never heard from her before. "You have to tell Mia it isn't true, and you just made it up because you're angry. You have to apologize to Mia for lying."

"I will do no such thing! I can say whatever I want to say."

"But, it isn't true."

"It is!"

"David!" Monica gave her father such a look that even her father suppressed his temper and backed down.

"Alright. It's not true, Mia. Your mother won't go to jail."

Mia, still sobbing, asked her father, "But why would you say such a thing about mama if it's not true?"

"Because I hate that woman! That's why!"

Her father stormed out of the living room, and Monica looked at him as if she didn't know him. Then she came to Mia and held her again. "It's okay, Mia. I am here for you. You are safe here with me."

With her father's stance against her mother being like this, it took forever to settle things between them. Mia noticed that there was hardly any money for her mother to take Mia out to an amusement park or go on a holiday. These fun things Mia did with Monica.

Mia's favourite time with Monica was when Monica took her to her parents. Mia's grandparents from both sides were either too far away—her mother's parents—or not close enough to visit often—her father's parents. Mia envied her friends when they went to stay with their grandparents and had a great time with them. Mia had only her mother and father, which was not a lot, but now she had Monica too.

Monica's parents lived in a nearby village with a famous ice-cream shop and a petting zoo. Whenever her father had to meet some important people from other countries for work at the weekend, Monica went to her parents with Mia.

Monica's parents were as good-natured as their daughter and took Mia as their own granddaughter. Every time Mia came with Monica, Opa ("granddad" in Dutch) Wim took her to the petting zoo and bought her an ice-cream afterwards, and Oma ("grandmom" in Dutch) Ginny made her favourite Dutch dish—the pancakes with apple, cinnamon, and syrup.

"Mmmm, this is really delicious, Oma Ginny! I think you make the best pancakes in the whole world!"

"I'm glad that you like it, moppie ("sweetie" in Dutch). Here, have some more."

Stuffing herself with the third pancake, even to Monica's surprise, Mia blurted out. "My mother doesn't make Dutch pancakes."

Oma Ginny smiled at Mia. "That's probably because your mother cooks something more delicious for you. What does she make?"

"Koreans. Always Korean stuff. She said she tried but was not good at making Dutch pancakes."

"Oh, but that sounds really nice, too, Mia. Pancakes you can eat anywhere."

"My mother can't cycle very well. When it rains, we have to walk to school with an umbrella. It takes ages. All the other children come on a bike."

Mia didn't know why she talked about her mother so negatively, but she couldn't stop for some reason. "And she always tells me to be polite to my teacher and the old people on the street. I don't do anything wrong, but sometimes she still apologizes to people. I don't even know what I've done!"

Oma Ginny and Monica didn't say anything and just listened to Mia's outburst.

"And, and," Mia was almost out of breath spilling out all the bad things about her mother. "She doesn't have enough money to buy nice things and do fun things."

Then Mia felt horrible after telling all these things about her mother to Oma Ginny and Monica.

The pancakes Mia had stuffed inside her tiny stomach must have disagreed with what Mia was doing. They came out all over her, like a science explosion experiment that Mia had seen on kids' television.

"Oh, oh the poor girl...." Mia heard Oma Ginny talking soothingly, "It's okay, moppie. You are okay."

She saw Opa Wim bringing the wipes, and Monica cleaned her face. Then she took Mia to the bathroom, and Mia had a warm bath. Monica washed her dirty hair with the pancake pieces stuck onto it. Oma Ginny found some clean clothing, a spare shirt, and jeans from Monica's nephew, one of her grandsons. Mia was too worn out after the bath to protest about it.

They left Opa Wim and Oma Ginny's home, and Monica drove to Mia's father's house. Mia sat next to Monica in the front seat, which would have excited Mia any other time, but not this time. After some silence, Mia whispered, "Mama is nice. I love mama."

"Oh, Mia, of course, I know!"

Mia burst out in tears. "I feel bad talking like that about mama."

"Sssh, it's okay, Mia. It's okay." Monica's right hand reached out and patted Mia's knee comfortingly. When Mia's sobs calmed down, Monica asked her, "Why do you think you wanted to talk about your mom?"

Mia looked down at her knees. Although Oma Ginny said that you couldn't see it was a boy's jeans, she hated wearing a boy's jeans. "I don't know. Sometimes I wish you were my mom, Monica."

Monica looked at her sharply while driving as if she didn't expect to hear what Mia had just said. "How come, Mia? I know how much you love your mother. I've always thought your mother was so lucky to have a daughter who loves her like you."

"I do love her."

"But then, how come?"

"Because you are so easy to love. You know, Dad doesn't hate you and talk bad about you all the time as he does about Mom. And you are Dutch and can do everything as Dutch people do. You don't have your strange way of doing things or eat different food than the rest. Mom misses her family, and she is sad because they are so far away. But you have your nice family here. If you were my mom, I would have had Oma Ginny as my grandma and Opa Wim as my grandfather, and I can communicate with them! If you were my mom, everything would have been so much easier."

Monica drove on without saying anything. Then she said, "But, Mia, easy isn't always the best."

Mia didn't understand what Monica said. But she feared rejection. "You don't want me as your daughter?"

"Oh, Mia! Of course, I'd love to have you as my daughter. I told you that your mother was blessed to have you."

Then she turned her face to Mia and showed her brightest smile. "But the thing is, Mia, as perfect as you are and as much as I love you, you have your mother. And she loves you more than anyone in this world, and no one can replace your mother."

"But I want an easier mother! A Dutch mother! A mom who isn't sad."

Then they arrived at her father's house, and Monica turned off the engine. She didn't move to leave the car but held Mia's hand.

"Mia, being different is not a bad thing. Being different makes you special. You wouldn't want to look the same and be just one of the pebbles on the beach. And your mother makes you the special girl you are. I am here, as your good friend, and I will always be there for you when you need me. But don't forget you have a mother who loves you very much and makes you different, good different. Okay?"

Mia nodded.

"And that your mother is sad sometimes, that's okay too. Everyone has a time when they are sad. You have it too?"

Mia nodded again, and then she looked at Monica, agonized.

"But what if mama is sad because of me?"

"Oh, Mia, I'm sure it's not you who makes mom sad."

"But then who did? Dad?"

Monica didn't smile now, and she looked more serious. "I don't know, Mia. Maybe, maybe not. I don't know what happened when your dad and mom were still married. Only your mom and dad do. Perhaps you can ask Mom when you are older. What I know for sure is that it wasn't because of you."

Mia was still not convinced, but she agreed weakly. "Okay."

Then, Mia had to ask again, "But *you* like Dad? Mama said she didn't love Dad anymore. Will you love Dad always?"

"Oh, Mia..." Monica squeezed Mia's hand that she was holding all the time. "I can't guarantee anything like that. No one knows what's going to happen. But I promise that I will try my best to make this work." Monica smiled and said it cheerfully. "Now, let's go in and see what your handsome father is up to."

Monica and Mia carried on having a lovely time together. Every time Mia went back to her mother after such a weekend full of adventures, she was ecstatic and told her mother what she had done with Monica. Mia knew that her mother was a bit sad because her mother probably wanted to do the same thing with Mia herself. Still, her mother never said anything that dampened Mia's joy and always said, "Say thank you to Monica from me, for looking after you so well."

So naturally, when Monica moved in with her father, Mia was excited and looked forward to going to her father's house. She even wanted Monica to marry her father and hoped they would give her a little brother or sister. Oh, how she wished for a new baby! Then she wouldn't feel so alone anymore. Mia craved the noise, chaos, and disorderly, crazily fun family life other children seemed to have. It was rather quiet at her mother's house, and even Mia felt her mother wasn't up for expanding their family. She always said she was happy with just the two of them and didn't need a boyfriend. Mia was sure that her wish was more likely to be fulfilled by her father and Monica.

But then, unfortunately, things changed. During the half-year that Monica was there, Mia saw how difficult her father was to live with. When her parents were together, Mia never observed them as a man and a woman. They were her mama and papa, and the interaction between them as two grown-up adults never caught her attention. Mia was barely seven years old when she and her mother moved out of their family house, so probably she was too young to scrutinize that aspect of her parents' relationship.

After Monica moved into David's house, Mia saw how she gradually lost her vitality. Monica used to be full of energy and had wanted to create a home for all three of them, including Mia. When Monica was just staying over for a few days in the first half-year of their relationship, she didn't interfere with David's ways and went along with his wishes. But now, after Monica had taken the step to live with him, she wanted to have some influence on their life, which Mia thought was only natural. Her father and Monica had surely discussed these things before Monica left her own place, right? Mia couldn't imagine there could be anyone better for them than Monica.

But Mia witnessed then her father's different side as a man. She heard David ask Monica to keep things as they were and do things as he did. Even folding the towels and rolling the socks after washing them had to be done in his way. Having a hot breakfast was a no-go, whereas Mia loved the English breakfast Monica made for them at weekends. Dinner had to be at six o'clock on the dot every day, and only one glass of wine was to be consumed at home. There was no flexibility in her father's life, and he refused to change it for anyone else. She had to take it or leave it.

The fun-loving, relaxed woman Mia had seen at the beginning of her father's relationship with Monica had turned into someone frustrated, humiliated, and nervous around Mia's father. They had many quarrels, and although Mia was there only for two weekends a month, she couldn't miss their heated arguments and yelling matches. It was then when Mia found out her father threw things when he was angry.

Mia was afraid that her father would hit Monica too. She asked herself what she should do if he did. Should she call the police? Call her mother? What if he hurt Mia too? Why was her father acting like such an asshole? Was he also like that with her mother? Did he hurt her mom?

Mia tried to cover her ears under the duvet, but they could scream really hard. She heard Monica shouting, "If I had known what you really are like, I would never have moved in with you!"

Then her father's favourite line, "This is my house! Don't try to change me!"

Even Mia was astounded at her father's arrogance. Why wouldn't her father take other people into account? Why couldn't he adjust? Because he was so perfect and brilliant? Who did he think he was?

Wait, Monica was saying something. Mia raised the cover of her duvet to listen to Monica.

"Do you know what you are? There is a term for someone like you. You are a fucking narcissist! That's what you are! You're so in love with yourself, only yourself. You are a manipulating, gas-lighting narcissist!"

Mia didn't know what gas-lighting and narcissist meant until she googled them on her mother's computer when she went back home. And Mia agreed that Monica had a point. Her father tyrannized people close to him. He was textbook charming to strangers, a gentleman, and he had a way of getting things done remarkably easily. Mia used to hear everyone say—neighbours, teachers, and her friends' parents—"What a lovely father you have!"

He bought expensive, quality stuff for himself, was always dressed smartly, and had an excellent public manner. No one would imagine him screaming like a rotten brat at his girlfriend, claiming everything was his, and he was always right, and she had to respect him.

"Respect?" Monica was perplexed. "Respect is what you lack yourself. If you respected me, you would never treat me the way you do. You demand a total surrender from your loved ones. You want them to be your subordinates and obey you. You are abusive and violent. You need some help and anger management!"

Mia had never heard anything like what happened next. Her father must have hit their bedroom mirror with his fist. She heard glass breaking, Monica screaming and crying, and her father groaning in pain. Mia opened her door and ran to their bedroom. When she opened their door, her father was holding his wounded hand, and everything was covered with blood.

Monica seemed to be in another world. Then she saw Mia standing at the door and came to cuddle her. "I'm sorry, Mia. But I can't do this. I tried as long as possible because I wanted to make this a good story for you, and I wanted to be here for you. But I can't stay here any longer. I hope he doesn't hurt you as he has hurt me. If you need me, you can always reach me."

"Don't talk to my daughter! You have nothing to do with my daughter! She will never reach you because you are nothing to her and nothing to me. Get out of my house! And Mia, you go back to your room!"

That was the last time that Mia saw Monica in her father's house. Mia didn't reach out to Monica because her father said if Mia ever tried to contact Monica, he wouldn't forgive Mia. Monica was a bad person, a horrible woman who cheated on him and stole his money. If Mia ever saw Monica on the street, she should not talk to her and run away with her because she might take her somewhere dangerous. Mia couldn't believe that Monica was what her father told her she was, but Mia was only ten years old and scared of being kidnapped. And Mia was afraid to betray her father even when she knew that he was wrong. A child's loyalty to a parent was a burden that she couldn't comprehend but nevertheless felt its weight in her inner conflict.

About a year later, Mia went to the supermarket alone, and someone called her, "Mia! Hi!" It was Monica. And then, Mia ran away. She didn't even say hi to Monica. Monica, whom she had even wanted to be her mother. Monica, who took her to her parents and shared her wonderful family with Mia. Monica used to buy her lovely little presents almost every time Mia came to stay with her. She still had the bracelet engraved with "M & M forever."

Monica also sent Mia a birthday card to her mother's address after moving out of her father's place. Monica wrote that Mia could always call her and put her telephone number down. She said she'd like to hang out with her sometimes if Mia wanted to. Monica added that she missed Mia and that Oma Ginny and Opa Wim missed her too. Mia was her good friend. And Mia ran away from Monica.

Mia couldn't forgive herself for that afternoon. She couldn't forget the look on Monica's face when she turned around and left. She had nightmares afterwards, still continuing often.

With David's other girlfriends after Monica, Mia never bothered to open herself up. Mia now saw a pattern. David had an exceptional taste in women and talent in digging up friendly, warm, and kind women who even looked great too. They got smitten by him, fell under his spell and in love with him. Then they would, one by one, follow the same route. Her father would claim their total surrender and demand they surrender their whole time only to him, eroding their freedom. They lost their friends and family because David consumed all their energy. The stronger ones fought, then lost and left in a fury. The weaker ones gave in and started to mimic him. They told Mia the towels and socks must be folded as David showed them. They told Mia that dinner shouldn't be a minute later than six o'clock and Mia shouldn't talk about her mother in her father's house. But in the end, they all left when his tyranny became unbearable, after they had lost themselves and lived in isolation.

Her father once said to Mia, "I've never laid a finger on any of my girlfriends."

Mia thought, "Well, maybe not a finger, but your manipulation did more damage to them than a slap."

So after witnessing the unfortunate fate of her father's series of girlfriends, Mia was wary around Serena, lovely as she was. How long would she hang around? What stage of his manipulation was she at? Unless a woman had infinite patience with a personality disorder, or zero self-respect, or was an emotional sadomasochist, no relationship with David was going to last.

Anyhow, Mia was not going to be around the two of them this weekend. Dad and Serena didn't need to be bothered by her. She was going to stay in her room and just talk to Daan whenever he was available.

***

Daan had been busy lately. He had started a part-time job at a supermarket near his house. He lived in a different village, not where their school was, and far away from Mia's father's house, so meeting up had been challenging for the last couple of weeks.

"But why do you have to work so hard?" Mia asked, annoyed because she just wanted to see him more often.

"For next year, you dummy." Daan pinched her cheek gently when she pouted her lips at him. "I want to move out when I work for my uncle, and that requires money."

"But when you work, wouldn't you be earning enough money for a place to live in?"

"Well, not in the beginning, probably. That's why I've started saving now. And if you come and live with me, I'll need to take care of you too."

"But I would work, too." Mia didn't know what kind of job she could get when she was only sixteen and didn't have a high school diploma, but she would find something, for sure.

"I know. But you are still very young and need to finish school. So I need to help you out."

Mia put her head on Daan's shoulder. His plan touched her, and she wanted to do the same for him, helping him out. "But how much money do we need to save?"

Mia was thinking of her saving account that her parents set up when she was born. She had heard about it from them but had no idea when she could take it out or how much there was.

"Thousands of euros." Daan laughed at her shocked face.

"Thousands? Do we need that much money to save? To live together?"

"Not only to live together. I need money for other things too."

The smile had gone from Daan's sweet face, and Mia sensed some tension in his body. "What other things?"

Daan sighed. "Do you remember what I said once about Simon? The thing is ... he lent some money to my family when my father got injured at work and lost his job. I owe him lots of money."

"How much?"

"Two and a half thousand euros."

Mia's mouth was agape, and she was lost for words. Two thousand five hundred euros! She'd never even seen that much money before.

"But you shouldn't worry, Mia. It's not your problem. Simon said I don't have to pay it back until he needs it. I'm sure, as soon as I start working, it won't take that long to pay him back."

Mia thought about how she could save money for Daan. Her father wouldn't let her get a job until she was sixteen, he'd said that to her many times. Even then, he said she shouldn't do it. He'd rather see her spend her time studying and get herself into a university. Her mother wouldn't have minded it as long as it wasn't anything dangerous, but her mother couldn't let Mia do anything David was so against. Like the time when Mia wanted to do gymnastics. When he was young, her father had seen a girl who was paralyzed after an accident during gymnastics training, and he'd sworn to himself that his daughter would never do anything so extreme. So even after her parents' divorce, their different approaches to Mia's upbringing continued to cause lots of tension. It led to some outrageous fights between her parents. Mia decided long ago that she didn't want to cause her mother trouble like that. Even so... wasn't it time for Mia to start living her life?

What else could she do to save money?

When Mia arrived at her father's house, she saw another brand-new racing bike in his garage. He already had two! She was exasperated and wondered why her father would need a third bike, but that's how he was. Nothing spared for his brilliant self.

Maybe she could sell his bikes. Mia chuckled when she imagined his outrage when he found his precious, high-cost bikes gone. His blood pressure would surge up to the height of his ego! And that would be the end of her father's tie to Mia. She might try it when she really needed to break away from him. How much would three brand new racing bikes raise? As soon as the dreadful dinner with Dad and Serena was over, Mia would google on Marktplaats, the Dutch version of eBay.

***

During dinner, Mia felt that her father and Serena were still safe from disaster. Serena was clearly in love with her father and laughed heartedly at her father's arrogant, often politically incorrect jokes. She seemed to be in the phase of "I can't believe how lucky I am to have this dashing man." Mia wished their relationship would last longer. Serena appeared to have a remarkably docile character, and she might last a little longer. Wait until you move in, Mia warned Serena in her head.

Her dad and Serena were watching a film and chilling out in the lounge. Mia quickly googled how much racing bikes cost before retreating quietly to her room. Oh my god! Mia almost clapped in excitement. She didn't know her father's exact models, but what she briefly saw cost more than eight hundred euros each! They would already be pretty close to the goal. Her father would kill her if she sold anything, but it was an idea, a last resort in case things got desperate for Daan.

She wanted to call Daan, obviously not to share the plan she was nurturing, because she didn't even know how to sell things on the internet. She would probably need to make an ID, and a bank account of her own, because if she used her current account linked to her parents, they would quickly find out who did it. She didn't care about herself, but Daan would get into trouble with her parents. Her father would shun her and Daan for the rest of his life. He might get Daan arrested too. Mia suspected her mother wouldn't shut her down, but she desperately wanted her mother to like Daan. Otherwise, they would have no one to turn to, and Mia would have no family. When she realized the consequences of getting caught out if she did this, Mia gave up on the idea. She would have to think of another plan to help Daan.

Then someone called her on the phone. Mia was puzzled because Daan knew that Mia was at her dad's and wouldn't have called. She didn't want her father to find out that she had a boyfriend, and they had agreed they would only send messages.

It was from Simon.

Mia answered the phone in a hurry and was short of breath. "Hello?"

"Hey, Mia." Simon's drawling voice sounded friendly, surprisingly enough.

"Simon. Why are you calling me?" Then she was hit by a panic. "Is Daan okay? Has something happened to him?"

"Ah, I find it really sweet that you are so concerned about him.

Daan is a lucky man."

"So he is okay?" Mia whispered now because she was scared to be heard by her father.

"He is okay, relax. Although I am calling about him."

Mia's shoulder started to quiver. She was nauseous, afraid to find out what Simon wanted.

"You know Danny boy borrowed some money from me?"

Mia closed her eyes. The worst was happening.

"Yes."

"Did you hear how much it was too?"

"Yes."

"Two. Thousand. And. Five. Hundred. Euros."

Mia stayed silent.

"And I want it back. Soon."

Mia squeezed her hand into a fist. And she asked the most stupid question.

"All of it?"

Simon's laugh was so loud Mia covered the phone with her hand.

"All of it? Of course, I need all of it."

Something was growing inside her, fear probably, and despair.

"And I thought you could help Daan since you are such a good girlfriend to him."

Mia swallowed hard before she could speak. "How?"

"You could work for me. Every time you help me a bit, I would deduct that money from Daan's debt."

"What... do I need to do….."

"I need you to deliver things to people. People would be much nicer if a pretty little girl like you turned up with the stuff than my ugly, big boys."Another loud and throaty laugh.

Mia didn't want to ask what the stuff was. She knew what it was, and pretending not to know made it easier to do it.

"And how much would you give me for that?"

"Aha! Now we are talking business. I knew you were not just a pretty face."

Mia waited.

"Ten euro. Every time you deliver something to someone, I will deduct ten euros from Daan's loan. By the time you've done 250 rounds, he is free. Then you could even save up more money and live together."

Did Daan tell Simon about their plan? Wasn't it a precious secret for just the two of them?

"Is that the only thing, delivery? You are not going to change what you said and make me do other things?"

"Like what other things, Mia?"

"I... I don't know."

Hurting people. Stealing from people. Selling things. She closed her eyes again.

"So, what are you saying, Mia?"

She kept her eyes closed until she felt dizzy and hung up on the call.

Mia stayed up all night contemplating Simon's offer.

It was gruesome what she had to. She was rather timid and always felt awkward meeting new people. Now she had to go around strange places to deliver some dubious and probably illegal stuff. How could she do such things?

But she knew she could. Because she loved Daan. And by working for Simon, she would also make their plan possible. They would get away from home and live together.

She didn't say yes yet to Simon. But she knew her answer. She would do it for Daan.

CHAPTER 10
JANE

After the unexpected phone call from Frank, Jane was in a turmoil of emotion. Many ghosts from the past surged up from deep in the ocean and floated in a circle. They all held up a picture in front of her, tapped her on the shoulder, and confronted her. "Look, Jane, don't turn your head. You have to see this!" Jane tried to close her eyes, but they came floating inside her head.

Jane knew that she was a survivor. She wasn't just sitting on a train wishing it would just go on and on, although there was a time like that. But the truth was that Jane got on the wrong train in the first place and didn't know where it was heading. She was alone with Mia on the train and could ask nobody. She looked outside, and because she didn't know where she was, she was scared to jump out. What if it was a desert? What if there was no water and food for Mia and nowhere to sleep with a child? Here Jane had at least enough mugwort and garlic to eat. What if Mia didn't like where they were and wanted to go back to the train? What if no one knew who she was and she didn't exist anymore? After seven years of wondering and contemplating, the time had come. The unknown outside world seemed more inviting than the safe, sealed train, and she finally jumped out, with Mia in her arms.

Most of the time on the train was in a blur. Jane wanted to forget about the endless despair that swayed her every day. After she jumped out of the train, there followed a long search for a safe place. First, it took some time to find out where she was. From the middle of nowhere, where she got off, she started to walk with a child. When she saw a village and met other people, she asked for water and food for them. She wasn't good at asking for help, never had been, but now she had to. She needed help to find a shelter where she could recover from the journey and get strong. Then she knew she had to look for a house, get Mia back to her school, and find work. She needed to build a life for the two of them, a safe life, and that was where she had to go.

When Jane asked for the way to a place that she could make a home, she made mistakes. She was an amateur in asking for help, and she thought, 'I'm not going to make it too complicated for myself.'

Where she needed to reach, say it was E, was a long way. She doubted when she asked the way to E if she would remember the complex itinerary. So she divided the distance into intervening stops. She thought she would only ask the way to A first. From A, she would ask the way to B, then to C, and D, and as the final bit to E. That must be more manageable, right?

It seemed like a great strategy. E was hundreds of miles away, and when Jane arrived in terminal A, she asked a passer-by who looked friendly how to get to B. She told Jane to get on the train and change at A1. Then get on the bus to A2, and she could walk the last part to Terminal B. Which she followed. At terminal B, she did the same. She asked the way to C, and she got on the bus and had to change three times! Mia complained, and Jane was exhausted. If just getting to C was so challenging, how difficult would it be until they reach E?

But she had to go on. At terminal C, she asked the way to D. People overheard her, and all started to give her a different route. Someone said the quickest way was to take the train and change twice. Someone else said it was best to take the bus and change only once. It took longer but was a more comfortable transfer with a child than the train. Someone said, no, no, you are all wrong. She had to take both the train and the bus. That was the quickest and easiest. They all went into a discussion, and Jane didn't know what to do. In the end, following the last advice, she thought she was going to save her time and energy. But somehow, she ended up in H, instead of D, and cried with a crying baby. Someone asked what was the matter. She said, still wailing, "I had to go to D, but now I am at H!"

The man looked nonplussed.

"But D is quite far from here. How did you end up here? Is D your final destination?"

Final destination? Jane was astonished when the man inquired.

She had been so obsessed with getting to B, C, and D, but they were not her final destination.

She shook her head and said, "No, I need to get to E. That's my final destination."

The man smiled, "Well, that sounds a lot better. You know, E is much closer from here. In fact, there is an express train to E. You don't need to change, and it's faster than anything."

Settled on the express train with Mia, the most comfortable journey so far, Jane realized that her strategy wasn't probably as great as she thought.

She was too focussed on getting to just the next stop, and she'd lost sight of where she was going.

When the man at terminal H heard that she came from A, he didn't laugh at her, but he thought what she did was extraordinary.

"I don't know why you just didn't ask the way to E from the beginning. You've taken an excruciatingly long and hard way. There was an easier way, taking the express train from A to E, which would have saved you so much trouble."

The next time, Jane thought, she wouldn't mess around. She would just set her eyes on her final destination and go straight for it. If you are going to E, just ask the way to E! Not A, B, C, D stops in between! She'd learnt her lesson. So when she arrived at E, she tried to put the journey behind her and focus on her new life. First, she found a house near Mia's school. Mia liked the little cottage they moved into, and there was a small garden to run around with her friends. Jane was grateful she lived in the Netherlands because even when you lost everything and fell hard, a social net received you. With the local government's help, she managed to survive for a few months until she started working for a Korean company. Life got more manageable, and Jane felt better. She didn't want to remember how different her previous life was. Jane held her head high and only set her eyes on the future.

Until tonight. What Jane heard from Frank made her doubt if she had done the right thing. If she had, Mia wouldn't have thought that she was the problem. Jane didn't want to go back to the past, but now she had no choice. She had to look back where Mia had got that baggage of guilt and responsibility from. Jane couldn't hide any more from the damage that her difficult years must have left on her daughter.

***

From the moment Jane found out that she was pregnant and David proposed to her, it was pure madness. There was just so much to do until the baby came. Getting married in a registry office in Amsterdam wasn't as straightforward as Jane imagined. They had to declare that they were legally unattached, and getting her documents from South Korea was a nightmare. They also had to prove they were in a relationship, using private photos of them together, the horrendous phone bills a few months back, and as a cherry on top, the ultrasound photo of their baby. Then they had to wait for a month until there came no objection to their marriage from anyone. When all this was sorted, they had a brief ceremony at the city's registry hall with Mariska and her boyfriend as Jane's witnesses. To their great sorrow, Jane's parents couldn't make it to the ceremony, and nor could all her friends in Seoul. David also kept his entourage simple for Jane's sake, and she was fine with that. Jane had always dreaded marriage in South Korea, feeling that it was an affair between two families rather than two individuals. Jane preferred it this way, although she didn't tell her disappointed parents.

After they got married, Jane went back to Seoul to wait for her resident's visa. She spent the next three months wrapping up her old life. It felt different from when she was leaving for study or work. This time it was for good. She caught up with her family and friends as if it was the last time they would see each other. She said goodbye to her colleagues in the office, and it was bittersweet because she didn't know when she would be back to work and what she could do in the Netherlands. Jane chose carefully and packed the stuff she wanted to take. They were mostly books and CDs, her clothes—she hoped she would fit into them soon after the baby was born—and presents for the baby—they knew it was a baby girl now—and for David from her family and friends. When Jane received the green light to enter the Netherlands again, she left her homeland to start a new life with her husband. She welled up when her parents took her to the airport, but her mother said she would come and help her once her granddaughter was born. "Take good care of your husband, too," her mother said to Jane and touched her now rapidly growing belly for a long time. Jane was sad to see how old her mother suddenly looked then. She was leaving the warm nest that her parents had given her all her life.

Husband… how weird to call David her husband. She never imagined her being married at twenty-five and coming to live in the Netherlands. It was a wonderful experience to work for a year and taste the place and culture, but living permanently in a foreign country was entirely different. It was unsettling and intimidating. But Jane tried to put a brave face on it. What was nobler than leaving everything behind for your love? How romantic this all was!

She could change her place in the world because she loved him and the baby. The last few months before her contract finished were challenging, and there was friction between them, but things got better since they were expecting a baby. She saw that David had made a nursery room in their new house and got everything ready for the birth while she was in Seoul. She visited the midwife and learnt about giving birth in the Netherlands. She felt overwhelmed by how different it was from giving birth in South Korea.

In South Korea, cesarean section was more common, and the babies were born at the hospitals. The Dutch went for natural birth unless there was a medical complication and lots of women preferred to give birth at their homes. In South Korea, a woman stayed in bed for at least three weeks after the delivery and kept themselves warm—no cold shower and food allowed—and ate seaweed soup religiously. Here, Jane found, a woman had a shower just after the baby was born and had cold juice with a biscuit and special sweets. They left the hospital on the day they gave birth.

'Superwomen!'

Jane was amazed by the strength of the Dutch mothers. No wonder they carried everything and went everywhere on their bikes! In the rain and wind!

Jane wasn't confident that she could perform such a wonder too. Most important was that she should learn to speak Dutch. And to drive because cycling with a baby felt too scary. In Seoul, she didn't have to drive because it was a lot easier and more convenient to use public transportation. No hassle with traffic jams and parking. It was cheap too.

Maybe all the worrying and the strain from switching her country caused the baby almost to come too early. As stressful as the situation was, Jane was secretly relieved she was now allowed to give birth at hospital rather than at home. David, also, because he didn't want his house to be splashed with blood. And other things that were too sinister even to mention.

Jane was bedridden for the last two months of her pregnancy.

When Mia was finally born, Jane was so excited that they could now start their life as a family. David would be a devoted father as he already was before his daughter was born, and Jane just felt so much love for her daughter. She'd never felt anything so overwhelming as that. But it was also frightening to be responsible for someone else, a little person's life. Mia entirely relied on Jane to drink, to digest, to sleep. To survive, to grow, for a chance of a good life. The stronger her love for the baby, the more vulnerable Jane felt as a mother. Jane felt the massive task she was in charge of, whereas she was still just a girl herself. But she would have to transform quickly from a girl to a mother because Mia needed her more than anything in the world.

The first three months after Mia's arrival flew in the blink of an eye. David went back to work two weeks after the birth, and Jane was left alone with a newborn. Jane found she couldn't do what the Dutch super mothers did. It took longer than a shower and orange juice for Jane to feel remotely close to human again. Every part of her body ached, she lacked sleep, and handling the baby was more rigid than her office job. Jane missed Korean food like crazy, especially her mother's seaweed soup. She wasn't one of those Korean people who couldn't go a day without eating Kimchi, but she suddenly craved it too. She wouldn't eat any spicy food because of breastfeeding, but the craving and homesickness just washed her out.

David loved his daughter, but he didn't know what to do with such a tiny bundle of a doll who couldn't say anything back. He tried to help Jane with feeding and changing her, but he soon lost interest in the tedious job and went back into his old life.

Jane wished she also had a life to go back to, but she didn't have any. She'd burnt all her bridges behind her when she left her home. Jane wondered if other mothers also felt the same way, that it was almost impossible to look after a newborn all by themselves. She had no family to support her here. No mother to tell her what to do when her daughter just cried for hours, and she didn't know why. No friend to take a walk with and have a grown-up conversation with in the fresh air. And David's Obsessive-Compulsive Disorder drove her mad. He wouldn't let the baby stuff be displayed in his sight and stored baby wipes, nappies, and bibs away every time Jane needed to use them.

"David! Please! Can we just leave Mia's stuff on the table! I've got a baby in my arms and have to look for the stuff all the time. We can't keep the place picture-perfect like before. We have a baby!"

"I can't stand our house looking like a ghetto. We don't have to turn our life around because of Mia. Mia is our daughter, and she will need to learn to live with us. She will have to keep the place tidy too!"

"We can do all that when she is older. For now, I need to keep her stuff handy. You have to accept that you can't keep things the same with a baby. I have accepted it, too."

The discussion went on and on. While David was at work, Jane did all she could, taking care of Mia alone. But before he got home, she had to store everything back in the drawers because otherwise, all hell broke loose.

One day Mia just wouldn't drink, and every time Jane put her in her cot, she would protest and scream. Jane had no time to clear up the house. She hadn't eaten all afternoon and was still in the same shirt that she slept in last night, stained with milk, and god knows what else.

David came into the mess of the lounge, and stopped, looking horrified. "For god's sake, Jane, what is going on here?"

Jane felt fury rising in her but kept her voice calm for Mia. "Nothing is going on. I'm looking after Mia. That's all I am doing."

"Couldn't you just tidy up the house while you are home all day?"

"No. I couldn't. If you'd seen me today, you wouldn't have expected it too."

"This is disgusting. You could at least try to be less lazy."

Jane put Mia down in her cot, and her daughter immediately started to wail as if there was a sensor on her back.

"Did you say, lazy?"

"Yes. I didn't know you could be so inert when you moved in before."

"You don't know what's changed since then? How about your daughter that came into your life?"

"Jane, not every parent has to turn into a slob when they have a baby. It is your choice, you know."

A slob. That was how David saw her now after accidentally messing up with his protection and getting her pregnant.

'I didn't want to be this person you'd made me!' Jane yelled inside her head.

"If you knew it so well, why don't you take care of Mia all by yourself."

"And where would you be?"

"Anywhere, but not here."

"You are abandoning your daughter?"

"She is your daughter too."

"But you are a mother. Becoming a slob is one thing, but at least, try to be a mother, will you?"

'I wish I could go back to my old life! I wish you didn't exist!'

Screaming and yelling seemed to be the only thing Jane was doing those days, although only in her head. Because she didn't know how to say that in Dutch, and she didn't want to scare Mia.

'I wish I'd never met you! I wish you'd just let me go!'

"You need your celestial robe back," the fairy whispered to Jane silently.

Perhaps Mia heard it. The screams in her head. Jane covered her mouth in regret.

Maybe she'd seen and heard everything that went on around her as a baby, and that was why she thought she made Jane sad.

'Oh please God, please let her not remember any of this....'

Mia must have been only a few months old then, but babies could feel things too, Jane was sure.

Did Mia also remember when Jane tried to run away with her? Jane only physically attempted it when Mia was seven months old, but that was not the only occasion that Jane wanted to go. Since that day, there were so many times, that was every day. She remembered the event that led to the dreadful day.

***

Jane's mother came to meet her granddaughter in the Netherlands. It was her mother's first international flight across the oceans. Jane knew her mother, and if it hadn't been for her granddaughter, she wouldn't have dared to take such a long, scary trip alone. Jane counted the days before her mother arrived. She missed her mother and her old home in Seoul so much, and the ache in her chest wouldn't go away whatever she did. Sometimes Jane wondered if the law of conservation of mass also applied regarding happiness and luck. When Jane counted all the blessings of her early life with her family, friends, study, and job, she was frightened to imagine how many difficult times she would have to experience to compensate for that. Jane feared that she was now in the middle of the big payback time.

Mia would now turn herself over on the rug when Jane put her down, and Jane played with her on the floor. Watching her baby trying to crawl and now showing more interest in her toys, a familiar feeling used to visit her. A dangerous mix of gloominess, despair, and loneliness overwhelmed her whole body and shook her to tears. She hid her face from her daughter. Jane was determined that Mia shouldn't see her mother crying. But sometimes, she couldn't control her emotions and had to hold Mia on her chest so the baby wouldn't see her face.

Jane's only hope was her mother's coming. Her mother would remind her who Jane was, and Jane would be able to find herself. Jane could remember how warm and content her mother always made her feel, and she would crawl out from this endless hole of depression. Her mother would make her right again. Because Jane found out, as much as she was wary of the law of conservation of mass, it was her mother's love that kept her going and fighting for sanity. That would be her only medicine. Otherwise, she didn't know what she would have done when she was yelling and screaming in her head like a crazy woman.

Jane's mother arrived with massive volumes of Korean food. Kimchi, seaweed, miso paste, and chili paste. Barley tea for the baby. Jane's favourite prawn crackers. Jane didn't want to open and eat them. They were too valuable. Just looking at them, feeling the package in her hands, and saving them in the kitchen cupboard made her feel like the richest person in the world. David's face crunched bit by bit every time her mother took the food out of her suitcase. Even in sealed packages, these had their particular odor, and David was not amused by these in his kitchen, to put it mildly.

Then the same thing started to happen with David and Jane's mother. The ingredients Jane's mother had brought disappeared when her mother wanted to cook for Jane. Jane went through every cupboard and fridge compartment, but they were not there. After a thorough search in the house without a result, Jane found them in the back garden. In the bin to go out the next day. Her mother was stunned when Jane brought them all back from outside and washed them in the sink, but Jane couldn't tell her mother where she had found the food.

Jane's mother was the most gentle and loving soul, but David couldn't tolerate her Korean way of doing things. Her mother was concerned that Mia was now crawling on the floor. Her mother had had an operation a few years ago with her problematic knee, but she still knelt on the floor for her granddaughter's hygiene and wiped it with a mop. When David saw Jane's mother on the floor with a bucket of water and cloths, he went bombastic. He shouted at Jane, "This laminate flooring is a special kind, and it needs a special cleaner! She's ruined it. Your mother's damaged my floor!"

Jane had never been so thankful that her mother didn't understand any English. Still, David wouldn't stop going on how expensive his floor was. Her mother must have felt the strain from his loud bouts and escaped upstairs with the crying Mia. Jane closed her eyes. The precious time with her mother, which Jane missed so much and waited for such a long time, had turned out to be more stressful and depressing because Jane had to watch out between David and her mother continually. It was her only hope to climb out of the ruins in her soul, but it had failed. Jane exploded, as she'd never done in her life before. "Stop!"

David stopped. He was astonished because he'd never seen Jane so enraged in front of him. David was unaware of her silent screams or that Jane only held herself in for Mia's sake. He didn't think that Jane was able to rage like that.

"I am so sick of it. Sick of you! If this floor is so important, I will give you money to fix the damage. Just stop going on about it when my mother is here!"

"Did you say you were sick of me?" David's eyes glared dangerously. "Sick. Of. Me?"

"Yes. I can't stand the sight of you. You're arrogant, imperious, selfish! You are such a jerk!"

"And that's coming from a woman who is lazy and worthless. You seem to have forgotten that you came here with nothing, nothing at all! You are not even a good mother because you are depressed, aren't you? You cry every day because you are so miserable looking after your daughter. I've never seen anyone so useless. I shouldn't have brought you here."

David's words throbbed Jane's brain. "You brought me here? Have I missed something? I neither asked nor wanted to come here."

"Ha! Don't kid yourself."

"Excuse me?"

"You can't deny this is a much better place than where you came from. You complained about the subway trains you had to take to work and how you had to stand like a bean sprout. You wanted to come here and live like us. I've saved you from a dump!"

Jane didn't even know where to start. South Korea was probably more advanced in some aspects than the Netherlands, and she missed nothing in life in Seoul. Jane would love to stand on the train like a bean sprout more than anything, and she'd fly to the train right now! She was just in shock to have found out finally what this man, whom she called her husband, honestly thought about her motives for marrying him.

"I didn't know anything about you." That was all Jane could mutter. "You didn't save me from anything. I didn't need saving from anyone. I was happy with myself and my life. Don't treat yourself with false heroism because you are not my hero, far from it!"

"Is that right? What about the first time that I saved you from that junkie? What would have happened if I hadn't helped you out? Huh?"

He stepped closer to her while gazing at her intently. Jane wasn't sure if he was entertained by the memory or angered by it. He looked both.

"I would have been fine," Jane whispered, suddenly anxious from the glare in his eyes.

"Don't lie. You know yourself that something would have happened to you. You'd have been taken by that junkie and maybe by more men."

Jane opened her mouth, but nothing came out of her.

The only thing she was repeating in her head was, 'I didn't know him. I didn't know.'

"You were a slut, going to club after club, looking for fun. I knew that you were playing around when I met you."

"I... " What was David even talking about? She was twenty-four, for god's sake, and single. What did she do wrong, just having harmless fun with her friend?

How she wished to go back to that carefree girl. She was swayed by that longing, having discovered who David was. "I'd rather have been taken by anyone but you. Anything would have been better than living with you now."

Her husband then changed into a stranger. Jane's words transformed the man in front of her into someone vile, who could hurt her viciously.

He threw her onto the dining table, and he took her from behind. Jane, numbed by the violence and shock, silenced herself with her sleeve. She bit into her arm. 'Mom and Mia are upstairs. They mustn't hear anything.'

When David left the lounge, she pulled up her trousers with her trembling hands, and her legs went like jelly.

Sitting on the floor, she heard the garage door being slammed. Mia started to cry upstairs.

Jane wobbled, walking to the sink. She turned on the tap and splashed water on her face. Then aggressively rubbing her face with cold water, she remembered the words.

David said just after he withdrew from her, "Don't even think about taking Mia. I will follow you to the ends of the world."

She heard her mother cajoling Mia in Korean. It was time to feed her. She adjusted her shirt and trousers and checked herself in the mirror under the stairs. Then she walked up the stairs slowly, one by one, to call her mother and daughter. She had to act like a daughter and mother.

Two weeks later, Jane's mother and Jane stood at Schiphol Airport. Her mother was going back home, and Jane wanted to hide in her mother's suitcase. Just like when she was eight years old, and her mother went to look after Jane's sister-in-law, who gave birth. She didn't want to be parted from her mother.

It was more excruciating to see her mother walking on tiptoe with her husband. Jane hated herself for putting her mother in such a degrading situation. She swore that from now on, she would go to South Korea to see her mother, not the other way around. Her mother didn't confront Jane with anything until they left the house in a taxi. Because David didn't want to come with her mother, he offered to stay at home with Mia, and Jane was relieved that they were alone.

Jane checked her mother in for the flight, and they had a coffee at the sterile airport café with no atmosphere. Her mother still didn't say much, just held Jane's hand and stroked her daughter's face with her coarse hand.

Then her mother had to go in. At the departure hall just before the entrance where Jane now could not cross with her mother, they stopped and stared at each other.

Her mother's face crumpled like a paper ball. Jane could see every line of her mother's wrinkled face. Her mother's gentle, loving face was covered with the saltwater that Jane couldn't see anymore because she was covered with it too. Her mother held on to Jane as if she was leaving her child behind in an orphanage. She held Jane like she knew that she was losing her daughter forever.

"Come back anytime you want, Jane. You have us. You have a home. You are not alone. Don't you forget that."

That was the first time that her mother acknowledged her daughter's unhappiness. Jane realised that all mothers had the same ability to feel their child's pain, as she now felt Mia's.

***

Jane covered her face with her hands. She wanted to cry, but nothing came out. She'd cried all her tears many years ago. She didn't shake anymore when she was confronted with those memories. But she was bringing up the memories now for a different reason. Mia. What if Mia had heard it somehow through the wall. Their charming, characteristic old house had thin walls. What if Mia had seen her crying above her bed when she was sleeping like an angel. What if... she'd heard them when David was taking her violently.

Sometimes Jane wanted to tell Mia. She didn't want her daughter to know, no way, but sometimes she wanted her to understand. Without telling her, Jane couldn't explain why she was so sad and that it wasn't Mia that made her so miserable. But Jane couldn't and never would tell Mia. She'd damaged her daughter too much already by staying with her father. Jane thought she did that for Mia, but it was the opposite. That was the mistake Jane had made, then still so shortsighted as aiming just to get to the next stop, rather than to where she had to be.

CHAPTER 11
FRANK

Frank kept his promise to Jane to watch Mia closely at school. Her grades had no sign of improvement, and to be honest, Mia didn't seem to mind it that much. Mia hardly hung out now with Nora and Esther. Mia used to sneak out during the breaks, but Frank saw her resting her head on her desk a few days ago. He was stunned to see her asleep. To his concern, Mia kept nodding off in his class, and he caught her asleep the following days as well.

Jane had asked Frank to call her anytime there was something up with Mia. He was about to call her that evening when Jane called him, beating him by a few seconds.

"Hello, Frank."

Jane sounded unsure. Frank was grinning like a child with a pleasant surprise when he heard her voice. How happy he was to hear from her!

"Hello, Jane, good to hear from you."

"Oh, it's kind of you to say so. I hope I'm not disturbing you."

"No, not at all. Is there something you want to talk about?"

He knew it would be about Mia. Jane still sounded hesitant.

"It's Mia. Since last week, she's been coming home really late. Well after nine."

"Nine? Did she say where she was?"

"She said that she had a part-time job at a supermarket and met up with her friends after work."

"Did she? Did you two discuss work before?"

"She did ask about it a few months ago. But her father told her she should focus on school."

"I see. So Mia just took the initiative and went for it."

"It seems so."

"Are you worried? Not happy that she's working?"

"Well, it's just that I don't know if she was telling me the truth. I really don't know these days. Maybe I'm getting paranoid. I think it's good that she wants to work. Only if her father finds out he will give both Mia and me a hard time. But maybe it's time for both of us to stand up for ourselves."

"Is he still a big influence on your life?"

"Well, old fear doesn't die so easily."

"Sorry?"

"No, what I mean is, he is such a dominant man. Whether I like it or not, he *is* Mia's father, and as much as Mia seems to despise him lately, I'm sure she loves him in her heart."

"All children do. Well, up to a certain point, I guess."

"Yes. There's only so much you can bear." Then Jane changed the subject as if she regretted what she just said. "I was wondering if you would talk to Mia sometime. To ask her what is going on with her job. I hardly see her at home, and she gets angry when I try to talk to her. She said I should stop interrogating her." Jane sighed.

"I did notice that she was tired at school. I also wondered if Mia fell out with her friends."

"Nora and Esther?"

"Yes. They were not really doing anything together at school."

"Oh, that's weird... Mia went out with them even this week. At least, that's what she said to me."

"I see." There seemed to be something that Mia was hiding. Now Frank was sure. "I will talk to Mia. And you are coming to next week's meeting, right?" He'd been waiting for it for the whole month.

"Yes. Did you send the email to David?"

"Yes. I'm sure it will be fine."

'What will happen if he indeed turns up against my advice? Could David be possibly that unreasonable?' Frank wondered then told himself. 'Relax. I'm sure I was clear enough in a polite way.'

He heard Jane saying, "Thank you for listening to me, Frank. I appreciate that I could call you and ask for your help."

"It's no problem." Then he realized that Jane was hanging up and he didn't want her to. "Oh, wait!"

"Yes?"

"How is the project coming on?"

Jane sounded puzzled. "Project? I don't know anything about Mia's project."

Frank smiled. Jane thought he was talking about some Chemistry project. "No, not Chemistry!" 'Although we could work on the chemistry that you provoked in me.'

"Which one then?"

"Our project. Remember what we said to do? To make Mia see

that you were not sad anymore?"

"Oh..." Jane was quiet for a moment. "I didn't know it was your project too."

Frank felt the heat on his face. "Well, it sort of is since I'm the one who came up with the solution."

Jane sounded even more staggered. "So it is our project now? Why would you want to be involved?"

"Because I like you." That must be his Dutch courage, literally and figurately speaking.

Silence from the other side.

"Jane?" Frank didn't plan to blurt it out like that. He had planned to to put some time and effort into earning Jane's trust and affection for as long as it took. But being impulsive as he sometimes was, it was out and done. What an idiot.

"Why?" Jane whispered.

Frank tried to dig out some more Dutch courage in him. "It sounds crazy, but I don't know why. I just liked you from the first time I saw you."

"You mean when I turned up at your place demanding an apology?"

"That's right."

More silence.

"That is probably the craziest thing I've ever heard." Jane said equally matter-of-factly.

"I'd probably agree with you."

"So, what is it that you want from me?" Jane's flat question reminded him of the first time they met.

Calm but deadly, that was what he thought of her. "I don't even know what I want from you. Haven't thought about it."

"You are not really good at this, are you?" Jane chuckled at Frank's clumsy answers in disbelief, which for some reason, made Frank ecstatic.

"No. Never been good at romancing a lady, I'm afraid."

"Me neither. It doesn't sound very promising."

"Well. I do know one thing I want, though." Jane stopped her sweet chuckling.

"I want to see you smile. A lot. All the time. I would really like that."

"Is it because..." Jane's voice was severe, and Frank could imagine her face dead-serious talking to the phone. "I look so hopelessly miserable and depressed?" Jane didn't sound upset when she said such a horrendous thing about herself.

"No!"

"No?"

"You do look pretty, if I may say so."

"Ha!"

Maybe she was getting angry now.

"I don't know how to explain. The last time we talked on the phone, you said, 'often we can't describe why love dies.' Do you remember?"

"Yes."

"Then could you also say, 'sometimes you can't describe why you love someone?'"

Jane didn't reply.

"I know love is quite a big word, we don't know each other very long either, but I am fascinated by you. How you think and how you see the world differently than I do. I want to get to know you if you'd let me."

Jane murmured something, but Frank didn't catch it.

"Did you say something, Jane?" Then she said it so softly Frank wondered if he heard it right.

"I hope you can handle it."

Was that what she said?

Frank wasn't 100% sure, so he asked her gently. "Are you afraid I couldn't handle you?"

Jane hesitated, then she admitted. "Yes. Are you not?"

Jane's notion about herself dazed Frank.

"Why do you think that I should be worried about that?"

"Well, don't you ever wonder why people get divorced? To me, everybody seemed to think like that. Whenever you find out that someone is divorced, you think, what could the reason be? Isn't that right?"

Frank recalled that he was wondering exactly that.

"See, you did too." Jane knew what Frank was thinking. "I'm not telling you off or anything. It's what we all do. I do too."

Frank didn't know what to say anymore.

"Sometimes other people notice what is not right in a relationship, even before the couples do. But sometimes it is hard to trace anything, and often the couples can't explain either."

Frank coughed to come clean. "That's what I thought too. When

I met Mia's father, then you, I wondered what would have happened in your marriage."

"Any idea?"

"No. Except that he was irate and nasty towards you. I couldn't imagine why he or anyone would feel that way about you."

Jane laughed softly. "Do you know what people tell me all the time?"

Frank waited for her to tell him.

"I think it's meant to be a kind remark, almost a compliment. I'm sure people say it because they like me."

"I don't understand why someone like you is divorced. You seem perfectly normal. You are not bad-tempered, you didn't let go of yourself, you are not stupid, I can't think of anything wrong with you! How come?"

Frank just listened, simply because he was ashamed to have thought that himself.

"So we all think whether we explicitly admit or not, that divorce is for people with some kind of malfunction. We try to look for the impairment, some obvious ones, and some invisible ones. Where are the faults and defects?"

"Jane, I didn't think....."

"It's okay, Frank." Jane stopped him rushing to deny such behaviour—which would be a lie.

"Because I am damaged, of course."

Jane's statement of doom exasperated Frank.

"Damaged? Jane, it is not the middle ages that we are living in! Nobody would think that you are damaged because you're divorced. Practically, at the rate it's going, everybody will soon be divorced, at least once."

Was it because she's a South Korean? Is divorce a big no-no, a taboo in her country? Is that why she sees herself so negatively? Frank was stupefied when Jane laughed at his bewilderment.

"Frank, I don't have anything against divorce! In fact, I'm grateful people can get divorced, that it is not a sin like in the middle ages. For some people, marriage is a prison, and you need to get out of it."

"Then why do you speak so about yourself, and why do you think I can't handle you?"

"Because I am damaged, Frank," Jane repeated patiently. "I couldn't start a new relationship for the last eight years because

I'm scared. I'm afraid to feel something for someone and then find out he isn't the person I thought he was. I'm terrified in case the other person would misjudge me and think I'm something other than myself. I would rather die than put myself in a relationship where I would lose myself. I have scars from my marriage to Mia's father, Frank. And I've been thinking about it since we talked last time. I've had to recall what happened. And I can see that as hard as I tried not to show it, Mia must have known. Of course, it wasn't her who caused the destruction, but she's seen the damage and blamed herself. I've damaged her too."

There was only one thing Frank could say to Jane. "You asked what I wanted from you, Jane."

It was quiet again on the other side.

"I know what I want. I have a goal—to have a meaningful life with a wonderful person like you. I have opinions—that you will find different from yours and mostly immature and stupid. I have a religion—well, I am Jewish, and although I don't practice the religion, I do believe in what some of us went through. In fact, Primo Levi is my god. And I have love—which I wish to be you. If I can be myself, I will be satisfied. And if you can be yourself with me, I will be satisfied too."

Frank heard Jane gasping and gulping. Why was she making such a strange sound? Frank remembered the conversation they had the first time and guessed that Jane must have also been familiar with what he quoted, Anne Frank.

"Jane, in other words," Frank concluded to Jane, who still said nothing, "I can handle it. A piece of cake."

Then he heard Jane burst out laughing, mixed with the strange sound she was making.

"Now, can I also ask you a simple question? To get to know you?" Frank asked.

Jane must have nodded. Frank could see.

"What is your favourite song?" he asked her.

Jane typed, 'The Greatest Love of All' on Youtube on her laptop.

Frank didn't know this song. He was familiar with Whitney Houston's other popular songs, mostly from the movie *Bodyguard*, but he didn't remember hearing this one.

Even after they had hung up, Frank played the song over and over. It could have been for an hour, and it was well after midnight. He thought it was one of the most remarkable songs he'd ever listened to and happily dozed off on the couch. It was then that Frank saw Jane behind his closed eyes.

In his dream, Jane was holding a baby girl in her arms. She was lulling the baby to sleep and singing the same song. She was repeating the words, and her face was covered with tears.

Then Frank knew that Jane had come far from where she had been. He had said so casually that she should be happier, but he realized it was too much to ask from her. It was such an attainment that she just stood here now. In his dream, Jane didn't look like the woman whom he'd fallen so hard for. He'd never seen such a sad face before.

***

Two days later, when Frank saw Mia again at her desk asleep, he gently woke her up.

"Mia? Are you okay?"

Mia opened her eyes with difficulty, startled, and sat up.

The break was about to finish.

"Will you come with me to the next classroom? I know it's empty, and it's the self-study hour. I'd like to talk to you."

Mia nodded in confusion and started packing her bag.

When she was ready, they went to the next room, and Frank closed the door.

"Are you alright? Do you need some water or anything?"

Mia shook her head.

"I was wondering if you were feeling okay. I've seen you sleeping during class too. Are you unwell or tired?"

"I'm just tired, that's all."

"I see."

"Now, can I go?"

"Well, let's talk a bit more. How come are you so tired?"

"Why are you asking? I could have been playing a game or watching Netflix all night."

"Were you?"

Mia stared at Frank like he was a mad man.

Then she gave up. "I started working in a supermarket. Filling the shelves."

"That's not a bad thing, having a part-time job. Well, it's positive. Only I would be a bit concerned if that made you so tired that you had to sleep at school. You seem to have forgotten to hand in lots of homework too. I remember you were working hard to make it to the next class a few months ago. What's changed?"

"Nothing. Nothing's changed."

"Some things have. You have a boyfriend, Daan."

"And what of it? Is that not allowed from school?"

Mia was indignant at the mention of Daan.

"How is Daan?"

Mia looked sideways, "Why don't you ask him yourself?"

"Do your parents know that you have a boyfriend?"

"Look, Mr. Bloom, I don't think you have the right to dig into my private life like this."

"You know you can always come to me if you need any help."

"Help with what?"

"Have you seen Simon lately?"

Mia stood up, grabbed her bag, and started to walk off.

"Which supermarket, Mia?"

"What?"

Mia stopped, and Frank saw a panic passing in her eyes.

"Which supermarket are you working at?"

"What do you want to know it for?"

"I might drop by and say hello."

"None of your business."

Then she turned around and left the room.

'That did go well,' Frank told himself satirically. It wasn't a waste of time, though, because Frank was now confident that Mia didn't work at any supermarket. He would need to investigate where she was going and what she was doing. He only hoped it had nothing to do with Simon.

As eagerly as he wanted to get on with his private investigation, he had other work to do. The parents' meeting was in a few days, and he had to prepare for a fifteen minute session with the parents of twenty-one students, including Jane.

While he was going through his students' files, he found himself whistling Jane's song.

It was funny, Frank thought, how Jane's song spoke to him. It could have been about a teacher too.

Yes, I also believe the children are our future, and that's why I became a teacher.

'Madness!'

He saw the blackbird again through the window and laughed at himself.

He was relieved that Jane knew how he felt about her.

It would be a bit awkward when they finally met each other at the parents' meeting. He'd seen her only once two months ago and never since. Since then, she'd been in his head all the time. The thought of her was growing and had taken all the space in his brain.

'I hope she won't feel uncomfortable coming to the meeting after my blurting out what I feel for her.'

Then he started to whistle the melody.

* * *

It was the evening of the parents' meeting.

Frank put Jane on the roster for the last slot, so he didn't have to finish in fifteen minutes.

It was the second and the last day of the meetings, and although he was exhausted, he felt full of vitality, looking forward to seeing her.

Then at half-past eight, Jane stood at the door which Frank left open.

"Hi," Jane stayed at the door and didn't just come in.

Frank jumped up energetically, and he thought he must look like a panting dog. "Hi! Please come in. Have a seat. Coffee or tea?" '

Jane smiled at his enthusiastic offer. "How good is your coffee?"

"As good as the school coffee goes."

"Then no, thanks. Just tea, please."

"Good choice. Sugar?"

"No, thanks."

They sat with white plastic cups in their hands, and Frank beamed like a fresh lightbulb.

He forgot this was a parents' meeting and just wanted to stare at her face.

She looked more beautiful than the last time which he had played over thousands of times in his head. Today she was wearing more colours. It was April and much warmer than February. Jane wore a yellow dress down to her knees and a denim jacket over it. He recognized the same black bag with the yellow ribbon and the ankle boots.

"You look nice."

"Do you always compliment what a parent is wearing?"

Frank laughed nervously. "No. Never. Only when I've told her that I like her. I've already made a fool of myself, so there's no shame left in me now."

A cautious smile started from her mouth and spread wide on her face. Her eyes were smiling too. "Shall we talk about Mia now?"

Frank coughed when Jane made this suggestion. He hoped that no one was listening to their conversation. He would have to behave now. Look serious. "Yes. About Mia. This term's report is here."

Jane took the paper sheet from Frank—with two hands—and studied it. "It's not looking very great, is it?"

Frank shook his head. "I'm afraid not. As I told you on the phone, Mia's grades have gone down quite dramatically. It would be difficult for Mia to go up to the next class if she doesn't do anything about it."

"I see." Jane sighed. "You know, I'm not even worried about the grades anymore. I used to, only because I thought it would make Mia disappointed with herself if she didn't make it to the next class. But now, I don't really care. I just wish I knew what Mia was occupied with. As long as she was feeling okay, I wouldn't worry about the grades."

"I understand. I'm worried about them too. I talked to Mia a few days ago."

"Did you? How did it go?"

"Difficult. Mia was sleeping on her desk again, and I asked her if she was okay. Mia said that she was just tired. I asked how come, and she told me about her job. But..."

"But?"

"My gut feeling as a teacher says that's not what she's up to."

"Oh..."

Watching Jane's face, Frank realized that this wasn't going to turn into a date night. Jane had lost her smile again.

"When I asked her which supermarket she was working for, she looked alarmed and didn't tell me."

Jane nodded in silence.

Then, Bob, the concierge of the school, knocked on the door and said to Frank.

"Still working? Everyone's left, Frank. It's nine o'clock."

"Okay, Bob! Thanks, we're leaving." Then Frank nodded at Jane. "We'd better go."

Without speaking, the two of them walked out of the room and school.

As Bob had said, the car park of the school was empty except for their two cars.

Frank walked with Jane to her car. "I'm planning to investigate the case if you want me to."

"What do you think she might be doing, Frank? Where did she go if she wasn't working at the supermarket? And why would she lie about it if it was something legitimate?"

Frank saw Jane's eyes were filled with terror. She was trembling, and the report sheet she was holding in her hands was fluttering too. He couldn't bear to see her standing like that. He stepped towards Jane and hugged her. "Maybe she didn't want to get into trouble with her father. Everything will be okay, Jane," He whispered in her ear.

At that moment, a car, a large sports car, came from nowhere and screeched to a halt next to Jane's car. Jane freed herself from Frank, and they stared at the interrupting vehicle.

"What the?" David yelled, opening his car door and stepping out like an angry bear. He looked furious.

"I thought I would take a chance and drive to school before you left! And what do I see here? Are you two an item? Is that why you told me not to turn up? How scandalous!"

Frank saw Jane was still shaking, although she lifted her chin. Her voice was miraculously calm, and he couldn't hear her trembling when she spoke, "And why are you here, David? When you were told not to turn up?"

"I can perfectly see what you two are up to. Is it even allowed? To have something with your student's parent? Maybe I should ask the principal about it. And the fact that you tried to exclude me from a parents' meeting where I've got every right to be as Mia's father!"

Frank wasn't intimidated by David's threat, just feeling disgusted with the person he was. God, to think that Jane had to live with this guy! Poor Jane, but how strong she must have been to go through that for so long! "Do what you want, Mr. Hollander. Is there a reason why you wanted to come like this?"

Frank wanted to punch David's face, but he held himself in check. Dating a student's mother was one thing. Fighting with the father was another matter.

"I don't know what you are doing as a mother. You do a rubbish job, as ever. Do you even know what Mia is up to? Any idea?"

Jane didn't reply to him because she didn't know. Jane couldn't disagree with his slagging this time because she was feeling like a rubbish mother.

"I don't think Jane deserves such a comment, Mr. Hollander." Frank couldn't stop himself; he had to interfere.

David laughed aloud and shook his head in disbelief. "It is Jane now, is it? God, you two are pathetic. And I will tell you why this woman is a rubbish mother. Her daughter was trying to sell my bikes on the internet. My brand-new racing bikes! Three of them! I just found out that she was googling the prices on my computer. You've raised a thief! It was always you who looked after her, so we all know who is responsible for that kid. Well done, you've done a great job bringing up a scamming daughter!"

Jane and Frank just stood there, not knowing what to say. Was that what Mia was up to? Selling her father's stuff to make money? But why would she need so much money? For what?

David was satisfied looking at the shock on their faces. He looked smug and pleased with himself bringing such news about his own daughter. "Tell her that she will have to explain herself if she wants to come to my house. But I've had enough of that girl. Good luck with her. She's all yours."

Then when he was almost sitting in his car, he came out again and shouted at Frank, "Wait! Aren't you that teacher who killed the gay boy? I thought your name sounded familiar. Aren't you gay yourself?"

Jane pulled Frank's elbow tightly as if she knew what he was thinking of doing.

"So are you into both men and women? Jane might not have noticed if I hadn't told her, she's so thick! But she is, of course, an expert herself in fooling around. A student abuser and a slut! You two deserve each other. Well done!"

Then the car screeched away, and Frank could see David's face as he laughed out loud in the car.

They stood still for a while after the car had disappeared.

A long sigh, more like a groan, escaped from Frank's stiff mouth. "I know."

Jane tapped his arm gently. Frank realized she was still holding on to his elbow.

"What kind of man would own three racing bikes, outrageous, right?" She shook her head.

For some reason, Frank started to laugh. "That was exactly what I thought. Three bikes, goodness me." Then he added, "Now I fully understand when you said that you couldn't work it out. I don't think anybody can."

Jane started to laugh too.

"I love it when you laugh. It makes me so happy."

Jane's laugh changed into something more subtle, a smile that Frank had caught the first time he met her and had missed ever since then.

'God, I want to kiss her.' He thought of the scandal if anyone saw them. Like, Bob or Ron if they were around somewhere. 'Damn it, why should I care when this asshole is going to tell everyone? I might as well kiss her.'

So he kissed her. And to his surprise, Jane didn't push him away or slap his face. She kissed him back. Feeling dizzy from euphoria, Frank had to support himself not to wobble.

Then he remembered what David said. "Oh, by the way, I'm not gay. Not that I would have a problem if I were, but I am just not."

"I think I could judge that perfectly well just now." Jane was smiling.

"And it wasn't like what he said. I didn't kill any student, for your information. It's a long and sad story. One of my students was struggling with his sexual identity, and I was close to him. He killed himself, and his parents blamed me."

"How tragic."

"Yes. He must have felt so alone. I wish I could have helped him better."

"And for you too. You must have felt so alone if that's how people talked about it."

"Yes." Frank realized that it was the first time anyone had acknowledged his pain, and he felt the long-awaited comfort releasing it.

Jane nodded, looking into his grateful eyes. "Believe me, if anyone knows about how it feels to be slandered, that's me."

"Well, then I am in good hands." Frank kissed her again.

"But who said that you are in my hands?" Jane challenged him when he stopped for breath.

"Am I not?"

Jane pretended to think about it. Then she smiled. Oh, that smile.

"I think you are. In good hands."

'We deserve each other.'

The only good thing that came out of that filthy man's mouth.

Jane shivered and said, "I know it's April, but I'm always cold."

"Come here. I will warm you."

He held Jane in his arms and kept her warm.

"How come are you so cold, my Jane?"

Jane tilted her head. "I don't know. I've been cold ever since I came here. Strange, because it gets even colder in the winter in South Korea. It goes down to minus ten or something, and we have so many ski resorts too. But it's a sunny and dry cold, and maybe that's different from 'waterkoud (damp cold)' here."

"Maybe. Or like cold hands, warm heart."

Jane looked up at him, and her eyes were dancing with a smile. "Maybe."

The refrain from the song appeared in his head. He hummed it to her.

Jane stiffened when he started singing the song, and then she relaxed in his arms.

So he carried on, until the end, and then this time, Jane stood on her toes and kissed him. It was the best parents' meeting in his fifteen years' career.

CHAPTER 12
MIA

Mia had been working for Simon for two weeks now. Six times, she had delivered something to people. Something. It was apparent what the stuff she took them was. She could see it from the eyes of the recipients.

Simon said he was cautious on her behalf. He didn't want her to get scared and do a bunk. Once it was in a park that she handed a white envelope to a man. Then it was in a car park around by the train station. A few times, she knocked on someone's door and handed in the small package. There seemed to be a party going on. So she'd done it six times. Sixty euros. It felt nothing compared to how much this was taking over her life. She was exhausted from being nervous and afraid. She hated the time she had to spend with Simon's gang. They all looked at her differently without Daan beside her. When she thought of how many times she would have to do the run to get rid of Daan's debt, she was overwhelmed by despair. It was soul-destroying.

When she wasn't working for Simon, Mia waited for Daan around by the supermarket he had worked for the last few weeks. It was forty minutes biking from his village to her house, and that made her tired too. She'd never felt so drained in her fifteen years of life.

Despising the prospect of hanging out with Simon, Mia thought she might have to give it up. It was evident that she would get caught soon. Her mother didn't seem to believe what Mia was saying, and Jane looked so distraught. And then there was this Mr. Bloom. Mia was staggered by the attention he was paying her. He's gone mad this term. Before he gave her a low grade for her assignment, he wasn't interested in her or any other student. Now it seemed like he was watching her and following her everywhere. That he'd noticed how tired she was and was asking questions was alarming. It wouldn't take long until he physically turned up at the supermarket if she told him the name of one. But she wouldn't be there, and that would be the end of the story. What a bummer... Why was he making her life even more complicated?

And there was Daan too. He had no idea what Mia was doing for him. Simon said she shouldn't tell him. It would hurt Daan's

pride. "Don't let the right hand know what the left hand does."
She hated Simon's hoarse laugh. Funny that he knew something
from the bible. He was the most unlikely person to be going to
church, in Mia's opinion.

***

Mia came home early that day. She'd said no when Simon called.
She couldn't be enthusiastic when she counted two hundred and
forty-four runs left. Mia felt annoyed with Daan too. Why did
she have to do something so horrible for him when he wasn't
doing anything for her? Well, he said he was saving money for
their future together, but why wasn't he doing the runs for his
loan shark himself? It hit her when she realized that she was
doing something that Daan disapproved of. Daan said Simon
asked him repeatedly to work for him, and he said no. It scared
Mia when she thought Daan would blame her for getting
involved with Simon.

Simon didn't sound amused at all when Mia told him she was
going home. "What about Daan's debts? Are you already giving
up on him?"

"I am not giving up on him. I just can't do it anymore."

"Can't do it, or don't want to do it?"

"Both."

Simon chortled, "Oh, oh, Mia, you don't understand, do you?"
Then his voice became stern. "It's not like you can just quit
when you want."

"Why not?"

"Because what you've been doing was wrong, you knew that,
didn't you? And now you are one of us. We could just give your
name to the police or let your parents find out. The moment you
pay off the rest of the money will be the moment you can quit."

"But it is not my debt!"

"You took it over with love."

As if he would know anything about love.

Feeling exhausted and angry with Simon and herself, Mia threw
herself on her bed.

She just wanted her mother. Mia hadn't seen her mother for ages,
hanging out with Daan and working for Simon. Last night it was
the parents' meeting at school, and when her mother came home
late, Mia pretended to be asleep. Her mother gently opened
Mia's bedroom door and called her name softly, but Mia stayed

silent, whereas she yearned to lie in her mother's arms and fall asleep like when she was a little girl. Her mother used to tell her tales from her childhood. She told the stories from her favourite books and sang the songs she loved. Mia wanted to tell her mother everything and get rid of the heavy load on her chest. But mom would be so disappointed with Mia. She would be shocked to find out what she'd been doing with Simon. She would be sad that Mia didn't confide in her and tell her everything about Daan. The last thing Mia wanted to see was her mother becoming sad. She dozed off, wishing she would never wake up.

***

"Mia? Are you alright? Were you sleeping?" Her mother woke her up, and Mia didn't know what time it was. "Were you home early? Have you eaten anything?"

"What time is it?" Mia's body was groggy, and her voice was husky.

"It's half-past six. I'll make some dinner. Will you come down in a bit?"

Mia nodded from her bed, and her mother left, closing the door behind her.

Mia wasn't hungry, although she hadn't eaten anything since the breakfast. She got up and opened the door, and shouted downstairs, "Mom! What are you making?"

Mom answered back from the kitchen, "The Japchae!"

Ah, Mia's favourite. In that case, Mia would come down.

After having a ridiculously long shower, Mia sat at the table. Her mother was almost done cooking and mixing the glass noodles with the beef and vegetables.

The smell of sesame oil made Mia suddenly ravenous. It was the first time in two weeks that they were sitting down together and having a nice meal. That was Mia's fault, though.

"How was the parents' meeting?" Mia remembered to ask her mother this. She had been totally abandoning her school work, and there couldn't have been anything good said about her.

"Well, it was interesting." Her mother smiled, and Mia wasn't sure whether it was a rueful smile or a mischievous smile.

"Interesting grades?"

"That, for sure."

Her mother brought plates, and she put the Japchae in front of Mia. "Let's eat first. I've got a dessert too."

"What is it?"

"Strawberry cheesecake ice cream."

Mia's favourite again.

Then it crossed her mind that her mother had prepared Mia's favourite things for a reason.

"Wait, is there something you want to coax me about?"

Her mother pretended to look hurt. "Coax you? What do you mean?"

"That you need to sugarcoat me with food about something."

Jane burst out laughing.

'That's strange. Mom is laughing!' Mia got even more suspicious.

"Hey, you think about it. If one of us needs to sugarcoat the other, would it likely be you or me?"

Mia thought about it. It was Mia herself—a good point.

Mia shrugged and started to eat the delicious food.

"So what else was interesting than my grades?" Mia brought it up after she'd stuffed herself with everything her mother had made. She felt like she could eat all night, so deprived she was to her surprise.

"The most interesting part was that your father turned up."

Mia's mouth was wide open. "Dad? He came too? But wasn't it your turn this time to come to school?"

"Yes, we thought so. But he turned up."

"Why?"

"He was informing us about what he suspected you of."

Mia's appetite was gone. "What did he say?"

"He thought that you were planning to sell his racing bikes on the internet."

Mia's stomach churned. Too much food, which she now regretted. "Why did he think so?" Mia tried to keep her voice calm. How the hell did he find out?

"He saw you were searching it on his computer."

Ah, that was it. Mia couldn't believe that she didn't think about this when she googled it at her dad's house. But searching it can't be a crime? She hadn't actually done anything. Only thought about it. 'Keep calm and carry on.'

"Well, I was curious about how much it would cost, seeing Dad had bought yet another one. I couldn't believe how much money he was spending on bikes, when he always finds it so difficult to spend any money on me."

"That's what I thought too."

"Thought what?"

"That you were just searching out of interest."

"Yes, of course!" Mia felt genuinely indignant about her father's suspicion as if she had nothing to do with it. "But how come Dad thought I was trying to sell them? He must think I was a scam or something."

If he only knew what she'd really been doing... Mia swore that she would stop working for Simon. The more she thought about it, it was such a risk for her and Daan as well.

"He seemed to think that you were trying to steal them and sell them all. Weird. I don't understand why he thought like that. He said you needed to explain if you wanted to see him."

Mia rolled her eyes in outrage. "I don't want to explain myself to him, and I don't even need to see him if he sees me like that. He can forget about it."

Her mother shrugged. "I wouldn't push you to do anything if you don't want to. But he is your father, even if he is such a difficult person."

"He's a horrible person. I wish you hadn't had a child with him."

Her mother was aghast with what Mia just spat out. "That child is you, and I wouldn't want to change you with anyone."

Her mother sounded so shocked and in disbelief, and it melted a bit of Mia's heart. "Even when he is such an asshole?"

"Even if so. You are worth it all."

"How can you think that?"

"Think what?"

"That I'm worth all that trouble. If you hadn't had me with Dad, you would have been much happier."

Her mother put her ice cream spoon down on the table. She had held it in her hand when they talked about Mia's father, and now her strawberry ice cream was pink liquid. Mia's half-eaten ice cream, too.

"Mia, this is probably a good time for us to talk."

"We were talking."

"No. A real talk. As a mother to daughter, and also woman to woman."

Mia had never seen her mother so determined. Except for the day her mother told her that she was leaving her father.

They moved to the lounge and settled themselves on the couch. Her mother wrapped Mia's legs in the blanket, and Mia rolled her eyes at her mother's funny habit. "Mom, it is you who's always cold! Not me!"

Her mother stopped her wrapping and smiled apologetically. "You are right. But it's comforting when you have warm feet." Then she picked her cup of tea from the coffee table. "Mia, why do you think it is because of you that I was unhappy?"

Her mother watched Mia closely while she sipped her tea.

"Well, I've just told you. If you hadn't had me, you wouldn't have had to stay in the marriage with Dad."

"But it doesn't always work like that. It is not as simple as that. I've tried telling you many times that you were my light in the tunnel. I couldn't have gone through the time without you."

"But without me, you wouldn't have had to go through the tunnel!"

Her mother sighed. "See, this is like the discussion about the chicken and the egg. We are like the chicken and the egg. Without me, you wouldn't be here. Without you, I wouldn't be here. We are here because of each other, and we are nothing without each other."

Mia sighed too because her mother didn't think logically. "But Mom, if you married someone else, you would have had a different child, and you would feel the same way about that child too. It didn't have to be me."

"It had to be you, Mia! You are the daughter for me. It sounds crazy and impossible, but I've always thought that you would be my daughter even if I married someone else. Because... I know it isn't right that I felt that way, but I've always felt that you were my child rather than our child."

Mia was quiet. She didn't think what her mother was saying made any sense. She tried hard to see her mother's point, but it just didn't work.

Mia's mother looked desperate for a way to explain her illogic. "Look, I'm struggling to make you understand, so I will have to borrow some inspiration from my favourite book, *Anne of Green Gables*."

Mia knew that it was her mother's all-time favourite book. Jane told her that she used to hide her favourite books under her textbooks at school and read them. She was caught from time to time and had to clean the teacher's room. Mom was fond of all the books from the series, but most people only knew the first one, and it used to infuriate her when the teachers said, "The same book again?"

"Anne admires Mayflowers and exclaims to Diana—her best friend—that she is sorry for people who live in lands where there are no Mayflowers. Diana is sweet but less imaginative than Anne, so she says, as practical as she is, "Perhaps they have something better." Anne thinks there couldn't be anything better than Mayflowers. Diana says if they don't know what they are like, they can't miss them. But, then, Mia, listen, Anne says that that is the saddest thing of all. Tragic, not to know what Mayflowers are like and not to miss them!"

Mia blinked at her mother in total bewilderment, thinking, 'What is she even talking about?'

"That the saddest thing is not to know their existence and not to miss them!" Her mother repeated stubbornly, but Mia gulped hard.

"So... what are you trying to say, Mom?"

"Don't you see, Mia? I feel the same way about you! That there couldn't be anyone better and it would be tragic not to know you! Isn't that clear now?"

Mia shook her head. "No. Not even a bit."

Her mother flailed her arms in more desperation. "Then what about when Anne says on one splendid day that she pities the people who aren't born yet for missing that day. They may have other good days but never this one? Does this make more sense to you?"

Mia shook her head harder. "Nope. Absolutely not."

"Oh, I feel the same way about you!"

"Mom! I have no idea what you are trying to tell me!"

"Then how about that I've always believed that even if I had married an African or Korean man, somehow you would have popped out of me because I chose you."

Her mother's thought was just too ridiculous. Mia burst out laughing and couldn't stop until she had tears in her eyes. "I don't know where you get these crazy ideas. You've read too many books."

Her mother admitted, defeated, "I probably have. I love books."

Then her mother's eyes got serious again. "So you could repeat that I could have had a different child, but I never wanted a different child. I don't. And don't force me to say that I should have wanted someone else."

"Do you really think so?" Mia looked up at her mother through her eyelashes from the other side of the couch. "That you would still have had me with someone else?"

Her mother nodded. "Yes. It makes perfect sense to me. I've always wanted to have a red-haired girl since I loved Anne of Green Gables so much. Oh!" Her mother exclaimed as if she remembered something, and then her face started to blush. "I have something to tell you."

'Oh dear, what is it this time?'

Mia's eyes got bigger when she spotted her mother's strange excitement.

"It is about Frank."

Mia tilted her head in confusion. "Frank? Who is Frank?"

"Oh, Mr. Bloom."

Now Mia couldn't close her mouth. "Oh my god! You are not going to tell me that you have something going on with Mr. Bloom? The bully?"

It had gone over Mia's head that Mr. Bloom hadn't really been living up to his nickname for the last few months. He'd been... actually, pretty nice. Did that have anything to do with her mother? Was she the one who had changed him?

"Now I get it!" Mia screamed in her enlightenment. "That's why he's been paying so much attention to me! He's been observing me all the time, and he's been unusually kind to me. That's why!"

Her mother's cheek coloured again. "I guess that could have been why. Although I find him just kind, a good person."

"You can't be serious, Mom! He's kind because he likes you. Oh my god, you lied to me!"

"I lied to you?"

"Yes! You said that Dad turning up was the most interesting thing, but this exceeds everything! What happened with you two, and how long have you guys been loved up?"

Her mother laughed. She did start laughing more often, Mia noticed. "We haven't been loved up, whatever that means. I saw him for the first time, well, because of your assignment, a few months ago."

"And was it on since then?"

"On? No, no. Somehow we started to talk, and it kind of hung around, what we've been saying to each other. I think we recognized that we had something in common."

Mom and Mr. Bloom have something in common? What can that be?

Her mother looked at Mia and smiled. "We recognized that we are both survivors. We have endured. And it started from there."

Mia thought about what her mother said. "What did you two have to survive from?"

"Oh, the usual. The misjudgment, incomprehension, prejudice, and injustice we all face in our everyday lives. Everyone is fighting their wars, as you are too, Mia, and Frank and I just recognized each other's wars."

Mia wondered if it was the same with Daan and her. She saw in Daan his determination to break out and stand on his own feet. He was kind and caring too. Was that also what Daan saw in her? Had they found each other?

"And now? What are you going to do?" Mia turned her thoughts to her mother and inquired.

"Oh, I don't know. I'm just telling you because you need to know. You are the most important person, and you should be the first one who finds out what is happening with me."

Mia swallowed hard when her mother said this.

Mia asked her mother again after a while. "Do you really like him, Mom? Does he fill your 2%?"

Her mother was surprised to hear Mia's question. "I do like him quite a lot, I think. We can talk to each other on the phone for hours, and I can tell him anything. We understand how the other person feels. And about the 2%....%

"I don't know if I still believe in it. I shouldn't expect anyone else than me to fill the 2% now, I think. I've managed on my own since I left your father, and I must be capable of feeling complete with myself. And," her mother carried on with her serene air, "I think missing 2% is probably not a bad thing. If you have everything fulfilled in your life, what is there left to search for anymore? The feeling of missing something gives you reason to go on. I'd rather have that in my life."

"I just hope... he is nice to you." 'Because Dad wasn't.' Mia added silently. "I hope he makes you happy."

"Oh, Mia! I am happy as it is. As long as you are happy, I'm happy."

"No, Mom, stop being a mother for once. You haven't only been a mother all your life. You were Jane before I came along, sorry, I apologize for that, and you must care about that Jane too. That Jane also needs to be happy. Whether the mother part was happy or not."

"But how can I be happy if you are not?" Her mother genuinely didn't think it was an option at all.

"Well, I don't know! But surely you can distinguish your mother part and Jane part and can feel joyful if everything else is going well beside me, right?"

Her mother pretended to consider the case. "No, of course not. Do "you" really believe that I could do that?"

Mia imagined her mother madly in love with Mr. Bloom, winning the lottery, her father suddenly being normal and decent towards her, or even living in South Korea. At the same time that Mia was delivering the drug to random people for Simon.

No, it wouldn't have worked. Knowing her mother, it would be impossible, Mia admitted.

Then she wondered, what should she do to make her mother happy?

Making her mom happy, that had been what Mia wanted most for as long as she could remember. She tried to find ways to do that. She told her mother the stories that would make her proud, things she did well at school.

Sometimes Mia just made up stories that her mother would like. She had a feeling that her mother knew that Mia didn't do all those wonderful things that she claimed for herself, but she wanted her mother to think that Mia was the most wonderful child. Mia performed her dance and sang her song to see her mother clapping and loving the show. She made the cutest present in her craft class at school and spent hours making her drawing perfect for mother's day.

But now Mia realized that she only needed to do one thing to make her mother happy.

Mia needed to be happy.

Mia felt her eyes were welling up, but she didn't want to cry. She changed the tone of her voice. "Just tell me if Mr. Bloom mistreats you. I would give him some horror teenager attitude."

Her mother laughed again.

"You laugh a lot, Mom. I love it when you laugh."

Her mother nodded in agreement.

"That's what Frank said too. That he loves it when I laugh, and he wants to make me laugh."

"Well," Mia's throat was choked, but she made an enormous effort to sound normal. "Then I think Mr. Bloom and I are on the same track about that."

***

Later that night, Mia was lying in her bed and thinking about what her mother had told her. Mom and Mr. Bloom... Who would have thought it? She wondered what her father was going to say if he ever found out. He had always been so possessive about her mother, even after their divorce. Her father believed that the reason her mother never had a serious relationship after him was that she couldn't forget him. He was the best man she could get, and now she'd left him, she couldn't find anyone as fantastic as him.

Her mother had asked Mia why Mia thought she had made her unhappy. Mia couldn't tell her mother that she knew. Why her mother had to leave her dad and what had been happening to make her want to escape.

Between the walls of their family home, Mia had heard sounds. Sounds that Mia wasn't meant to listen to; sounds that were always muffled. It was never explicit, and Mia didn't know what it was until she was older, not until she was almost in high school. All the pieces of the puzzle came together when Mia realized what her mother was going through.

"I've never laid a finger on any woman in my life."

After the many fights with his girlfriends when he threw things, her father used to say this to Mia. He was abnormally obsessed with his precious stuff, so it made him more enraged after he had destroyed them in a fit of anger. But Mia wished her father had hit her mother instead. Then people would have known. Maybe her mother would have got some help sooner. She could have left before she was damaged so much.

'Perhaps you never have laid a finger on a woman. Instead, you put your dick into a woman. You hurt Mom. I heard everything!' Mia wanted to scream at him.

Mia was five years old when she woke up one night and went to the bathroom. When Mia opened the door, the light was on, and her mother was crying under the shower. She was pressing her mouth with her hand not to make a noise.

Mia could never forget that picture of her mother. Her mother saw her standing there and stopped crying. She came out and hugged Mia and Mia got all wet. The water was dripping from her mother's hair, and Mia didn't know if it was water or tears running down her mother's face.

"Are you hurt, mama? Shall I get a pill for you?" Mia was worried. Maybe her mother had a bad stomachache, or a cramp like Mia had—growing pains, her mother said, massaging her legs—and needed to have some medicine.

"No, Mia. I'm okay." Her mother tried to smile.

"Then, why were you crying?"

Her mother was struggling to find something to say to Mia. "Sometimes you cry because it makes you feel better."

Mia didn't understand. "Do you feel better now, mama?"

"Yes, Mia. You make me feel better. You are my medicine."

Her mother saw that Mia was wet under the embrace of her own water-dripping body. "Come on, let's have a warm shower together and put on new pajamas. Shall I sleep with you tonight?"

Mia wished that her mother would sleep with her every night to make her mother feel better when she needed it.

But her father wouldn't have it. Because Mia was a big girl now and she had to sleep like a big girl, on her own in her room. "I bought that lovely bed for you! Do you know how much it cost?"

After that night, Mia woke up often, as if to check whether her mother was okay. Mia never saw her mother again in the bathroom crying under the shower, but she did hear noises.

The rustle in her parents' bedroom and then silence. The noises weren't loud, but still, the rustling felt dangerous, forced, and ruthless. The silence afterwards was deadly. It scared Mia. Sometimes she heard her mother walking around the house like a ghost. She was worried in case her mother became a real ghost, so she followed her mother.

Her mother was startled to see her. "Oh, Mia, have I woken you up?"

"Are you hurt again, mama?"

"No, Mia. Besides, I've got you. Even if I get hurt, you are my medicine, remember? Don't worry about me. Little girls like you are not supposed to worry about a big mummy like me. Okay?" Then her mother made some tea for herself and warm milk and honey for Mia, and they giggled at the shadows they made with their hands on the kitchen walls. Mia's favourites were the bunny and a dachshund.

One night, when Mia couldn't stop laughing because her mother was giving a finger puppet show with the finger puppets they found in a draw, her father opened the kitchen door in a fury. "What are you two doing in the middle of the night? I can't sleep with all the noise you two are making. Mia! Go back to bed. I don't ever want to see you downstairs after you go to bed. Jane! Are you out of your mind? What kind of mother are you to let your child stay up like this? You really need to think better as a mother and change your behaviour!"

Mia then stopped on her way out of the kitchen and turned to her father. "Don't say that to mama! Mama is the best mama in the world. Don't hurt mama!"

Mia thought her father was going to hit her.

But he couldn't because her mother ran to stand between them and pushed Mia out of the kitchen. "Go to your room! Go, go!"

The following day Mia's father told her that she was not to talk to him like that.

Surprisingly he was in a good mood, and her mother was quietly preparing their breakfast and making Mia's lunchbox.

Mia didn't say anything, but she knew what happened in the kitchen after her mother closed the door. She stayed behind the closed door and heard what her father was doing to her mother. Mia knew that her mother was hurt, but her wounds were invisible and Mia couldn't find any. Nobody could see what he'd done to her. That's when Mia fervently wished that her father would hit her mother. That was when Mia realized that her mother got hurt because of Mia, and that she couldn't always make her mother better and be her medicine.

***

It was past midnight when Mia finally fell asleep after remembering those years before her parents' divorce.

A phone call woke her up. It was quarter to one in the morning. Who was calling her at this time?

She checked the caller, and it was Simon. She put the ringtone down and ignored the beep until it stopped. But when it went again, Mia got anxious in case something had happened to Daan. "Hello?"

"Hey, Mia," Simon laughed as if he had forgotten that he was annoyed with her earlier that day.

"Why are you calling me so late?"

"I couldn't wait since I've got this brilliant idea. It's a business proposal."

"A business proposal?"

"Yeah, I've been thinking since we talked today. I know that you were frustrated because you're earning only a small amount of money."

Mia didn't say anything and waited for Simon's so-called business proposal.

"I know what you can make better money with. You could lend yourself as a service."

To Mia's silent confusion, Simon asked her, "Do you know what I mean?"

"No. What are you talking about?"

"Awww, you are such a baby. How cute!"

"What I mean is," Simon changed his tone and became more serious. "You know there are lots of men who would want to spend some time with a girl like you. I can arrange that for you if you think you could do it."

"Do 'what'?" Mia's tongue was dry, and her palms were sweaty.

"It could be anything. You could even ask more money for the things you'd let them do."

"You are asking me if I want to sell myself?"

"Well, there are enough girls out there who'd do that for money."

"And you thought I was one of them."

"I know how much you love Daan and want to help him."

'And you are using my love for Daan to get me into this business?'

That was when Mia truly felt how dangerous and vile Simon was. He wasn't just a dealer, a cool dude that sorted things out for his mates. Simon was a pimp! He was a loverboy!

Then Mia realized that she loved Daan, but she loved herself more.

She thought about what her mother had gone through. For years her mother had stayed in a manipulative, destructive relationship to be with Mia. Her mother kept what she was going through to herself. She endured it because she wanted to spare Mia from damage. Her mother did all that because of Mia, and Mia had to admit that her mother was right. If Mia had been exposed to what was happening at the time, it would have destroyed her. As much as Mia wanted her mother to have left there and then, she realized that she was more important to her mother. Because of her mother's sacrifice, Mia had become who she was. Protected, loved. She was precious.

'My mother loves me more than herself. My mother would give her life to me!'

Even when her father stabbed her mother in the back, her mother put a smile on her face to Mia.

'I'm worthy of that much love.' Mia silently told Simon in her head. 'How dare you suggest that I ruin myself? How dare you think that I could throw away my mother's love? You and a man like my father should bloody well be punished!'

Mia wiped away her tears. Thinking of her mother's suffering gave her a reason and the courage to love herself. "Can I think about it?" Then Mia hung up the call.

Mia went out of her room and walked to her mother's bedroom. She knocked on her door. Her mother sounded disorientated. It was two in the morning, and Mia had woken her up. "Mia? Come in! What's the matter?"

Mia crawled into bed beside her mother. It was warm from her mother's body heat, and Mia snuggled against her mother.

"You alright? A bad dream?" Her mother stroked Mia's hair.

"Yes, a horrible dream." It was the worst nightmare, what she had done for the last two weeks and what Simon had just suggested to her. She wanted to wake up from that dream now.

"Your hair seems to have changed its colour again. It's become more reddish."

"I wondered where that came from. I only found out tonight when you told me that you wished me to be red-haired, like Anne of Green Gables. You ordered it from the catalogue?" Mia laughed.

Her mother looked ridiculously serious. "I think I might have ticked that box, indeed. I thought, how lovely to have a daughter that looked like Anne!"

"So, it's all your fault."

"I accept full responsibility!" Her mother held her hand in surrender. "It's been ages since you came to my bed. I have missed it."

Mia watched her mother's face. The difficult years before and after the divorce would have left some scars on anyone, but her mother's skin was still young and shiny. "How come your skin looks so good?"

"My skin? Is it good? I guess, because I use Korean cosmetic products?" Then her mother giggled.

Mia gaped at her mother in wonder. 'I've never seen Mom like this. She's become like a teenager, thanks to Mr. Bloom!'

"Mom?"

"Yes?"

"I just remembered to tell you something. And I have two questions to ask. What do you want first?"

"Oh, okay. Tell me something first."

"I have a boyfriend."

"Oh!" Her mother sat up in bed. "Is he nice?"

"Yes. He is. His name is Daan."

"Daan."

Then, when Mia didn't fill her in anymore, her mother asked, "Are you going to tell me more about him?"

"No."

"Oh." Her mother's face became disappointed.

"You can meet him yourself. Is it okay if he comes here next weekend?"

"Of course! You have to tell me what he likes. I will do the shopping and make something nice."

"Calm down, Mom. I'm sure he will be more nervous than you are."

"How exciting! I'm looking forward to it."

"Yeah."

"And the questions?"

"Okay, I will start with an easy one."

"There is a tough one too?"

"Well, sort of. So. Do you remember Monica, one of Dad's girlfriends?"

"Monica? Of course, I do. She sent you a birthday card, didn't she?"

"Yes, she did. I wonder if you still have her address?"

"Oh... well, I think I do. It was a few years ago, but I kept her card."

"Really? That's great. Do you think she still lives at the same address?"

"I don't know... You could always try, I guess."

"I think I will. But how come you kept her card all these years?"

"Oh... It's because I couldn't throw it away when I read it."

"Did you read it?"

"Well, she wrote to me too."

Mia was stunned to hear that Monica wrote to her mother as well. Why? About what?

Her mother nodded to Mia. "I was surprised too when I received her letter."

"What did she say?"

"She apologized to me."

"She did? For what?"

"For believing what she was told about me. Monica said when she met your father, he was very bitter after the divorce, and it broke her heart. Listening to his story, she couldn't believe how unlucky he'd been to have married me. How unfair a charming man like David had to suffer from a woman who cheated and took his money. She felt for him and wanted to make him happy again, she said. Monica said she loved you, too. She never wanted to have children before, but she enjoyed the time that she spent with you so much she wanted to create a family for you."

Mia felt a tear dropping on her mother's pillow. She wiped her face with her elbow.

"That was why she stayed and tried hard to make it work, but Monica found out that David was overly jealous of her social contacts. He manipulated her to believe she made him suspicious. When she left, he told people that she took his money because she lived rent-free in his house. She said she'd never experienced such darkness afterwards. She fell into a deep depression and lost a great deal of weight. Her family and friends had been worried about her. Monica discovered that David spread the same stories about her. Then Monica realized that she had been wrong to believe the stories he told about me and wanted to say sorry."

"Did you talk to Monica after she sent you the letter?"

"I wrote her back."

"You did? What did you write her?"

"That there was nothing to apologize. That I know what she had gone through and how she must have felt. I wished that she would recover from the trauma and find herself again. And I said, when you wanted to have contact with her, I would give you her address. That I had always been grateful that she was there for you and gave you love when you were there."

Mia stared at her mother. Her mother always said that she wasn't one of the Dutch super mothers. Her mom could never carry her and the groceries on a bike in the rain. She was always cold, too, even in the summer. Mom didn't have green fingers, having lived in an apartment all her life like everyone else in Seoul. But Mia felt her mother's strength lay somewhere else, in her heart. How could she be so understanding and forgiving when she had suffered so much herself? Even her mother couldn't say that her father was a decent person, but she never badmouthed him for the sake of badmouthing either.

"Mom?"

"Yes?"

"I have to confess you something."

"Oh. What is it?"

"There were times... when I was small... that I wished Monica was my mother."

Her mother's eyes stayed into Mia's eyes. Mia looked for signs of hurt, anger, or disappointment, but there weren't any.

"Did you?" was all her mother said.

"Yes. I'm sorry."

"You don't have to be sorry."

"It's just... I think because it was a difficult time. Do you remember? When we moved out of the house, I think we were in some kind of survival mode. You had to sort out so many things, and it took so long until we felt even remotely settled. There was no money, I know, that's because Dad made it so tricky for you. You were always so worn out and looked drained. I didn't feel that I could ask you to have fun with me. And Monica did all those lovely things with me."

"I understand, Mia. I am sorry that it was so tough then, for you as well. I wish I'd had more energy and money to help you better. I should have looked after you better. But thankfully, Monica was there."

"Yes.... and it just seemed so much easier with Monica. You know, her being Dutch and having her family with her. It's awful that I thought like that, and I am so ashamed now, but it just felt less hassle to have a Dutch mother like all my friends. I'm sorry, mom. I feel guilty about those times."

"Oh, Mia, please don't! You were a kid, and your father and I, as parents, should have provided a safe and carefree childhood for you. We failed to do that together, and I did all I could to make it work for us, but sometimes I felt lost. Please don't think it was any of your responsibility. I'm just really proud of you to have got through it so bravely."

Feeling much better now she had told her mother and her mother didn't blame her, Mia exclaimed to her mother. "How can you be so zen about these things?"

"These things?"

"About Monica, and Dad too. Were you not bothered that I was so close to her and someone else loved me so much too?"

"Oh, why would I?" Her mother looked confused about Mia's amazement.

"Were you ever jealous, ever in your life?"

"Of course, I have been jealous many times in my life. In fact, I was painfully jealous in the beginning when Monica came into your life. I wasn't bothered at all by the fact that your father had a relationship, but I felt torn that you had a new relationship with someone else. That I had to share your affection with her. But soon, I realized that the more love you had in your life, the better, even if that came from other people. At some stage of your life, I would have had to let you go your way. I would have had to share your affection with others, like friends, boyfriends, and your own family. I'd better get used to it, I thought. Otherwise, I would turn into that woman in the film "Misery." I could see and hear from you what a kindhearted person Monica was, so I was relieved too."

Mia thought of what her mother said. Why couldn't other people in the world be more like her mother? Where did her mother's wisdom come from?

"Where do you get these thoughts from, Mom? Is there a book that you read that's helped you to have such a state of mind?"

"A book?" Her mother looked surprised then smiled at Mia. "There were so many books and songs that kept me going over

Jane, Frank and Mia   179

the years. They were my only friends, my only consolation except you."

Mia remembered that her mother used to read and listen to music in the lounge every evening until Mia fell asleep. She had felt safe knowing her mom was sitting there.

"I used to read old Buddhist Wisdom a lot. Especially when I had a troubled mind at night and couldn't get rid of it, thinking about the gossip I heard about me."

"What is that wisdom?"

"You shouldn't want to clear your name when you are upset at being mistreated. If you do, you come to cherish a grudge. That's why the Great Saga says you should regard being mistreated as the door to finding patience."

Mia tried to repeat what her mother had said. She wanted to memorize these pearls of Buddhist wisdom. "Mom, can you let me read all those words of wisdom? I'd love to keep them close to my heart too."

"Of course, I'll look for it, along with Monica's address."

"Thank you."

"And... What was the other, tougher question?"

"Oh, right." Mia had almost forgotten about it.

"You don't have to tell me if it's a difficult thing to talk about."

"What is it, Mia?"

"How did you manage to leave Dad? I mean... I can't imagine that he just let you go seeing he is still so obsessed with you. How did you get out of his clutches?"

CHAPTER 13
JANE

It was when David almost hit Mia, then a five year old. Jane realized that she'd stuck it out too long. Until that moment, Jane didn't see how she could explain anything to her daughter. Mia was still David's little angel, and Mia looked up to her father. Jane wanted to keep that picture as long as possible for Mia. A child needed a proper childhood. The reality could come later when Mia was old and strong enough to deal with it.

By the time Mia was five, the woman that Jane had once been was gone. David was a champion in gas-lighting, and after years of being criticized, deceived, and humiliated, Jane was brainwashed and couldn't remember who she was. Jane was not even allowed to get a job. Jane realized that the reason why David didn't interfere with her career at the beginning of their relationship was only because he didn't consider her job as a career at all. Jane wouldn't earn enough money to pay for childcare. Mia would suffer from her mother's absence, and David didn't want to send his daughter to a crèche. He didn't need that stress. Jane, David pointed out, might get funny ideas and might want to go back to the time before she was a mother, her "playing time." Jane shouldn't forget that she was a mother, which was the prime function of her existence.

As if Jane could ever forget that she was a mother. She knew only too well that she existed wholly for her daughter. But she wished that she was something else than a mother—an au pair or an escort girl, one of the two.

Once a mother from Mia's class mistook Jane as one of the au pairs, common in the wealthy Amstelveen residences. The mother approached Jane when the girls wanted to play together at her house. "Are you the girl's au pair? Can you tell her parents that they can pick her up at five o'clock?"

Jane was shocked that she didn't look like Mia's mother and murmured uncertainly, "I am Mia's mother."

"Oh, I am so sorry!" The mother looked horrified at her misjudgment.

"I didn't... You look so young, and Mia doesn't look Chinese...."

"I am Korean."

"Oh, I'm sorry!"

It could have been because of the mother's embarrassment that the girls never played together again. But Jane thought, I'd rather be an au pair for Mia! Because then she would have to work strictly for Mia. The parents would tell her what to do, how to look after their child. Jane would love the girl with all her heart, but she wouldn't have to decide anything and get blamed. Like, when Jane spent a bit more money than usual on the groceries and had to defend herself by saying that Mia needed to try different food types as she grew up. Or when she bought a pricy birthday present for Mia's best friend who'd also given Mia an equally expensive gift. Jane didn't want Mia to appear stingy to her friends, but she was scolded for wasting David's hard-earned money on others.

'Just give me the fucking list of what I can buy for your child!' Jane screamed back to David in her head as she always did.

"How can you throw away so much money—my money—so easily? You're not bringing in any income yourself. You should be ashamed living like a parasite, sucking my money out."

She would have felt much happier as Mia's au pair, but now she was also an escort girl for David. She had to play the role of his wife when he needed her, be presentable when he showed her to his colleagues, nod and look engaged when they occasionally met his family or neighbours. And she had to let him have her as you would oblige a paying client. But then.... she would at least have got paid for that.

When he threw her on the dining table and took her the first time, he left the house afterwards. Jane fed Mia—then a baby—and cooked for her mother, who was visiting. When David came back, he didn't say sorry, but he was nice to her. He murmured something like, "You shouldn't have said such a horrible thing to me. When you said that you'd rather be taken by other men, it made me snap. Don't say things like that anymore."

It was always Jane who said sorry. To have said something that made him angry, to have done something that triggered him. He always punished her in the same way. She wished that he hit her. She wanted to get bruises and wounds so she could go to a doctor and be separated from him. But he never hit her. He threw things around the house, but unfortunately, they never landed on her. She preferred to be taken from behind because then she didn't have to see his face, and he wouldn't see her crying. If she had to face him, she closed her eyes, and her hair and pillow got wet. He never noticed that she was crying while he was taking her.

When Mia came into the bathroom once and caught Jane, Jane broke down naked under the shower. But then her little girl was worried about her mother and wanted to take care of her, and it broke her heart. It shouldn't be that way, Jane thought.

So she trudged on. No, she just sat on a train going round in circles. A day passed, a month, a year. She tried to produce a smile when Mia stretched her mouth with her tiny fingers, but Jane knew there was no smile, twinkle, or life in her eyes. She watched her daughter singing and dancing and clapped and laughed with her, but she was empty inside.

There was no vestige of warmth in her, and she frequently thought about ending everything. Whenever it was too much to bear, she wanted to just walk into the North Sea and drown herself. But her daughter... How would she survive after her mother's death? It would be an even worse crime to leave Mia alone with her father.

Jane noticed that things changed as Mia grew up, and she thought hard about protecting her daughter from her father. Now Mia was six years old and able to say what she thought. She didn't know how scary her father could be, so she wasn't on her guard, which could escalate the situation and make him flip out. Jane saw that the little girl wanted to protect her mother, too.

"Don't talk to mama like that. She is the best mama in the world."

When Mia almost got hurt that night in the kitchen, Jane knew she had to get out of this life. No, this couldn't be called a life at all.

Even when Jane made up her mind to leave David, she still didn't know how to take the plunge. If she just ran away with Mia, she knew, 100 percent, that David would find them anywhere in the world. He was a man of means. Getting caught somewhere outside of her comfort zone and Mia being confronted with the consequences were both dangerous. She couldn't go to her parents because then they would find out what kind of no life Jane was living, and their hearts would be irreparable.

David never let go of his things. Jane and Mia were his

possessions. But what if... Jane was not his anymore? If she was ruined and contaminated, would he still want her? He always said that he disproved of people who had affairs.

'So it is okay to do what you do to me while you judge other people's love life.'

He didn't seem to spot the hypocrisy and irony himself.

Jane couldn't think of any other way of unlocking herself from David than throwing herself at someone else and getting ruined. David would want to discard her then.

But how could she do that? And with whom? She didn't want to use anyone and didn't seek to destroy anyone else's relationship, but how could she find a casual one-night stand that meant nothing more than one-time sex? The only places she went to were the supermarket and Mia's school.

It was a riddle that Jane wrestled with for almost a year.

Since the night when Jane pushed her daughter out of the kitchen, and David took her like a madman, Jane was anxious in case Mia heard anything. She almost suffocated herself with her sleeves and pillow. Her chin hurt because she gritted her teeth so vigorously.

Once, Jane felt ill. Every muscle in her body ached, and she had a temperature and terrible migraine. She didn't have dinner because she had no appetite but swallowed a strong painkiller before going to bed. When David came on to her, she shook his hands off. Maybe the painkiller doped her brain from measuring the likely consequences. When he reached out to her again, she was so infuriated that she threw his hands away. It led to the most vicious taking so far. David grabbed and pulled her hair back and sneered in her ear, "Stay still."

And she did as she was told every time. For her to let it happen and just close her eyes was the best way to get through it. She'd learnt the hard way, and now she'd made the fatal mistake of refusing him. She was punished more brutally.

But this time, a thought came up, and it kept being played in her bruised brain. 'This is my body, "my" body!'

But David wouldn't let her rule her own body.

'Who's given him the right to destroy my body and soul? I have! But I don't want this anymore. He's not my husband. He's a monster!'

That was the first time in years that she'd felt rage rise in her, and once it surged, she couldn't get rid of it. Ever.

* * *

Jane had wanted to learn to drive for a long time, but she couldn't take lessons until Mia was a few years into her elementary school. Before preschool, Mia only went to nursery school twice a week for two and a half hours. Jane used this time to tidy up the house and do the grocery alone. David wasn't so enthusiastic about Jane driving, but now he had to agree that Jane needed to get around with Mia. Jane only went to places where she could bike or walk, but it was important for Mia to try other extra activities. And Jane had more hours to study for the theory exam when Mia went to school.

Jane passed the theory exam at her second try. It was confusing to remember all the rules about bikes, trams, and different traffic systems. David complained when she failed the first time because it was a lot of money to take the exam, so she studied really hard to pass the next time. The day after she took the exam for the second time and passed, she was preparing dinner, and Mia was watching television. They heard a loud claxon outside the house.

Mia jumped out of the sofa and ran outside to look, and Jane followed her. David, who went to work on his bike, was back with a brand new sky blue Mini Cooper.

"Papa! Is this yours?"

Jane gasped at the car and saw Mia running to her father in excitement.

"It's mama's new car. She can take you to the hockey club once she gets her driver's license."

"It's so pretty, papa!"

David walked over to Jane, who stood still at the door in shock and put his arm around her stiff shoulder.

"Do you like it? I thought you needed a car that suits you. You will look pretty in it."

Jane came out of her anesthetization and nodded at him absentmindedly. "Yes, it's lovely. How nice. Thank you."

David went to their neighbour, who was also a car fanatic, and the couple came to check out the car.

"Oh, how lucky you are, Jane, to have such a generous husband! How much he must love you, buying such an expensive gift for you...."

Jane was on autopilot, nodding yes with soulless smiles to the wife. "Yes, very lucky. Yes, thank you, I love it."

Finally, after a lengthy period of admiration the neighbours went home, and the three of them sat down for dinner. Jane heard David's boasting all evening, and although she tried to look enthusiastic, he noticed that she was rather quiet.

He frowned at her when Mia was excused from the table and went back to her television programme. "What's the matter? You don't like the car?"

Jane shook her head quickly. "No, no, of course not. It's beautiful."

"Then how come you don't look it?"

"No... I mean, I'm just worried because it is a new car. I thought since I was just starting driving, I'd better drive a second-hand car until I felt confident enough. That's all."

"Ha!" David snorted and put down his napkin on the table, irritated. "I don't understand you. Anyone else would be jumping up and down in joy and lie at my feet in gratitude. No wife of mine will ever drive an old sack of a car, I won't allow it! It's never good what I do for you, is it?"

"No! I didn't mean that...."

David left the dining table in a rage, and Jane knew what would happen later that night.

***

Jane's driving instructor was a young man named Henk. Like most people in the Netherlands, Jane was learning to drive a manual car. Jane struggled with the concept of changing the gears, and it took her some time to get the hang out of it.

Once she got a bit more comfortable with driving, the two of them got to talking. Jane learnt that he was twenty-eight and started working as a driving instructor a few years ago.

"How old are you, Jane?"

Jane, her eyes on the road, answered, "Thirty-three."

"You don't look it, you know."

"Really? That's good."

"Try to hold the wheel like this. There, you are sitting so rigid. Doesn't your shoulder hurt when you drive like that? And your arms. You need to relax a bit. I know you are nervous as a learner driver. It's only natural."

Jane didn't tell him that she was always nervous. In her head, she constantly prepared for what she needed to do next, and worried whether David would approve of her actions or not.

"When did you come to the Netherlands?"

"Seven years ago."

"What brought you here?"

"I married a Dutchman."

"Ah, for love. That's nice. Children?"

"Yes, a daughter."

"Your Dutch is pretty good."

"Thanks."

"How did you learn Dutch?"

"Well, we speak Dutch at home."

"Does your daughter speak Korean, too?"

"Unfortunately not."

"How come? I've always envied bilingual children. It would be the best way to learn languages, I believe."

"I think you are right."

"So why did you decide to speak only Dutch to her?"

"I didn't decide it. My husband decided."

"And you were fine with it?"

"Where do I go now? To the right or straight?"

"Go straight. We will stop soon and practice parking."

Jane looked straight ahead. She didn't want to show her frustration when asked why she hadn't taught her daughter her mother tongue. She was angry with herself that she'd just given in to David's outrageous language ban. She felt like the Koreans under the Japanese invasion when they were not allowed to speak Korean. They were even forced to change their names. Now Mia couldn't speak Korean, and she would struggle if Jane took her to South Korea and sent her to a Korean school. Another lost chance. Jane turned to the right when Henk gave the direction, and after driving on a quiet road a while, they arrived at an empty parking lot in the industrial area.

"It's the perfect place to practice parking. It's much easier to start with when there's no car around you."

For the next half an hour, Jane did all kinds of parking, and she found the parallel parking most difficult. Then it was time to go back.

When they were driving on the familiar road, Henk asked, "How old is your daughter?'

"She's six."

"She must be so pretty. Mixed children are gorgeous."

Jane didn't know what to say. "It's to the left, right?"

"Yes. Let's park the car there. You did well today."

"Thank you."

***

In the beginning, Jane was scared of every roundabout and intersection, expecting misjudgment and causing disaster. But after three months of driving, nothing like that had happened. As Jane felt more at ease with driving, talking to Henk came more easily too.

He asked about her life but didn't interrogate her when she didn't elaborate on her replies.

Jane learnt that Henk was single. His long-term relationship ended a few months ago.

"What happened?" Jane was brave to ask him the question. She was used to the Dutch way of speaking, "You can ask me anything, and I will either say yes or no."

Henk shrugged, "She fell in love with someone else."

"Oh."

After a few seconds of silence, Jane said, "I'm sorry."

"Well, I'm not sorry."

"You are not?"

"No. I'm glad I found out before we bought a house and had a child together and all that. I've seen it with my mates and family. Divorce sucks. It brings out the worst of people, you know. It would have been a disaster."

Jane smiled mischievously, "Do you know what we say about marriage in South Korea?"

Henk looked at her, surprised by her rare smile. "No? Tell me."

"That it's like Lotto. You never get it right."

Henk and Jane laughed aloud for the first time.

"I wonder why it has to be like that, though."

Jane sighed softly at the end of their laugh.

Jane was now a confident driver, and she would soon be almost ready to take the test and pass, Henk had said the previous week. Jane wasn't that exuberant when she heard this, because she enjoyed her lessons with Henk. It was the only time she talked to anyone other than Mia and David. She would fall back into days and weeks of stillness in the house once she passed the test.

Today, they just stopped in the middle of nowhere in a nearby farming area and talked.

"I wonder that too. Very rarely, the couple breaks up on amicable terms, but that's when there's no child or money to fight over."

"I wouldn't want any money."

"Wouldn't you?"

"No. I just want out. To breathe. To be free." Jane was shocked by what she was telling Henk.

He didn't know anything about Jane's marriage and had never met David. Maybe that was why Jane could talk to him.

"Are you not happy, Jane?" Henk's voice was neutral, and Jane sensed no judgment.

"No." The simple truth. "I don't know who I am anymore. I don't know where I'm going. Sometimes I am so miserable that I wish I were dead."

"That's pretty intense." Henk's face turned solemn and his voice concerned. "Did you ask for any help? Like marriage counseling or therapy?"

Jane shook her head. "I haven't, but it wouldn't have worked. It would have made it worse."

"So, what is the problem, do you think?"

Jane, despite her devastation, had to smile faintly when she replied. "Is it an awful, ignorant thing to say that he is the problem?"

"Well, not to me if that's what you think."

"You can say whatever you think," Jane and Henk said at the same time and laughed.

"Exactly. And why shouldn't you?"

"I came to like that logic. Only I couldn't speak to my husband."

"What happens if you do?"

"He gets angry and... humiliates me."

"Humiliate you? That's emotional abuse! Does he ever hit you?"

"No. I wish he did."

"You wish he did? What do you mean?"

"He hurts me in a way that no one can see the scars."

Henk fell silent. He was probably trying to figure out what Jane meant.

"It's no use. I've thought about leaving him for as long as I've been married. I realized that I didn't know him at all. But I have my daughter, and he used to say, if I ever took her away, that he would do everything to find us and destroy us."

"That's blackmail... Unbelievable that you are living with someone so ghastly. It sounds like he's been mishandling you. Are you sure you don't want to ask for help? You could also go to your family doctor. They deal with this kind of thing too. It's about your mental health."

"I don't know what I can do. When you've been oppressed and belittled for so long, you don't believe in yourself anymore. But recently, I got scared that he would also manipulate my daughter. I could see he was going to bully her as well. I am wondering what I should do."

Henk didn't say anything. He reached out and put his hand on her elbow. The weight of his warm hand wasn't pressing her. It comforted her.

After a while sitting like that next to each other in the car, Jane smiled and started the car. "Thank you for listening. It does help me to talk to you."

* * *

It was the last lesson before the test. They went through every point that the examiner could make difficult during the driving test and, as their customary ritual, stopped in a remote car park and talked.

"So. The last lesson. You will pass it, no problem."

"I'm quite nervous about the exam. But to my surprise, I like driving."

"I'm glad that you had at least one thing that you had fun with. I've enjoyed driving with you too."

"That's kind. You were a great instructor."

They smiled at each other. Jane had grown fond of Henk, who was down to earth and calm.

"I've been thinking about what you told me last time, Jane."

Jane turned to Henk and raised her eyebrows, "Thinking about what?"

"About your marriage."

"Oh. I'm sorry that I burdened you with my story."

"Don't say sorry so easily, Jane. I've noticed that you say sorry about almost everything that wasn't your fault at all. Even during driving." He smiled.

Jane smiled back apologetically. "That's the Korean in me. We say it often to make the atmosphere better."

"I thought maybe that was why your husband married you."
Jane's smile disappeared from her face. "What do you mean?"
"That he was looking for an easy victim. So he could control the person. You are soft and gentle. You grew up in a culture more prone to adjust to others. I think he was taking advantage of that."
Jane thought about what Henk said to her. "I would prefer to think that it was love when it started. I don't want to feel like a pathetic prey that he hunted with a purpose. There were times, years ago, that I believed we were in love."
"I'm sure that's what you felt ages ago. But I just can't imagine any Dutch woman, who grew up here, would put up with someone like him for so long, even for the sake of a child."
Jane let out a tiny laugh, and told Henk what she had learnt from her long period of suffering. "Oh, Henk, I've stopped believing in stereotypes. Domestic violence exists everywhere, even in this country, and happens even to the most emancipated of women. Anyone can be a victim, but I agree with you that I score a higher degree on the pain scale."
"You're right about that, Jane. It happens everywhere. And I don't even know if it makes any difference now how it started. The important thing is, Jane, that you are suffering and what you are going to do about it."
"What 'can' I do, honestly?" Jane was aggrieved at Henk's inquisitiveness. "Do you think I've never thought about leaving him? Just running away with Mia and going back to my parents? Well, I've considered it every single day for the last seven years. But how can I explain to Mia why I left her father? I can't tell her that her beloved father is an abuser. I just can't! Mia needs to have a normal childhood!"
Henk didn't get heated by Jane's outburst. He just smiled gently at the rare exhibition of her emotions. "But is it normal, Jane? Are you giving her a normal childhood? Jane, think about what I'm saying to you. By sticking it out with him, what kind of example are you giving your daughter? What messages will she get from this abusive relationship? Maybe she will grow up thinking this is normal and it's okay for her father to treat her mother like this. And maybe she will accept such a man as her partner and tolerate such behavior. Is that what you want for her?"

Jane inhaled sharply in shock. She'd never thought like that. Since she talked to no one about her marriage, she had only a tiny thinking box, and her thinking box had shrunk to nothing along with the size of her brain, she thought ruefully.

All the time, Jane had been telling herself that she needed to stay for Mia. But Henk was right. What he had just pointed out to her was absolutely right. What am I showing Mia, what messages am I giving her?'

The thought that Mia would grow up believing her parents' marriage was a normal relationship frightened Jane.

'No! No! You shouldn't stay with a man like your father. You should be happy with yourself, and you need to be loved as you are. You have to leave if someone tries to destroy you! You have to!'

Jane was pleading with her daughter in her head. Jane and Henk sat in silence for a long time.

"What would be the worst thing that can happen when you leave him, Jane?"

Jane just shook her head resignedly without a reply.

"Would he harm you?"

Jane thought about it. "I am sure that if I just run away with Mia, and he catches us in the middle of nowhere, then anything could happen. I think, in a civilized environment, he would be too self-aware to harm me physically. He would find another way to hurt me, though."

"Would it be any worse than now?"

Jane remembered all those nights when he had taken her and left her humiliated.

She shook her head.

"What about your daughter? Are you going to let her see him if you leave him?"

That was a more complicated matter. "I think I will have to because Mia would want to see him. And I can't take her father away from her."

"You don't want to tell her why you are leaving him and what he's done to you?"

"Oh, Henk!" Jane looked at him in her despair. "She's only six! How can I tell her what he's done to me?"

"Then... you don't think he would hurt her when she sees him?"

Jane had thought about it before, of course. "Not when I'm the only one who's betrayed him, not Mia. As long as Mia adores him and loves him, Mia would be safe with him. He's a narcissist and needs to feed on affection from others."

"But what about when Mia gets older and sees what he's like?"

"I can't stop it, at that point. Then Mia would have to break away from her father, but it would be her own decision."

"Is it a risk worth taking? Isn't it safer to run away to a place where he can't find either of you?"

Jane slowly moved her fingers along the edge of the steering-wheel. When she'd made a few rounds, she said, "It's a risk that I'd prefer to take rather than running away and having to explain the reason to Mia now. It would destroy her childhood. It would take away her trust in people and the world. I would be here, not going anywhere, watching her like a hawk. Mia might end up as her daddy's little girl forever, which is also fine, as long as he's good to Mia and Mia's happy. And if the time comes that Mia finds out for herself what her father's like, I would be here to help her. But at least, by then, hopefully, she would be older and stronger to deal with the truth."

Henk looked at her, clearly agonized. "But Jane, what kind of life would that be for you? You won't ever get rid of him from your own life until that time comes!"

Jane assured him with great fortitude, "I can do that, Henk. What is for Mia is for me."

"But you are still so young and have a whole life ahead of you!"

"Henk," Jane smiled gracefully. "Life is short, and suffering is brief too. You can't have everything, and we have to choose our priority. And mine is my daughter."

All the way back to her house and Mia's school to pick her up later, Jane thought of what they'd talked about in Henk's car, and she told herself, 'I have to do this for Mia. I have to save myself for Mia. I am running out of time because soon, Mia will be old enough to see things. I have to do it before she finds out, with me still stuck in the marriage. I wouldn't be able to help her then because I would have lost all my sense and intelligence under his tyranny.'

***

Jane passed her driving test without any issues.

The examiner, a silver-haired man with a generous smile, complimented her. "Not many people pass at their first go. You were good. Congratulations!" Jane felt an unfamiliar wave of pride, and it startled her. It'd been a long time since she'd felt anything like that.

The previous week, when they were saying goodbye, Jane had asked Henk, "If I pass, can I still book you for one last lesson? Just one. I wouldn't ask for more than one."

Henk gazed at Jane, and she couldn't see what he was thinking.

"And if I don't pass…"

Henk smiled at her and said, "Then it is business as usual."

The week after the driving test, she was meeting Henk. It was the first time that she wasn't seeing him as a student.

Henk said, "Congratulations, I knew you would pass the first time." Henk asked if Jane wanted to drive the car, but Jane shook her head to indicate "no" because she was very nervous. So Henk went on in his gentle, unassuming voice, "Where do you want to go?"

"Let's go to that car park."

He just nodded, and Jane looked out of the window, both in silence.

When they arrived, there was no other car, as always.

Jane sighed in relief.

Henk kept gazing at her without saying anything, until he finally accepted that she wasn't starting the conversation. Jane looked like a frightened bird. "So, how are things going?"

"Good. I mean, better. Your marriage counseling has worked wonders."

She relaxed when Henk laughed at her sarcastic answer.

Jane took a deep breath. "I've been thinking about this for a long time. And I think I will ask you. Because we won't see each other anymore after today."

Henk raised his eyebrows, still saying nothing.

"You can say yes or no, right? I'm asking something crazy, but please don't take pity on me; just say what you want to say."

Henk nodded slowly.

"I want... If you want... I want to have sex with you."

Henk's blue eyes got bigger, and he was… Jane couldn't say if he was smiling or grimacing. Jane couldn't look at his face anymore.

"You… really don't have to say yes, if you think I'm mad or disgusting."

"You mean now, and here?"

Jane was relieved by his practical question. Thank god Henk didn't get angry and tell her off, saying she'd insulted him, thinking he would accept such an offer and she was his student and so on...

She nodded. "Yes. As I said, I want it just once. No more, not after today."

"Even if you really liked it and were impressed by my skills?"

Jane let out a nervous laugh. "Is that yes? And yes, even if you took me to a place I've never been to before; just this time."

"That's a shame." Then a wide grin appeared on his young yet wise face. "I would be crazy not to say yes to you. And no, there's no pity involved, for the record. I'm accepting your offer with two hands because I wanted to do that with you."

* * *

Jane waited for another two months until Mia's school broke for the six weeks summer holiday. Mia had become seven in the meantime, and she'd had the most fantastic birthday party with her playmates at the horse riding centre. Jane had booked a holiday house at the other side of the country and secretly packed a bag for herself and Mia when David was at work. Only the essential things would come with them, and she was rather glad that she didn't want to take anything from the house. Jane just needed Mia. She still had the money that she had saved when she was working in Seoul. She would use it for real this time, and if she ran out of money, she would ask her parents for help. There was no other way, no going back.

She sent Mia to Mia's best friend's house for a sleepover and promised the parents that she would come the following day to pick Mia up. The parents were stunned when she said they were to release Mia only when she came, not to David.

Then she waited for him. Their bags and Mia's stuffed toy animals—all except Gomi that Mia took with her to her friend's—were all packed in her car. At the last minute Jane took the framed photo of Mia off the wall. Tonight she would sleep in a hotel near Mia's friend's house. She had her mobile phone at the ready in case she needed to call the emergency number.

When David came home, she told him as calmly as a sea without waves that she had slept with someone else.

Jane didn't blink when he started screaming. She almost nodded when the regular bouts of abuse began to arrive. Jane was a disgusting slut, and he'd known that all along. She was a lazy, worthless mother and a parasite who lived off him. He also grabbed the vase from the top of the china cabinet and smashed it on the floor. When he came close to her, she was stiff with fear and held the phone tight, ready to press the number, but he yelled that he didn't even want to touch her dirty body. She'd never felt so happy to be called dirty.

Then she stood up when he finally said the line she had been waiting for, "Get out of my house! Count on it you won't get a cent from me! You sleazy nothing!"

She ran outside before David remembered the new car and came out to stop her from taking it. When she started the car in a hurry and drove away from the house, she realized that David didn't even ask where Mia was. He didn't spot the empty place on the wall where Jane had taken Mia's photo from either. After so many years, she was still astonished how he could be occupied only with himself. In any other circumstances, Jane would have tried to be reasonable for the sake of the child, but really, how could you remain in a reasonable relationship with an unreasonable person? It had to come from both sides, and Jane knew the contemporary divorce model, aka "modern family" style divorce, would never be possible in their case.

The best thing she did all these years was learning to drive. She turned the radio on and was absorbed in a strange mix of disbelief and relief. She was free! She didn't have to go back to his house, always his house, not theirs. She didn't have to feel despair choking her throat whenever she returned home after a school run or grocery shopping. She couldn't decide whether the sound coming out of her mouth was a laugh or a cry. Then after the brief period of euphoria, she felt the clouds of fear being drawn down on her. What had she done? How could she have thought that she could manage on her own in a country still foreign to her? What about Mia? Was it right to take Mia away from her familiar, comfortable environment and jump into the unknown, scary world of single motherhood? Oh god, what had she done…. Should she go back and beg for David's forgiveness? What would happen then? How would he punish her now that he didn't want to touch her anymore? Would she even survive his new way of punishment? Then she heard the song on the radio and stopped crying to listen.

Jane wiped away her tears. It can't be only her in the world who had failed and stood up again. And as Coldplay told her, she'd never know what she was worth if she didn't try.

"I will fix you, Mia. And I will fix me, too," Jane whispered in the car. Then she sang "Fix you" aloud with Coldplay.

* * *

"Things can only get better from here," Jane told herself every day since she left David.

As soon as she arrived at the holiday house that she'd rented for the summer holiday, she had to think hard about building their new life. She would have to find a solicitor to represent her because the last thing she wanted was to talk to David. Being the smooth talker that he was, she wouldn't be able to negotiate anything even when she was not going for a divorce war.

'Call me naïve, but I don't want to live another day as his wife.'

She only needed to keep the car for Mia's school runs and eventually the commute to her work—which she had to find urgently—and enough money so she could rent a small house near Mia's school. Mia would have to see him too, as long as she wanted to, so Jane would find a place not too far from David's house, but not in the same village, no way. This was going to be their new home.

She would have to learn to ask for help when she needed it and not close herself down as had been her habit during her marriage. Henk had helped her see that she couldn't have saved herself and Mia by sticking it out. She was grateful that he had also helped her out with her mad request. It was liberating because it was her body, and 'she' made that decision to make love with someone. She didn't love Henk, and Henk didn't love her, but they had become friends for a brief but critical time of her life. She saw it as a gift. People say, that good books find you when you need them; in the same way, a good friend found Jane when she most needed them.

Jane finished her story and looked down at her daughter, eight years on. Jane had started full of hope, but it wasn't easy to build a new life with a small child on her own. She struggled with things that she hadn't had to struggle with when she was with David. Finance, house, school, work, it was all on her. The most excruciating struggle came when Mia went to her father's. Ever since Jane had given birth to Mia, they had been one, and for the first time, she had to part with her daughter.

And at the crucial moments of Mia's life, Jane was alone. When Mia got her swimming certificates. When Mia performed a solo at her dance school. When Mia graduated from her elementary school and was doing the traditional end of school musical. Jane looked around the hall on those occasions. Everyone had someone to sit with and to share their pride and joy in their child. They laughed and cheered together. Whether they were parents and siblings, grandparents, friends, or even ex-partners, everyone had at least one another person to share their love with.

But Jane didn't. Sometimes David was sitting somewhere in the hall to watch Mia, but they were not on such terms as to sit together or talk to each other. There was no one else other than Jane and David in the world who remembered Mia's birth and what she was like as a baby. When she walked first and which word she said first. And they couldn't remember those moments together. There was no other person than the two of them who could look at Mia with parents' eyes, and they couldn't look at her together.

These moments were when Jane realized the consequences of their break-up, and it was heart-rending. She never missed David as her husband, but sometimes she missed him as Mia's father. Just to clap and cheer for Mia together, only to share their pride and their joy in Mia together, would be enough for Jane to feel content, but it was never going to happen. On the other hand, if that had been possible, they wouldn't have broken up the way they did.

But thankfully, after every weekend that Mia went to David, she returned to Jane—despite Jane's ungrounded fear of losing her, and she ran to her mother's arms with her every milestone and achievement. Then Jane's wounds healed. Every two weeks, Jane got new wounds, and every two weeks, they recovered. As the process repeated year after year, Jane was conscious of the scabs on her heart, but even these days, her scars flamed when Mia was gone.

Besides these rare moments of regret and often sadness, being divorced was, in general, a struggle. There were people happy to help them when Jane asked and a few who wanted to take advantage of her. A divorced, single mother was in a vulnerable position, Jane soon found out, but Jane never wanted to depend on anyone. She left for their freedom with so much at stake. So here in her new life, she still had to grit her teeth hard and endure things that her new life threw at her.

'Yolo[6] is highly overrated, and endurance is a part of life,' Jane often said to herself. You can't just live in a perfect world where nothing bothers you. Jane didn't mind it at all, unlike how many would think. She was willing to endure many things as long as it was for herself and Mia.

Her daughter looked up at her from the pillow where she was listening to Jane's story. She came up to Jane with tearful eyes and threw herself into her mother's arms.

Jane stroked her daughter's back and whispered silently, 'Thank goodness that I had her. Thank goodness she's here with me and has become a beautiful, sweet and wise young woman.'

"Mia?"

"Yes?"

"I wanted to ask you...."

"Yes?"

"What would have happened if I'd taken you away from your father when we got divorced? Like if we went to South Korea."

"South Korea?"

"Yes."

"Because you wanted to go back, right?"

"Yes."

"But you stayed here because of me."

"Just think about how it would have been for you?"

Mia fell into deep thought. "I would have despised you."

Strangely enough, Jane looked relieved.

"Because I didn't know what Dad was like and didn't know the reason why you were leaving him, I would have been traumatized if you'd taken me away from him. At the time, I still loved him a lot. I would have blamed you for breaking the bond between us and would have been miserable, missing him. For me, Dad would have remained my hero, and you would have become the devil. And I liked my school and friends so much

---

[6] Yolo: you only live once

too. I wouldn't have adjusted well if you'd taken me to South Korea, not speaking the language and missing my normal life."
Jane nodded and felt the years of her heavy loads lightened.
"I see, Mia."
Mia nodded at her too. "I can see why you wanted me to think about it."
"You can?"
"Yes. Were you worried if you'd made the right decision?"
"Yes. There were times when I doubted I'd done the right thing for you, especially when I saw that you were being affected by him. I was worried that letting you keep the bond with your father I had exposed you to danger, the possibility you'd be damaged by him."
Mia thought about what her mother said. "But I'm not damaged by him, Mom, at least not the way he damaged you. It's because I've seen it myself, what he is like, otherwise I wouldn't have understood your decision. Losing my father when I wasn't ready would have been more damaging to me, Mom. I can see that now. You made the right decision. I just feel sorry for you that you had to sacrifice yourself like that."
Jane was stunned and shook her head at Mia.
"No, no. You should never think like that. It wasn't a sacrifice. It was the only thing I wanted. I did my best to protect you, and I just wished it was the best for you. That's all."
"It was the best way, Mom, believe me."
Then Mia smiled her most lovely smile. "Mom?"
"Yes?"
"How did that song go? The song you always listened to when I was small."
"The Whitney Houston song?"
"Yes. You know, it just came up lately in my head out of the blue. I still remember some of the lyrics. And while I was listening to your story, the song came up again."
"Really? You remember it?"
"Yes. Shall we look for it on Youtube?"
"Let's."
The mother and daughter, in the bed, watched the music video together.
"Wasn't she very young when she sang the song? And so talented!"

"Yes. I used to think she was one of the best artists in the world. I still do."

"Such a shame she suffered so much too."

"Yes, such a shame."

Then Jane thought, 'Life is really too short, and—as the Dutch artist Youp van't Hek sang—no one knows what time it is. I'm so glad and proud that I didn't waste any more time of our life there.'

Mia sang along to the song with the young, beautiful Whitney Houston on her phone.

"This should be the United Nations anthem for all the children in the world."

Jane smiled, "I can't agree more. This song has saved me so many times in my life."

"That we must learn to love ourselves is the greatest love of all. Wow... That's just like, an essence of life's wisdom in one sentence!"

"I'm glad that you remembered the song all this time."

"I'm glad that you sang it to me."

"It was a matter of life and death."

Mia played the song again, and then she moved to other Whitney Houston songs.

"My other favourite was 'Run to you.' I went to see the film with my first boyfriend in Seoul." Jane winked at her daughter.

"It is amazing! Better than some of the songs that you hear today." Then Mia looked into Jane's eyes. "And Mom? How serious is this thing with Mr. Bloom? Are you running into his arms too?"

Jane laughed. "We will see. I just think I must be ready now for some good things in life. Fun. Love. Maybe even lovemaking."

"Mom! That's just so gross!"

"Well, for me, it's a victory to feel this way."

"I know. I'm proud of you."

"And I am of you."

Jane and Mia stayed in bed listening to the music, until they saw the dawn had arrived. Mia went down to the kitchen to make hot milk with honey. When she was waiting for the milk to warm up and stirring the honey, she remembered the night ten years ago, at her father's place. How lucky that they were not there now. Her mother did the most challenging thing for Mia. She'd taken her daughter away from that oppressive environment and given her a safe shelter. Mia wouldn't let anything or anyone destroy her after her mother showed her how to be strong.

Mia took the mugs upstairs and drank the milk with her mother. Now Mia found the songs she liked and let her mother listen to them. Then they fell asleep in Jane's bed, next to each other. If anyone had seen them together, one with red hair and the other with black hair, they would have been struck by the resemblance. They were two fairies, two survivors, and a mother and a daughter.

Jane and Mia had never had such a peaceful night's sleep in all years past. They both used to have repeated nightmares. Jane about losing Mia in a playground. Mia about Jane crying under the shower. But the nightmares disappeared that night.

A few miles away, two people were arguing in a picture-perfect house. The fight was getting nasty, and things were being thrown at each other. Serena, whom Mia had analyzed as passive and docile, threw her mobile phone at the screaming, angry man, and it hit him just next to his eye. His handsome face was covered in blood, and he moaned like an injured pig about the bloodstains on his luxurious, Bali-silk, white duvet.

CHAPTER 14
FRANK

For their first proper date, Jane suggested watching a film. "I want to watch *Room* with you. I read the book, and to be honest, I was a bit scared to watch it alone."

When the film started, Frank soon understood why Jane was afraid to watch it on her own. The details of the captivity were gripping. Frank held her hand while Jane was as focused on the screen as if she was the one kept captive in the room. Finally, the mother, Joy, escapes from her kidnapper with her son Jack, and Frank let out a long sigh of relief. Out of the room and exposed to the outside world, the mother and son struggle with anxiety, anger, and depression. In the middle of the movie, when Joy returns to her family, Jane suddenly stirred in her chair and sobbed silently.

Joy discovered that her parents had got divorced while she was lost, and her father failed to accept Jack as his grandson. He couldn't see Jack without thinking of the boy's biological father, his daughter's kidnapper and rapist. Joy broke with her father. Joy chose her son.

Frank held Jane's shoulders tightly, and Jane soon resumed her self-composure. She squeezed his hand hard, and they sat like that throughout the remainder of the film. When the movie ended, Frank realized that Jane saw her life with Mia as similar to Joy's in her room. Jane must have recognized her own struggles. She understood Joy's regret and guilt, too, wondering if what she did—to escape from her own "room"—was the best decision for her child. Frank imagined that what Jane was trying to do during her difficult years was to keep sane in an insane environment. Frank and Jane stayed in their seats for a long time until everyone had left the theatre.

They went to a pub for a drink near the cinema and settled themselves in a corner seat. Frank had his arm around Jane's shoulders, and they just sat there, with a glass of wine, in compatible silence. They didn't need to talk.

"I understood how Joy felt." That was all Jane said after she had been nursing her wine glass in her hands for a while.

"I know you did."

"I... was so angry with Joy's father."

Frank remembered that that was when Jane broke down. "Why were you angry?" Frank had some idea of what her reason was, but he asked Jane the question to help her pour her heart out.

"Because he couldn't distinguish the boy from the kidnapper. He was Joy's son, you know, only Joy's." Then Jane had a first sip of her wine.

"Was that how you felt about Mia?"

Jane looked up from her wine glass and stared right through Frank's eyes. "Is it wrong if I did?"

Frank shrugged. "It's not about right or wrong, I believe. For you, Mia was your daughter, yours only. I can tell you, from my experience as a teacher, Jane, that many parents see their partner in their child and despise what they see. They identify the traces of their partner that they don't like and blame them on the other person, or worse, on the child. Is it wrong if you saw Mia only as your child and gave all the love you had in you? You could easily have acknowledged Mia as David's daughter and despise Mia whenever you were reminded of him. For me, that would have been a lot more detrimental. Don't doubt yourself, Jane. You are a strong person to have done what you have done."

Jane smiled weakly. Frank saw that the stoic expression he had spotted when he first met Jane had changed into a softer, more vulnerable face. He loved the effect when Jane opened herself.

"What happened with your student?"

Frank put down his glass on the table. "I'm glad that you asked. Do you know I've been wanting to tell you ever since we met? The very first time, when you came to my place."

"Then already? How come?"

"I don't know. It was unreal. I've never talked about it, and suddenly I was dying to tell you all. I felt that you would understand."

"That's weird."

"It is. Or it wasn't weird at all because when you mentioned Primo Levi, it was like a sign. I felt that I could talk to you. Anyway, it was five years ago. Jesse was the previous year's student, one of the cleverest, and a football player. The ideal son of the Christian family where he grew up. Then Jesse developed a crush on his classmate—a boy—and got confused. He'd had a girlfriend before, and now he wondered if he was gay or bi. He confided in me, and I gave my advice. "Focus on the last year of school, you're going to university to study Science, and you will have all the time and freedom you need then to explore your sexual identity." I thought it was a piece of sound advice, but no. Of course, it didn't work out like that. Love just overwhelms you. It doesn't wait because it is the last year of high school. Jesse fell in love with his football teammate. It's a very macho world, apparently, and they were shunned by the group. The boy broke up with Jesse due to this pressure, and his parents also found out. Jesse strangled himself with the football team muffler."

Jane covered her mouth with her hand. Then she reached out her hand and touched his face.

Frank sighed and held her hand in his. "I fell into shock and wondered if I'd done enough to help him. Was it the right thing to say to him? Should I have said that he had to come out there and then? Or wait to come out? But Jesse wasn't sure who he was. What should I have done? I didn't know anymore."

Jane nodded. "We can only do the best we can. And you did the best you could. At least Jesse had you to come to and talk about his feelings."

"But then his parents found out that he was talking to me. And they blamed me for encouraging him to play with fire. They were religious and believed homosexuality was a disease. I'd made it worse than if they'd sent him for treatment. They raised suspicions about my friendship with Jesse, and I was involved in a police investigation."

"Oh no, Frank... How unfair the whole thing was for you!"

"Life is unfair, and don't we know it well." Frank winked at her.

"The worst thing was, though, that everyone, including my girlfriend at the time, who was living with me, believed there must have been something. That I had feelings for him and was hiding my own sexuality. I wouldn't have had a problem if I was gay. But no one really listened to what I said. I lost lots of friends then."

"People are cruel, aren't they? We only believe what we want to believe."

"Yes. I learnt it the hard way too."

"I can understand that you didn't like the school anymore."

"Yeah. And it was a shame, as you said. Because I did like my job as a teacher before all this happened. But I didn't want to put myself in a situation like that again and distanced myself from the students."

"I didn't know anything about you when I said that. I shouldn't have said it to you. I realized later that it was what I was telling myself, because even after the divorce, I struggled to enjoy my life. I'm sorry."

"Don't. It was what I needed to hear, and it came at the right moment from the right person. When you left my place, I had so many questions about myself, and it made me evaluate my life."

Jane put her head on his shoulder. "Funny that you felt that way when we first met. And what a coincidence that we both read Primo Levi."

"Was it a coincidence?" Frank gazed at Jane with curiosity.

"Some people might see it as a destiny." Jane's dark eyes turned more intense as she thought hard. "You know, Frank, I've been very cautious not to look for a sign from what was happening around me."

"Have you? Was there a reason?"

"Because what we perceive as a sign of destiny can easily be produced by wishful thinking and mislead. We are desperate for confirmation from above and hastily accept it as a yes."

"We do indeed."

"There was also a moment for me that I wondered if it was a sign. Out of the blue, you cited one of the notable quotes in my life. Then I asked, was it also a sign, but I'd made similar mistakes many times before."

"Which one was it?"

"The quote from Anne Frank."

Frank's eyes got wider. "Was that quote for you significant?"

Jane nodded.

"How extraordinary." Frank shook his head in disbelief. "But Jane, I couldn't have wished to meet here someone from South Korea and expect her to share my Jewish heritage. It must be the same for you. You couldn't have hoped for a lukewarm Jew who is your daughter's Chemistry teacher. I don't think our wishful thinking misled us."

"In any case, I'm glad that we got to know each other."

"I am too. I have congratulated myself for giving Mia one for that assignment."

Jane giggled, and that sounded like music to Frank's ears. "Or perhaps we should thank the rubbish wifi in the Netherlands?"

"Oh, that too! Although I've never thought that I would be grateful for that."

"Me neither!"

They fell into another comfortable silence until Jane lifted her head in excitement. "Oh! Mia told me about Daan."

"She did? That's good. What did she tell you?"

"Not much. She's bringing him home next week."

"Ah! So you'll meet him. That's quite something!"

"I'm so nervous. And excited too. I'm curious about who Mia likes so much. I hope he'll like my food."

"Well, he'll have to pretend to love anything you give him if he wants to win you over. Don't be nervous!"

"Will you come too, Frank? You know Daan well, don't you? It might be easier for him if there was another familiar face there."

"I'd love to come. And I'll pretend to love everything you give me, no worries."

***

When Frank was back at school the next day, Ron, the principal, called him to his office. "Hi, Frank, please have a seat."

"Thanks."

"How are you doing? I see you a lot more involved in school these days, and that is positive."

"Thanks. I am doing and feeling good too."

"So, any idea what I have called you about?"

"I have a vague suspicion."

"Good. I will come straight to the point as you and I are on such good terms. Are you seeing Mia Hollander's mother?"

"Yes."

"So that is true."

"Yes."

"Do you know how I know?"

"I can guess it. From Mia's father."

"Yes. Mr. Hollander called me and enlightened me about the inappropriate relationship between a teacher and a parent."

"Is it inappropriate?"

"Well, we don't encourage such a relationship if we can help it."

"Can you help it?"

Ron gazed at Frank for a long time and shook his head. "No, I guess not. But you know how people talk. And this father of

Mia... didn't seem very understanding."

"No, he's not."

"It can't all be true what he was saying about the mother? That someone could be so... faulty as he described her? I couldn't imagine that you'd fall for someone like that."

"All I can say is, Ron, that it says more about the person who says such things than the person he is slandering so shamelessly."

"I agree. I would be careful, though. He didn't sound like an amiable man."

"I will be, Ron. Thank you for your trust in me, again, as always."

"You are a good teacher. I don't want to lose you."

Frank stopped standing up from the chair when Ron said that.

"I've wanted to ask you for some time... how were you able to keep your faith in me? You only know me from school. Even the people who know me longer and better don't quite know what to believe."

Ron smiled and stood up to put the kettle on. "Well, from what I'd seen of you at school, I wanted to believe you. I saw that you had faith in yourself. And it helps if there is at least one another person who has faith in you too."

Frank nodded.

"It helped me. You helped me a lot. I feel devastated that Jesse didn't see that I had faith in him."

"Yes. It is devastating. You can only help people who want to be helped, though. Frank, don't let the past take away what you used to love to do. As long as you keep holding on, something good will come out of it."

Frank had almost forgotten about David by the time he left Ron's office. He had had a busy day teaching and checking on his students in class. Then, finally, it was time to go home. As Frank reached his car, he spotted a flashy sports car in the parking lot. David opened the door, and Frank could now see that it was garish red in the daylight.

"I thought I would talk to you."

David was wearing an expensive-looking silver-grey suit. He looked as posh as he did a few months ago when Frank talked to him at the parents' meeting, except for one thing.

"What happened to your face?"

There was a piece of white gauze plastered next to his right eye. "That's none of your business. And what's also not your business is…" Frank saw that David was getting out of breath with impatience "…. my daughter."

Frank inspected David's cold eyes. He tried to look for some kind of affection when David mentioned his daughter, but he didn't spot any.

"This is a critical time of her life. Whether she does well or not at high school will decide her future. I wouldn't accept a child of mine not being able to enter university. Never! And how she is doing now is hopeless. All because her mentor and mother are having an affair! I'm not going to tolerate it!"

'Right,' Frank wondered. 'How can it be an affair when the two people involved are both eligible for a relationship?'

"So what are you saying?"

"Stay away from my daughter. Otherwise,"

"Otherwise?"

"I will make your affair public, and you won't be able to keep your job."

"I wouldn't waste my time and energy if I were you." God, what a revolting man. Frank was almost in awe of this man's vileness.

"Waste my time? You don't think it would work?"

"No. I know it wouldn't work."

Frank's calmness seemed to trigger David's anger. "And why is that? Do you think you know everything about Jane? You know nothing about her. I'm sure she hasn't told you why we got divorced. I'm sure she doesn't tell!"

Frank turned around and opened his car. He wasn't going to give David the opportunity to badmouth Jane.

"She cheated on me! That dirty slut slept with other men. She just offers herself to random men, did you know that? You will get contaminated when you touch her. God knows what she carries!"

Frank turned around again and watched David's sweaty face. David wasn't as good-looking as first impressions at all, and he was just old and bitter and unable to control his temper.

"You know, anyone who knows Jane a bit wouldn't believe a word you say about her. So stop going around telling people what you think about her. I can't believe that someone like Jane had to live with you. She didn't deserve this bullshit. And you know what? Even if it's all true what you told me, I don't care. She's still the most amazing person I will ever meet."

Then Frank got in his car and drove off. Frank was fuming inside. If he'd stayed there longer, he would have punched him. Beat him out of his crazy head. That wouldn't have worked out very well, even if giving David what he deserved might have been worth losing his job for. God, what a jerk! How could people listen to him and let him talk? Where is dignity?

He stopped the car at the petrol station. He needed to cool down before he went back to school and punched him anyway.

Ten minutes later, Frank called Jane from the car. "Jane, are you home?"

"Hi, Frank! Yes, I just got home. Where are you?"

"Is it okay if I come to you? You don't have to feed me or anything, but I just want to see you for a bit."

"Really? Sure, Mia is seeing Daan and coming after dinner. You know where I live?"

When Frank appeared at Jane's doorstep with the flowers and a bottle of wine from the petrol station, Jane was pleasantly surprised.

"Here, sorry that it is from the petrol station. Next time I will get a livelier bouquet and decent wine from a proper shop."

"Are they for me? The flowers are pretty! You didn't have to bring anything."

"I had to see you. You look lovely, by the way." Frank stepped into Jane's modest but cozy house and kissed her.

"Thank you. Are you okay, though? Why the rush?"

"Can we sit, and would it be terribly rude if I pour myself a glass of this horrible, cheap wine?"

Jane chuckled.

"No need to drink that wine, if you know it's so horrible. I might have something better in my kitchen. I've made some simple pasta, with tomato sauce. We can eat and talk if you want."

"That's just perfect, Jane."

So they sat at Jane's dining table in the kitchen, and Frank poured the wine that looked more drinkable than the one he'd brought. Jane scooped the pasta and delicious smelling sauce from the bowl.

"So tell me, Frank. What's the occasion?"

"Mmm, can I finish this first and tell you about it? This is so tasty, and I didn't know I was so hungry."

"Of course, there's more, serve yourself."

Frank had a second serving, but he made sure there was enough left for Mia. Jane said that Mia was eating with Daan, but he knew how much teenagers could eat. He didn't want to upset Mia at all. "I've just had the most annoying conversation with David."

Jane opened her mouth when Frank finally told her about the encounter, and she frowned in disbelief. "Seriously? He's never done that before. I mean, going after a man I see."

"Really? I can imagine him turning up at every boyfriend's doorstep to scare them away."

Jane seemed to think what Frank said was funny, although her face became serious again. "Did he give you a hassle?"

"Well, he called the school first and told the principal that we had an inappropriate relationship."

"Oh, dear. Did you get into trouble?"

"Not really. I mean, neither of us is under age or married. We are just two people who like each other."

"Exactly. Only David would disagree, though."

"Obviously, but we don't care. But then he came to school to talk to me."

"What? He came to see you physically?"

"He was saying that I shouldn't see you for the sake of Mia. A bad influence on her school-work, and so on."

"What bullshit."

"That's what I said to him." Frank smiled at Jane. "Then he started to slag you. Like the first time at the parents' meeting. Then it was about you being a worthless mother for not showing up there and not caring about Mia's schooling."

"And this time, it was about something else, I guess. He's got a regular repertoire."

"Yes. An awful, vile man, he is. I just had to come and see you. To tell you how sorry I was to see the man you had to put up with for so long. It must have been... unbearable. I wanted to hug and kiss you."

"That's so sweet of you." Jane smiled, but she seemed to be distracted by something.

"You okay, Jane? Did I upset you by telling you that he turned up?"

"No. I just know what he would have said. In fact, do you know that I designed it? To escape, it was the only way."

"What was your plan?"

"To make him think that I cheated on him, I cheated on him. Are you disappointed in me, Frank?"

Frank was beginning to get over the shock and murmured, "No, of course not, Jane."

Then Jane started to tell Frank her story. "It took me many years to realize that what he did to me was abuse. Before then, I only knew that I was unhappy and miserable. David blamed it on my post-natal depression, and I was depressed, for sure, but it was more profound than that. I married David when I had hesitations about him. He was possessive and controlling. I was twenty-four when I met him and took his obsession as a sign of affection. But it was more than I could bear, and I wanted my freedom back. After my one-year contract finished in Amsterdam, I was going to go back home. Then I found out I was pregnant. He was in charge of contraceptives, that was his initiative, but still, I got pregnant. But as he pointed out, it was my responsibility as well, and without any doubt, Mia was my baby from the moment that I found out. I couldn't think of my life without her."

Frank imagined a twenty-four year old Jane. She still looked not much older than that, but he was sure that she must have looked a lot more carefree than now.

"So I knew about his possessiveness, but I still didn't know him enough, what he was capable of. After we married, things got more difficult. He didn't want to change his ways and disproved of everything I did. According to him, I was a lazy housekeeper, a worthless mother. He called me a parasite because I didn't earn any money. But he didn't allow me to work either." Frank felt the blood was drawn out from his body. And pain took the place where the blood had been. He was feeling sick listening to what Jane had been going through.

"I was not even aware that I was emotionally abused. When you hear every day how useless you are, you start to believe it yourself. You lose who you were and can't remember it anymore. I had no friend or family to talk to and was completely alone, except for Mia."

Jane smiled at Frank. Frank wondered if she could see how much pain he was fighting inside him.

"And I lived for Mia. I stayed with David because I thought that was for Mia. He repeatedly told me there was no way I could take her away, and I believed him. But then when Mia was about five, she started to see how he was hurting me."

Frank froze. 'I should have gone back and punched him! I don't care if I go to jail for it!'

"Did he hit you, Jane?" Frank heard his voice sound as if it belonged to someone else.

"No. Never. He hurt me other ways."

"How... other ways?" Frank felt shaky.

"He took me brutally. There was no love, no tenderness, no consent from me. If I tried to refuse him, he got even more violent. I had to grit my teeth and wish it would be done quickly."

Frank felt something coming down over his face. It was hot and unstoppable.

"When I saw Mia getting worried about me, I thought I had to leave him. But I didn't know how to and was frightened. The only way I could see that David would let me go was to ruin myself. Then he wouldn't want me anymore. Still, it took almost two years until I brought myself to do it.

I learnt to drive, and the instructor was the first person I was able to talk to in years. He became a good friend and told me that David had chosen me as his victim. Because I tended to adjust to others' needs, and had no one to turn to. He asked if I wanted to show Mia that this was a normal relationship, leading Mia to accept such behavior from men herself. It was an eye-opener for me. I really had to leave him then."

Frank nodded. Jane wiped away his tears with her fingers.

"In the end, it was the friend who opened my eyes whom I asked for help. I couldn't make decisions about my body, with David, but this time I decided for myself. I asked him if he would sleep with me. Not out of pity, but as a friend. I didn't ruin myself, as it liberated me. I prepared to leave with Mia and told David that I'd slept with someone else. And ever since then, he has called me a dirty slut. A small price to pay for my freedom!"

Frank opened his arms, and Jane came to sit on his lap and embraced him. "He can say what he wants to say. As long as I am out of his life."

"You, strong, amazing woman." Frank couldn't go on because

his throat was too choked.

Jane looked perplexed when she heard what Frank said. "If I were that strong, why did it take me so long to leave?"

"Everything you did was for Mia. You did all you could, no, more than that, for her. That was your strength."

"Some people have asked me why I tolerated what David was telling others. Some even suggested suing him and making him stop. But you see, I don't mind. I don't need him to praise me or approve of me. I just don't care. I'd rather be slandered as a whore than live like one in my marriage with him. I've tolerated worse things with him."

They just stayed in each other's arms, and Frank buried his nose in Jane's hair. "I saw you in my dream the other day."

Jane lifted her head and looked into Frank's eyes. "You did? When?"

"When I was listening to your song."

"Oh."

"I saw you holding baby Mia and singing the song. You were crying."

"Oh..." Jane's eyes got bigger then changed watery. "I can't believe you saw that. I was like that."

"I thought so. It was so vivid, like I was there."

"I used to cry holding Mia when she was a baby and listening to the song. I was worried in case it made Mia sad too. It was such a relief, the other day, when she told me that she loved that song."

"I saw that."

After a minute of silence, Jane intoned. "Even in this place one can survive, and therefore one must want to survive, to tell the story, to bear witness."[7]

Frank kissed the top of her head and carried on. "We are slaves, deprived of every right, exposed to every insult, condemned to certain death, but we still possess one power, and we must defend it with all our strength for it is the last—the power to refuse our consent."[8]

---

[7] Primo Levi, *If this is a man*, London, Abacus, 1987, pp. 44-45.

[8] Primo Levi, *If this is a man*, London, Abacus, 1987, p. 45.

"That was what I'd lost, the power to refuse my consent. But I got it back. And I refuse to be bitter about it too, no more."

Frank nodded at Jane. They embraced each other again and stayed still as if time had stopped until it was dark outside and Mia came home.

When Mia saw them locked together like sculptures at the kitchen table, she almost shrieked from fright. "For god's sake! What are you doing here in the dark? Why is the light off?" She indignantly turned on the wall-switch and saw their faces. She stopped in shock. "What is going on? Are you guys okay? Have you two been crying?"

Neither Frank nor Jane could say anything to Mia.

"Mr. Bloom? Are you okay?"

Frank searched for his voice. "It's Frank. Call me Frank."

"O-Kay." Mia turned to her mother. "Mom? Are you sure you are okay?"

Jane nodded and pointed to the pan behind her. "If you are hungry, there's some pasta."

Mia looked exasperated at her mother. "Ha! As if I would want to eat now! By the way, I've eaten too, I told you I was going to!" Then Mia breathed out slowly and sat down with them. "So tell me, Mom. What's up?"

"Your father called the school and turned up to talk to Frank. He thinks we should not see each other for your sake."

Then Mia murmured something Frank and Jane couldn't quite get the gist of, but it undoubtedly sounded offensive.

"Mia!" Jane looked helplessly at her daughter. "I don't even know what that means... but that sounded rude."

"Never mind what I said." Mia rolled her eyes again, up to the ceiling. "I mean, how would that be for my sake?"

Frank decided to answer that question. "Well, he thinks you would be too distracted or too embarrassed if we were together."

Mia snorted aloud. "He doesn't even have the decency to admit it's for his sake."

Frank smiled and queried Mia. "Why do you think he cares, Mia? When your parents have been divorced for so many years?"

"Because he is a narcissist. He can't stand that Mom would be happy without him. Actually, Mom, that would be the best revenge, being bloody happy!" Then Mia stared at them, horrified. "Oh my god, I hope that was not why you two were crying. You were not considering anything remotely close to what he suggested, were you?"

"You don't think we should?" Frank prompted her gently, just for the record.

"As if! Don't ever quit something you like because of me, Mom. Don't sacrifice your well-being for me anymore. I won't let that happen, ever again."

Frank and Jane looked a lot more relaxed and relieved from Mia's somewhat aggressive blessing.

They both grinned like idiots, and Mia seemed desperate to change the atmosphere. "Mr. Bloom, eh, Frank, do you want some water? You guys must be dehydrated from all that crying."

"Oh, yes, Mia. That would be nice."

"Mom? You too?'

"Yes, please. Will you also put the kettle on for me?"

"I will make tea if you want. You two just sit and take it easy. You seem to need to recover."

While Mia was busy preparing some kind of high tea, opening every cupboard and taking out everything sweet, Jane asked casually. "So, is Daan also excited to come here?"

Mia nodded, not turning around from her tea setting. "Yes, he asked what you'd like, some flowers or chocolate, and I said maybe a book. We chose a book today together, but it's a surprise until he comes."

Frank and Jane exchanged a glance with each other.

'How nice to be looked after by my daughter,' Jane seemed to say.

'What a wonderful job you did with Mia. What an enchanting woman you are,' Frank's eyes seemed to whisper.

Then he kissed Jane so passionately that he didn't notice that Mia had brought the tea. Jane and Frank laughed at Mia's horrified face.

Frank left after they had all shared a cup of tea and biscuits. Mia's mother sent him off at the door, and when she came back, she hugged Mia tightly.

"What? Why are you being so clammy? Is it because of Frank?"

"No... I mean, yes, probably as well. But I just want to thank you."

"Thank me? For what?"

"For the person you are. I couldn't wish for a wiser and sweeter daughter."

"I don't feel at all wise or sweet... that's funny."

"And modest, too. You don't know how wonderful you are."

Mia couldn't take on this rubbish anymore, so she went up to her room.

She had been hatching a plan for the past few days, and today she'd met Daan and given him some instructions. She just needed to polish off a few last things, like finishing the letters that she'd started, and prayed that it would all work out. It was probably the boldest thing she'd ever taken to in her life. She felt petrified, even to nurture this plan in her head. Would she be able to pull this off? Was she brave enough? Then Mia thought about her mother. How courageous her mother had been, how she took a risk for Mia. She was heartened by remembering her mother and decided to go on with her plan. First, let's finish the letters. Writing these three letters was probably the most challenging part of Mia's plan so far.

She was just done with her first letter when her phone rang. Mia thought it would be Simon, but she was startled to see it was her father. He hardly called her unless he needed to announce something.

"Hello? Dad?"

"Mia. I'm disappointed in you."

'Oh, how are you, Dad? Nice to hear from you.'

Mia murmured in her head sarcastically, 'Why are you disappointed in me?'

"Didn't your mother tell you that I found out what you were up to?"

'She did, but Mom knows me better than you do. Ha!'

"No. She didn't," Mia lied.

"That's just so typical of her. What does she do as a mother? Your grades are like a joke too, but this time it's about something else."

"What is it?" Mia knew, but she acted just like she was in a play.

"I saw on my computer that you were checking the prices of my bikes."

"Oh, that! Yes, I did."

"Why? Were you trying to sell them for money?"

"Dad! How can you think that?" Mia went on with her acting. She didn't realize that she was so good at it. Maybe an option for her career?

"Because you googled 'price new racing bikes?'."

"I googled it because I was curious how much such a bike cost. You've got the coolest bikes, Dad, and I want to have one like that later. So I googled the price."

"You mean you weren't thinking of selling them?"

"No! How could I sell them? I don't have an account on the site, and you would have found out straight away. What's the point? I'm not that stupid, ha, ha!"

Her father contemplated what Mia said. Anyhow, just typing 'price bikes' didn't mean that she was going to sell them. Mia's father sighed and went on to the next issue. "There's another thing. Are you aware that your mother is having an affair with your mentor?"

"Is she?" Academy award-worthy acting, Mia clapped herself silently. "I didn't know that!"

"Isn't that scandalous? What would your friends and their parents think of them? All that gossip and uproar would distract you from your school. I strongly feel that they should stop seeing each other."

"Why don't you tell them yourself?"

"I did! But your mentor didn't seem to care about your school life. He was actually shockingly rude to me!"

'Dad, you are the rudest person in the world!' Then Mia remembered her plan and suppressed the hostile feeling about her father. "So, what do you want me to do?" Mia asked her father in her most sugarcoated voice. She needed to keep her dad as an ally, for now.

"I want you to talk to your mother. Put some sense into her head.

After all, you are my daughter, and you must be more sensible than your mother. Tell her that it would affect your schooling too much and you can't afford for it to happen. She will listen to you and do anything if it's for you. She's always been like that."

'Well, great that you are acknowledging how Mom has always been good to me!" "I'll try, Dad."

"That's a good girl. I knew you had more sense than you look like."

"And when do I see you, Dad? Can I drop by tomorrow? I've missed you." Mia grabbed her neck and imitated a gag.

Her father was pleasantly taken aback by Mia saying such a sweet thing. "Tomorrow I won't be home, going to this party for my work. What about Friday?"

"Going to a party? I really wanted to see you tomorrow. Can't you just see me even for half an hour? After your work?"

"I have to leave home at six. I only have time for a shower and to get changed after work. The party is boring and never-ending, but it's good for work, for networking. So I can't see you tomorrow. Friday?"

"Yes. Friday. See you then."

"See you, Mia. I'm glad that you understand and are on my side."

So it should be tomorrow, her grand plan. That meant that she didn't have much time to prepare, but talking to her father now had made writing her second letter much more effortless. She just had to get on with it and start taking action tonight.

She called Simon. "It's going to be tomorrow."

"Hi, Mia. So, tomorrow? Alright. What time?"

Her father wouldn't be home until late. But for the second part of her plan, she needed enough time after they left her father's house. "I will be there at half-past six. You should come around quarter to seven." She told Simon her father's address.

"Alright. What about the other business? You haven't forgotten about it? This business is even more important. Now is the opportunity for Daan to save real money. For your love-nest."

"I haven't forgotten it. Simon, you swore this was the way I could make money for Daan, right?"

"Of course, this is the fastest and easiest way to make lots of money. I promise you."

"Are there really so many girls doing this for you?"

"Yes, loads! You wouldn't believe how many girls are in trouble and need money. I help them out, and they also make money for me, so it's a sound business. Relax! After you've done it once, it will get easier."

"Okay. If you say so."

"Good girl. Then tomorrow, it is. I will send you the details tonight."

"Yes. Don't forget to put down everything about this arrangement, including money, so that I wouldn't mess up. Oh, Simon?" Mia almost forgot. "I am going to print out the paper for Daan, and we can sign it tomorrow."

Mia wasn't going to leave it to Simon and risk him turning up without the paper and claiming that he forgot. Mia was sure that he would do something like that.

"I knew that you're a good businesswoman. Alright, but I will only sign it when I have all the stuff that is worth that amount."

"I know. See you tomorrow then."

* * *

The next day Mia finished school at three. Frank saw Mia running out of the classroom as soon as the lesson ended. Then she came running back again and said to Frank, still panting.

"Mr. Bloo… Frank, will you do me a favour?"

"What's all this hurry? Are you okay? What is the favour?"

"Can you call Daan around eight-thirty?"

"Tonight? Is something going on?"

"No. Just call him at eight-thirty, and if he doesn't answer, will you keep trying until he does?"

"Daan? You're not going to explain to me what this is all about?"

"Not now. Please don't frighten Mom with this, Frank. I will explain later, I promise. Have you got Daan's number? Here, you'd better save the number." Then she ran out of the school like a thunderstorm.

Mia finally finished the last letter, the most difficult one of the three, after she came home from school. She'd already written the first two letters last night. The first one was for Monica, and Mia was going to post it in a little while. She would take the second one with her, and the third one was for her mother to open later. Mia left a note for her mother before leaving the house. That she was going to see Daan and would be home before nine. Mia also wrote down Daan's number. She added,

"Will you call Daan if I'm not back home by then?"

Mia checked to see if she had got the printed papers and letters with her. Two identical documents with her signature and two letters.

Mia dropped Monica's letter in the postbox on the way and arrived at her father's house at six-thirty. When she saw her father's house, Mia got so nervous and shaky that she almost fell off her bike. His pompous house with a secluded driveway was out of sight from his neighbours. To her relief, her father's car was not there. Just to be sure, she rang the bell. She tried four times, and when there was no sign of her father, she opened the door with her key and turned off the alarm. She opened the garage and saw his three racing bikes.

Then at a quarter to seven, a white van appeared on her father's driveway. Simon and another young man jumped out of the truck.

Simon whistled, looking at the house in front of him. "Hey, Mia, a big day, huh?"

Mia skipped the pleasantries and went straight to the business. "These three bikes."

Simon glanced around the garage, saw the vast volume of various vehicles, and whistled again, "Daan's done well!"

'As if any of this is mine!'

"So, two and half thousand, right?"

"No, no. That would be the price if they were new. I'd say one and a half for these three."

"Ridiculous! These are all brand new!"

'I haven't seen him riding any of those, to come to think of it!'

"Two Thousand then," Mia tried.

"No, Mia. I will be nice and say a thousand and seven hundred. Alright?'

Mia nodded. What could she do? Cancel the deal? She'd better wrap this up and leave her father's house a.s.a.p. "What else can you take then?"

Simon looked around. "Lovely cars."

"Forget it." Even Mia knew the price of those cars was up above there.

"How about..." Simon stopped. He pointed to her father's boat.

"That will do. The engine of the boat. That will do nicely."

Simon looked satisfied.

Simon's man, who had already stored the three racing bikes in the car, moved to the boat.

"Wait! Sign first." Mia took the papers out of her inside pocket.

"Here, and there."

"Why two?"

"Just to be sure."

Simon laughed like Mia was mad.

"I read that we both need to keep a copy each."

"You've done your homework."

When Simon had signed the papers and given one to her, she folded it carefully and put it back inside her pocket.

"Done here?"

"Done."

"Now go away, and I will be there at eight."

The van, full of her father's precious possessions, was gone in a second.

Mia closed the garage.

She left the second letter on her father's boat next to where the engine had been.

It said. "Dad, I just want to say that I think you are the most horrible person. You hurt Mom when she was married to you. I know it all. In fact, you should be in jail! And you continued to hurt Mom even after the divorce telling everyone your distorted stories. Shame on you! For all you've done, this is a small price to pay. I know you'll carry on with your life as in the past. Please don't hurt anyone else. No one will take your abuse because no one can do what Mom did for me. You will end up all alone in your life when people see how you really are. If you call the police, which I am sure you would do otherwise, I will tell everybody you are a fucking rapist. You know how people talk, don't you? How people just believe what they're being told? Except that this is true. So I've sold a few of your things and consider it as a modest pay-back. Or a one-off inheritance deal because I don't want to see you anymore.

It's taken me all this time to break off with you because I've been sad for you. You used to have so many blessings in your life, a gentle and loving, dignified wife and a daughter who loved and admired you. We would have done anything for you and kept loving you if you hadn't manipulated us and seen us only as your possessions. Even with your money, house, and statues, you won't be able to buy what you used to have with us. But I am not sad anymore. You can't cure narcissism. I hope you are sorry, but I know that's too much to expect."

She turned the alarm on, locked the door, and jumped on her bike.

As she cycled towards the town center, Mia saw that she didn't have much time to think about what she was doing. There was no going back now. She'd got the first part of her plan well sorted, and she was relieved about that. Now Daan didn't owe anything to Simon. She'd paid his debt with her father's stuff. Whatever Daan earned now, he could use it for himself. And Mia would finish high school and find out what she wanted to do with her life. The possibilities were endless.

She thought about her letter to Monica. It was like finally submitting an assignment that she hadn't been able to complete for five years.

"Dear Monica,

I hope you remember me.

I hope you don't hate me.

I know it's too late, but I want to say sorry to you.

For not saying hi to you and for running away when you saw me at the supermarket.

I also wanted to apologize that I haven't reached out to you when you've only been so loving and kind to me.

It wasn't because I believed what my father said about you.

I knew you tried very hard to make it work for me too.

But I was too young to hold on to what I knew. I was scared of my father and didn't dare to stand up for you and myself. I was only ten.

But I haven't forgotten about you. I still feel so bad about the day when I turned away from you. I still have the bracelet you gave me. I still wish we were friends.

But more than anything, I hope you are happy, much happier now.

You were my favourite person next to my mother, which is quite something because I really love her very much. So please forgive me, Monica, and thank you for being there for me at the time.

P.S. I now have a boyfriend, Daan, and he looks just like the boy in the film that we used to watch together. Which film was it, Monica? I can't seem to remember the title. Well, bye Monica, I missed you. And please give Oma Ginny and Opa Wim my love too."

At seven-thirty, Mia passed the police station. She stopped cycling and tried to catch her breath. She'd been running around like a headless chicken all day, and this was a crucial moment. Mia stared at the grey, nondescript building. She could turn her bike back and go home. If Mia went on, she couldn't undo anything anymore. She thought of what Simon was arranging for girls like her. She knew Simon tamed and often forced other girls into this. Maybe they also loved someone very much, more than themselves, and Simon used their love. How Mia almost went for it in her desperation. She would do this for other girls too.

Mia cycled on until she found the street where Simon had told her to go. It was now a quarter to eight. She hesitated for a moment when she got her phone out but then pressed the three-digit number determinedly.

It took some time before the lady agent on the other side understood what Mia was trying to tell her. Mia had to repeat it a few times, "I'm fifteen years old, and it's been arranged for me to meet a man for money. And I'm scared." Mia explained Simon's text message with his instructions. "It's almost eight o'clock. And I have to go in. Will you please come and help me?"

The lady agent realized that Mia would not follow her advice and was about to hang up. Mia told her the address again and pressed the "end" button.

Mia walked to the house number on Simon's text message. She could imagine how Daan would panic when he saw the police car. She felt disoriented that the plan in her head was unfolding in front of her. It was like Mia was acting in a film. She called Daan, and he answered straight away.

"Mia! Are you okay? What's all this?"

"Are you already where I asked you to be?"

"Yes, I'm here. What's going on?"

"Is your recording app on?"

"Yes. Mia! Are you okay?"

"Yes. Just start to walk to the address that I told you. It's only two blocks away. Leave the phone on but never say a word, even if you are desperate to do so. If I shout your name, then talk to me as hard as you can. You will see the police too. Please come now!"

"Mia! Mia!"

"Shhhhh! Don't say anymore and just come here."

When Daan was quiet on the line, she placed her phone carefully in her pocket, still turned on. She breathed deeply and knocked on the door. There came a voice asking for the password, and Mia said, "Delivery," as Simon had instructed her.

The door opened, and she went in.

The man smiled at Mia, and she saw his greasy hair and crooked teeth. Mia couldn't say how old he was.

"You're pretty."

Oh god, oh god, please don't let him kiss me. She avoided his face and held out her hand. "Money, first."

The man snorted but still reached out for his purse from the jacket on a hanger in the hall. "Forty?"

"Fifty." She received the money, folded it slowly, and put it in her pocket.

"For god's sake, come inside." The man pulled her hand and walked into the lounge.

Please, please let them hurry!

The man sat Mia on his lap on the dirtiest couch she'd ever seen. She prayed that the police would come and get her before she had to fight this man. If things got too horrendous, she would scream to Daan, which would hopefully stop the man. The man started to feel her breast, and Mia closed her eyes.

"You have pert tits... I like girls with those tits. Do you like what I do to you?"

Mia gritted her teeth.

Mia regretted her stupid plan now. She must have lost her head to have come up with this. She thought she was strong enough to pull this off, but she wasn't. She felt ruined already by the man's touch. Even Daan hadn't been so intimate with her. She tried to swallow her tears, but they must have dropped on the man's hand, fumbling her breast.

"For fuck's sake!" the man exclaimed in incomprehensible excitement as if he'd hit the jackpot. "What's this? Are you crying? Have you never done this before?"

Then he grabbed her neck, pulling her face to his mouth.

Mia twisted her head to get out of his grip and screamed as hard as she could, "Daan! Daan!" And she cried too, "Mom! Mom!"

Then an explosion made Mia's head numb. Her ears hurt and she couldn't hear anything.

Everything stopped. There was glass everywhere, and Mia felt pieces of it in her hand.

It seemed like the air in the man's lounge was vacuumed away, and for a few seconds there was surreal silence. Then as if the play button of a film was pressed, Mia suddenly heard shouts and screams and sirens, and she heard Daan's voice too. Mia thought it was from her phone, but Daan was there. He was now holding her in his arms. One of the agents who'd broken into the man's lounge ushered them out of the house to the police car. Mia couldn't remember what her plan was anymore. It felt as if she'd left her soul behind on that dirty man's couch.

* * *

It was well after midnight when everyone got home.

Mia, who had a bandage over her hand, was still quite dizzy but in a much better condition than a few hours ago.

Frank, who was also stunned, supported and held her mother in the police station all the time.

Her mother was so hysterical, it kind of calmed Mia, but now she looked like she'd died.

And Daan, whose face was also a mess, had been speechless all night, she noticed.

Mia gave Daan the paper when they were coming back to her house in Frank's car. He opened it and read it again and again. He still didn't understand what it meant.

"That you don't owe anything to him," Mia whispered in his ear. He tried to say something but he couldn't. He just shook his head and closed his eyes. To Mia's relief, he still didn't let go of her hand. Mia felt that it would all come later, what he wanted to say. The important thing was that Simon was caught. Mia didn't understand fully what would happen and how long it would take for everything to settle down, but for now, he couldn't exploit anyone anymore.

Her mother got a phone call, breaking the stillness in the car. From the shouts and abusive tone, Mia assumed it was her father; but she didn't care. She'd broken off with her father and was not going to be bullied by him anymore.

At home, her mother made some tea for everyone.

The nausea Mia had felt all night was catching up with her, and she started to doze off on the sofa.

She heard Frank saying that he would take Daan to his house.

Mia murmured, semi-conscious, "Can't you all stay here tonight? I don't want you to go."

Frank, Daan, and Jane looked at each other.

"I guess Mia can sleep with me, and Daan can sleep in Mia's bed. If you don't mind sleeping on the sofa, Frank, you're all welcome to stay here. It would be nice if we could have breakfast together. We've hardly had any time to contemplate what's happened...."

"I don't mind sleeping on the sofa, Jane. Let's do what Mia wants. If you're okay, Daan?"

Daan must have agreed since Mia didn't hear anyone leaving.

Somehow, probably by the two men present in the house, Mia was effortlessly transported from the sofa to her mother's bed. She briefly thought about offering her place in her mother's bed to Frank, but she was too wiped out to say it. Besides, it was really lovely to snuggle against her mother on a night like this.

She felt her mother stroking her hair, and Mia murmured, "Good night, Mom."

Her mother whispered, "You scared me so much, Mia, but I'm proud of you."

"I learnt it from you." Then she fell into total unconsciousness.

In the middle of the night—or was it early morning at dawn?— Mia felt the emptiness next to her. She saw that her mother was not there. Mia became terrified, like when she was a little girl and tried to listen to the sounds.

Then Mia heard something. Her mother and Frank on the sofa. Mia stopped breathing because it was shocking, your mother and teacher together.... Then she realized that it was different from when she was a little girl. Her mother was laughing and sounded, well, happy. Like she was having fun. Mia closed her eyes and tried to sleep again. There was no need to check on her mother. She was fine.

Mia was fine too. She'd found the greatest love of all; the love that was inside of her. Unlike any other love, her love for herself would always be there whatever she did and wherever she went. It was such a comforting thought. And tonight, she'd found her name again. She'd felt lost while carrying out her audacious plan, but when the police told her she'd helped many other girls as well as herself from exploitation, she was glad she'd taken the risk and opened herself up, made herself vulnerable. Her newfound strength made her feel beautiful. Mia had learnt that feeling lost came from looking for something, and as her mother said, she'd rather miss the 2% and choose to have a purpose in her life. She embraced both meanings of her name, and she loved both. She was sometimes lost, and most times, beautiful. She'd always derive love and dignity from her name.

She was "Mia."

EPILOGUE—BEGINNING

"Dear Mom,
Please don't go into shock when you read this. You are the most zen person as anyone could see, but I know this is quite a big deal what I am going to tell you. And you come out of your usually tranquil zone whenever I'm concerned. But, I think my plan will work, and if everything goes as it should go, I will be fine, and we'll all be home together soon. Just remember that I didn't want to hurt anyone but wanted to do the right thing.

I will start with a positive note. I've written a letter to Monica. You know, when we were talking about her letter, there was something I didn't tell you. About a year after she and dad broke up, I saw her at the supermarket. I was alone, and she called me and said hi. She looked delighted to see me. And do you know what I did, Mom? I ran away. I didn't even say hi.

Dad used to tell me if I bumped into her on the street, I should say nothing and run away. He said that Monica cheated on him and stole his money. Sounds familiar, huh? He also said that she would kidnap me if I went with her. It was not like I genuinely believed all he said, but I guess I was scared. I knew she wasn't like that, but still. Is that normal for a ten-year-old?

So I've lived with this guilt ever since that day. Also, with the shame of the way I behaved. I don't know if Monica would want to hear from me or even remember me. She might have moved somewhere else, and my letter might get returned. But I wanted to take a chance and try to fix it. Even if she doesn't want to have anything to do with me, I at least wanted to apologize. And this courage came from you, how you handled difficult situations with only good intentions and dignity. Monica used to tell me that I was lucky to have you as my mother, and she was right. I am so fortunate to have you as my Mom.

And now... I have some horrid things to tell you.
I kept it from you for some time that I had a boyfriend. I think, in the beginning, I was just stunned that somebody liked me because I didn't like myself at all. I felt different from the rest more since I entered high school, and I didn't have enough self-assurance to embrace the difference. And I felt lost too. I hated the father I came to know as I got older. I didn't tell you, but I knew what he did to you. I remember the night you were crying

under the shower and other nights walking around the house. I remember being worried and wanting to take care of you. And I felt angry with you too, that you hadn't left then. I knew it was for me, but I despised the fact that you sacrificed yourself for me and made me responsible for your suffering.

So when I fell in love with Daan, I loved him more than I loved myself since I was in such a mess.

That's when this Simon came in.

He lent Daan two thousand and five hundred euros when Daan's family was in trouble. Daan is going to start working next year and was planning to save for our future (sorry, Mom, I wanted to leave home), but Simon demanded the money back.

He approached me without Daan knowing about it, and I decided to help Daan. I delivered Simon's stuff to his clients for him— and I was sure it was drugs. I know. Shocking. I'm really sorry, Mom.

I did it six times, which deducted only sixty euros from Daan's debt, and I said to Simon that I wanted to quit. I saw the risk, and more than that, I didn't want to lose your trust when you found out.

Then you told me about Frank. Probably the most unexpected news I could ever get from you. It was such a shock, and maybe that's what made me open up, too, haha. You tried to explain that it wasn't me who made you sad, which I understood, well, kind of. But it was something else I understood—that when you love someone, as you love me, sometimes you choose to go through a difficult path if that's what it takes to love the person. You take the risk and carry hardship with you, but it's not always a terrible thing. If you love someone more than a life without suffering, you would do it.

When I understood that and Simon suggested next that I offer myself to men to make more money, I thought, how dare you? My mother loved me so much and chose to walk along a thorny road for me. I am worth that much love. I love Daan, but I love myself more.

Then I got so angry that some people take advantage of this kind of love. I couldn't let Simon go on exploiting girls like me who just loved someone. Daan also loved his family and had to use Simon's money to help them. I loved Daan and wanted to help him. And that's what Dad did, too, wasn't it—exploiting your love for me. So please forgive me for punishing Dad just a tiny bit. You know he deserves at least that.

And I'm sorry, Mom, that it took me so long to see what you've been through. I think, though, that I've always felt it in my subconscious when you were having a difficult time. But I'm grateful that you were there for me and still loved me when you couldn't have been happy. I've felt nothing but love from you even when you were suffering the most. I wish I'd shown my gratitude to you more.

I didn't fully realize until now how sad you were when I went to Dad, and how it broke your heart. I am amazed that you kept that all to yourself and still let me go. When I heard the Buddhist pearl of wisdom you hung on to, I understood why you did what you did. You didn't want me to cherish a grudge against Dad. Everything you did was to raise me undamaged as painlessly as you could.

Do you know that I am so proud of you too? You came to a foreign country leaving everything behind—a comfortable life with a warm family, good friends, a job you were content with. For love. I feel sad that the love wasn't what you thought and deserved but how many people can do what you did, Mom? It just shows how courageous you are and how much love you have in you, Mom.

I know because I still remember our evening ritual from when I was little. I always begged you not to sleep until I fell asleep. I felt safe knowing you were out there reading and listening, watching over me. And I had what you called the "worry tummy." I always had severe stomachache if I was nervous and couldn't sleep. Then you said, "Tell me everything you are worried about, Mia." I could tell you anything, and after I'd confided in you about the friends I'd fought with, school that was so boring, and the toys that I wanted to have, I could sleep. Do you remember?

When this whole Simon thing was lurking around like the worst dream, oh, how I wished that I could go back to that time.... But you've raised and fed me with the stories and songs vital to you. Everything I've learnt has come from you, and I decided to do what I believe is right. From now on, I'll be honest with you because I know how much we love each other, no matter what.

And one last thing...

Jane, Frank and Mia   231

It's the chicken and the egg question like you said, Mom. If you aren't happy, I can't be happy. If I'm not happy, you can't be happy, I know.

I promise I will love myself as you taught me with that song. I promise that I will keep my dignity even in the most challenging situations. I will always carry the greatest love of all inside me.

Mom, so please promise me that you will do the same. Go for your happiness. Don't give up on anything that makes you happy. Please find someone who deserves you, and whom you deserve. If that is Frank, keep him.

And one day, you will smile like nothing bad has ever happened to you. Or you will smile the smile that concentrates everything you have read and listened to and lived through.

Whatever we do, let's always find each other.

Love you, Mom, and see you in a bit. I'll be alright. I told Daan to pick me up from the address—he doesn't know about my plan, though—and Frank will call him too. By the time you're reading this letter, I will be safe.

P.S. I would have chosen you as my mother from the catalogue too. Or don't I get to choose as a child? Well, anyhow, we would have ended up together as you believed. I told Daan the story, and he bought you the book *Anne of Green Gables*. Isn't he sweet? Oh, now I have spoiled your surprise. Sorry!"

* * *

Jane finished the letter and sighed, as she did the hundreds of times that she read it.

Mia had also inherited Jane's tendency to say sorry too often, Jane noticed from her letter.

But that wasn't why she felt stupefied, even after reading it so many times. She still couldn't believe what her daughter had planned.

When Jane called Daan just before nine that night because Mia wasn't home, Daan said there was a letter for her in her bedroom, and she was to come to the police station.

She found the letter in her bedside drawer, and she was shaking so violently she had to call a taxi to go to the police station. She burst into tears when she saw Frank was already there. They heard that there would be a lengthy legal process and further investigation—it appeared that Simon was involved in several crimes—but Jane decided not to worry about it too much now.

That Mia was safe and she was unharmed was the most important thing. As frightened as Jane was that night, she felt proud of her daughter, who managed to think for herself and wanted to help others.

Jane let out another long sigh.

She saw the time and stood up to prepare baking.

Daan and Mia would be there in three hours, but Frank would come early to keep her company and give her a hand.

Jane smiled at the thought of Frank. They laughed a lot, talked endlessly and read each other's favourite books.

She knew the last fifteen years had changed her, and she would never be able to go back to the old Jane. But with Frank, she felt she didn't have to. She didn't want to be twenty-four years old again. Because then she wouldn't know what she knew now, and that would be such a waste of the lessons she had learned. With Frank, it was okay to be this Jane with her damaged years and all the pain she had experienced. She rather loved herself now.

Their most precious moment was when they fell asleep together after listening to music for hours. No need to talk, just walking through the lyrics into blissful dreams. She'd never known such contentment in a relationship.

"Sooner or later in life, everyone discovers that perfect happiness is unrealizable, but there are few who pause to consider the antithesis: that perfect unhappiness is equally unobtainable... Our ever sufficient knowledge of the future opposes it, and this is called in the one instance: hope."[9]

It was now Frank and Jane's most treasured quote. They needed neither perfect happiness nor overwhelming suffering. Because they knew it was difficult to be destroyed when you had dignity, they also believed in hope. And slowly, Jane felt she was becoming lighter at heart. There were more and more moments when Jane wasn't constantly worried about Mia. When Jane ran into the police station in panic and asked for her daughter, she saw a young woman there with a mission. She discovered that Mia had her own mind and would live her life according to it. Until now, Jane had clutched Mia to herself with all her life. But

---

[9] Primo Levi, *If this is a man*, London, Abacus, 1987, pp. 17-18.

it was time for her to let go of her grasp. Jane could just be there and support her daughter when Mia needed her. With this realization, there were increasing moments she felt free, as a woman, not only a mother. So life was good, as the Korean electronics company LG advertised. "Smart arse," Frank always said when he heard the commercial.

"Of course," Jane always answered.

Indeed, life was good for Jane, Frank, and Mia.

Jane, Frank and Mia   235

Jane, Frank and Mia   236

ADVANCE COMMENTS

If you're a fan of Korean Soap Operas you'll like this one. It's a take on the family drama of a mismatched multicultural couple, one with a zen approach to life, being Korean, while the other, being a very straight-laced Dutchman, has a touch of borderline personality disorder. Throw into the mix the stress that having a child brings into their lives, the stress it imposes upon their bi-racial child, a far too empathetic driving instructor and a teenage pimp, and you get a medley of self-absorption that cannot possibly end well unless someone picks up a Kimbap roll and uses it to slap some sense into the characters. This book will either make you despair for humanity that such characters are so recognisable, or give you hope that the dramatic misery they make for themselves is a lesson to all those who harbour such attitudes.

—**Lawrence Gray**, Founding President of the Hong Kong Writers Circle, prize-winning novelist and short-story writer

There are two types of great stories. One brings you somewhere you've never been to. The other requires you to open your eyes and face reality. *Jane, Frank and Mia* is the latter. I have Janes, Franks, and Mias around me. This is a story of the people I know, who suffered, struggled, decided not to stay still, and survived. It was impossible to separate myself from this gut-wrenching and life-affirming story.

—**Jeenkyung Chloe Kim, Zurich, Switzerland**,
    former reporter at JoongAng Ilbo, author of *Old Europe* (Medici Media, 2021), columnist for Korean media.

Jane, Frank and Mia is an extraordinary story about love. It is also a story about suffering, abuse, redemption and revenge. It is about finding oneself, understanding one's past and controlling one's trajectories. More than that: it is resoundingly about social, cultural and cross cultural prejudice. In the heart of even the most liberal of societies, bigotry is close, ever close, to the surface. The often tragic consequences are revealed in the ripple effect on the lives and choices of Jane, Frank and Mia.

The story itself unfolds layer after layer, scenario after scenario of embedded bias and stereotyping: religious, cultural, racist, socio-economic, sexist, body-shaming, homophobic and xenophobic.

It demonstrates how the roots of alienation begin in childhood, with the perpetuation of traditions like folk tales and nursery rhymes, seemingly benign influences that are fraught with hidden prejudice and hate-driven subtext.

Through plot, the author challenges these archetypes, often referencing literature and history with insightful erudition. She shows that there is a correlation between how people are treated and how they feel: that differences – just differences – tend to be perceived as threatening in almost any micro-environment, and that discomfort with differences seems to be the genesis for prejudice, alienation and even vitriolic hatred.

Even in a tolerant society, the greatest danger is complacency: "I've realized that our country's biggest problem is not the racism and discrimination itself, but our belief that it doesn't exist here. We consider ourselves open-minded and tolerant... but we should not think that we are untouchable. We are as faulty as everyone else in this world."

The plot itself is intriguing, has many moments of tension, extreme joy, fear, pleasure, insight, injustice and confusion. Most satisfyingly, it has a good dose of resolution and revenge.

The environment is multilingual and multicultural, covering topics like assimilation versus identity loss, idealism, disappointment, growth and courage. Empathy is a central thematic element, with evolution through insight being preeminent.

A wonderful, nuanced book, thought-provoking, heartening – especially at the end – and interesting.

—Hayley Ann Solomon, New Zealand,
Proverse Publication Prize winner, 2016, 2017.

All forms of art can reflect the true nature of reality. In the novel, *Jane, Frank and Mia*, the author describes a multitude of difficult situations that she might have experienced as an East Asian female immigrant in Europe. Through the subtle description of everyday life and the dialogue between the various characters, the author reveals the wounds and scars that she bore, guiding the reader to encounter a world that is both unfamiliar and familiar at the same time. But ultimately, this novel will allow you to see a life with value beyond the pain and difficulties.

—Yi Seung-Jun, Seoul, South Korea,
Documentary Director, including *Planet of Snail* (Best feature length film at IDFA 2011) / *In the Absence* (Nominated for the Oscars in 2020).

Jane, Frank and Mia   240

FICTION PUBLISHED BY PROVERSE HONG KONG

NOVELS

A Misted Mirror. Gillian Jones.
A Painted Moment. Jennifer Ching.
Adam's Franchise. Lawrence Gray.
An Imitation of Life. Laura Solomon.
Article 109. Peter Gregoire.
As Leaves Blow. Philip Chatting.
*Bao Bao's Odyssey: From Mao's Shanghai
    to Capitalist Hong Kong*. Paul Ting.
Black Tortoise Winter. Jan Pearson.
Blue Dragon Spring. Jan Pearson.
Bright Lights and White Lights. Andrew Carter.
Cemetery miss you. Jason S Polley.
Cop Show Heaven. Lawrence Gray.
Cry of the Flying Rhino. Ivy Ngeow.
Curveball: Life Never Comes At You Straight. Gustav Preller.
Death Has A Thousand Doors. Patricia W. Grey.
Enoch's Muse. Sergio Monteiro.
Hilary and David. Laura Solomon.
HK Hollow. Dragoş Ilca.
Hong Kong Rocks. Peter Humphreys.
Instant Messages. Laura Solomon.
Man's Last Song. James Tam.
Mishpacha – Family. Rebecca Tomasis.
No Boundaies for Lucifer. Gerard Breissan.
Paranoia. Caleb Kavon.
Professor Everywhere. Nicholas Binge.
Red Bird Summer. Jan Pearson.
Revenge from Beyond. Dennis Wong.
The Day They Came. Gerard Breissan.
The Devil You Know. Peter Gregoire.
The Finley Confession. George Watt.
The Handover Murders. Damon Rose.
The Monkey in Me. Caleb Kavon.
The Perilous Passage of Princess Petunia Peasant.
    Victor Edward Apps.

Jane, Frank and Mia   241

The Reluctant Terrorist. Caleb Kavon.
The Thing Is. Andrew Carter.
The Village in the Mountains. David Diskin.
Three Wishes in Bardo. Feng Chi-shun.
Tiger Autumn. Jan Pearson.
Tightrope! A Bohemian Tale. Olga Walló
    (translated from Czech).
Tree Crime. Melody Kemp.
University Days. Laura Solomon.
Vera Magpie. Laura Solomon. (Novella.)

SHORT STORY COLLECTIONS

Beyond Brightness. Sanja Särman.
Odds and Sods. Lawrence Gray.
The Shingle Bar Sea Monster and Other Stories.
    Laura Solomon.
The Snow Bridge And Other Stories. Philip Chatting.
Under the shade of the Feijoa trees and other stories.
    Hayley Ann Solomon.

FIND OUT MORE ABOUT PROVERSE AUTHORS, BOOKS, EVENTS AND LITERARY PRIZES

Visit our website: http://www.proversepublishing.com
Visit our distributor's website: www.cup.cuhk.edu.hk
Follow us on Twitter: twitter.com/Proversebooks
"Like" us on www.facebook.com/ProversePress
Request our free E-Newsletter
Send your request to info@proversepublishing.com.

Availability

Available in Hong Kong and world-wide from our
Hong Kong based distributor,
the Chinese University of Hong Kong Press,
The Chinese University of Hong Kong, Shatin, NT,
Hong Kong SAR, China.
See the Proverse page on the website:
https://cup.cuhk.edu.hk/Proversehk

All titles are available from Proverse Hong Kong,
http://www.proversepublishing.com

Most titles can be ordered online from amazon
(various countries) and other online retailers.

Stock-holding retailers
Hong Kong (CUHKP, Bookazine)
Canada (Elizabeth Campbell Books),
Andorra (Llibreria La Puça, La Llibreria)
United Kingdom (Ivybridge Bookshop, Devon).

Orders may be made from bookshops
in the UK and elsewhere.

Ebooks
Most of our titles are available also as Ebooks.

Audiobooks
Some of our titles are available also as audiobooks.

Printed by Amazon Italia Logistica S.r.l.
Torrazza Piemonte (TO), Italy